Murderous
Means

Murderous *Means*

A Southern California Mystery

Lida Sideris

First published by Level Best Books 2023

This novel is entirely a work of fiction. The names, characters and incidents portrayed in it are the work of the author's imagination. Any resemblance to actual persons, living or dead, events or localities is entirely coincidental.

Author Photo Credit: Kenny Young

First edition

ISBN: 978-1-68512-500-4

Cover art by Level Best Designs

This book was professionally typeset on Reedsy.
Find out more at reedsy.com

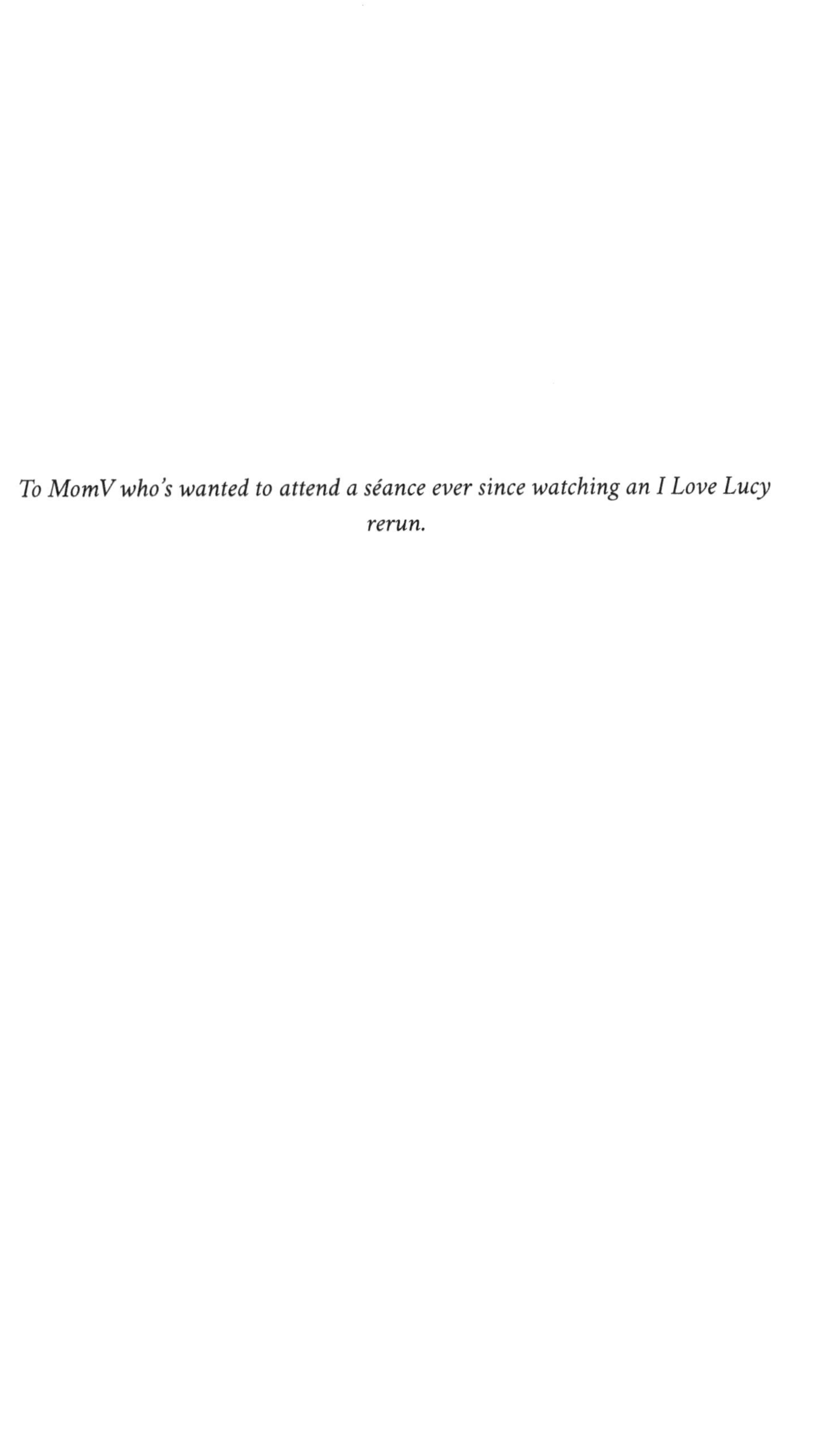

To MomV who's wanted to attend a séance ever since watching an I Love Lucy rerun.

Praise for Murderous Means

"The characters are hilarious and this series is a must-read for fans of Stephanie Plum."—*Kings River Life Magazine*

"What could be better than a sassy P.I, snappy dialogue and a plot line that moves like a locomotive on steroids!"—J.C. Eaton, author of The Sophie Kimball Mysteries, The Wine Trail Mysteries, The Charcuterie Shop Mysteries, The Marcie Rayner Mysteries

"Author Lida Sideris has served up another clever tale of mayhem that never ceases to entertain."—Paul Martin, author of the Music & Murder Mysteries

"If you are a mystery addict, then I highly recommend this book...5 stars."—Nana's Book Reviews

Chapter One

Most people think the worst when they spot a shadowy figure lurking outside in the middle of the night. But there's often a perfectly reasonable explanation. Take tonight, for instance. I was previewing my next job at a time carefully selected to avoid interruptions.

It was the quiet hour, halfway between sunset and sunrise, when sharp-fanged critters weren't the only ones in stealth mode. Although breaking and entering was one of my favorite pastimes, I carried a key for tonight's visit, provided by a prospective client. Except she wasn't expecting me till much later, like in twelve hours. I was checking out the place to determine if the job was worth taking. Plus, I did my best thinking and investigating in the dark, when hunches flowed freely, fully formed, and primed for action.

I knelt behind an overgrown shrub at the bottom of a driveway leading to Means Well Ranch. The house was one of three structures on twenty-nine acres at the end of Old Canyon Road in Los Ranchos, population 1300. The tiny town was nestled between two powerhouse communities with small-town vibes of their own: Calabasas and Malibu. Just far enough away from Los Angeles to make residents forget the worries and bustle of city life, but close enough to grab a bite at a top-notch Italian eatery in Century City. Los Ranchos was a hidden pocket of relief in the massive overcoat of L.A.

Crouching, I crept my way up the pebbly dirt driveway to an old but sturdy Victorian home sitting dead center of fenced-in pastures. The siding was painted a stark white; gingerbread trimmed the eaves. I inserted the key and stepped inside a tall, narrow, and dark foyer, with my penlight leading the way. Floral wallpaper stirred up the interior. The antique furnishings were the real deal, fashioned by expert craftsmen. From Windsor chairs to walnut corner pieces, it was like stepping back in time, circa 1900, except ladies back then didn't dress in black sweats or don suede ankle boots. Nor did they stash pistols in their crossbody bags and Japanese throwing stars in their belt buckles. Well, maybe the pistols.

A mission-style, upright player piano pressed against one wall in the living room. Oriental rugs scattered around tongue and groove floors, quieting my footsteps. Not that anyone would hear me. The house sat unoccupied ever since…I dove behind a small velvet settee and froze, penlight off. A floorboard creaked on the porch, a weighty creaking that lasted a tad too long. Was somebody out there?

After a respectable silence, I straightened and slid to the window, edging open a heavy curtain to hunt down ripples in the night. Maybe a roving raccoon or a bear walked the porch. I shuddered.

Spotting nothing outside, I resumed my inspection of the house. The homeowner, an energetic and fit seventy-two-year-old woman, died here almost a week ago. Three days ticked by before anyone noticed. Finally, a worried tenant on the property called a mutual friend who broke into the place. Josephine Joelle "JoJo" Means was found in her nightgown, lying peacefully on her four-poster bed. Heart failure was noted as the cause of death. No sign of foul play meant no police involvement.

Why was I snooping around? I wasn't a cop, but I was pretty darn close to becoming an official private investigator. My job was to cast aside any lingering possibility that JoJo's death wasn't all that peaceful. A possibility her sister had wanted me to explore.

"JoJo was as fit as an Olympian athlete competing in marathons and whatnot," Marti Means had said when she'd called. There was a certain toughness behind her low, crackly voice. "She climbed up and down ladders, mended fences, and fed and watered the livestock every single day. JoJo baked, she cleaned, she even sewed her own clothes."

Sounded like she died from exhaustion.

"My sister traveled the world. She wouldn't just up and die like that."

I thought she probably would since it wasn't entirely up to her, but the private investigator in me was willing to snoop around. Unfortunately, the next bit of information didn't inspire much confidence.

"Heidi insists JoJo's death deserves another look. 'There's more to it.' Those were Heidi's exact words."

"Who's Heidi?" I'd asked. A police detective? Medical examiner?

"Heidi Honeyman. She's my personal psychic."

As a hardcore skeptic of fortune tellers, I should've dropped the call right then, but I had two reasons for staying on the line. One, a strong desire to prove Heidi was a fraud, and two, I needed the job.

"That's why I'm hiring a full-fledged private investigator to take a closer look. When I heard you had a staff psychic, it was a done deal. You're perfect for this case. I'll get into the nitty gritty at our meeting tomorrow."

We didn't exactly have a staff psychic. Our in-house seer formulated his deductions based on logic and evidence, which might have made him appear to have psychic abilities on our last investigation when he really didn't. Who was I to argue? We got the job done, and everyone lived happily ever after.

While I wasn't a full-fledged private investigator, meaning my license to investigate hadn't been issued yet, I had plenty of real-life experience, thanks to my P.I. father. I'd worked with Dad, and handled a few freelance gigs on my own, which had sharpened skills already in place, when I wasn't at my day job, that is. Private investigating is what we did when we weren't skirting around the legal department of Ameripictures Film Studios. *We* being my legal assistant, Veera Bankhead, and me, ace junior attorney. At least, that's what I called myself. Outside of the legal department, we were a small-time start-up. Ant-sized actually, with only a name, and no office or professional staff, not counting my mother.

What was I looking for tonight, anyway? A clue that someone else had been in the house while JoJo was sleeping, thanks to a psychic vision. From Marti's account, her sister locked the place up tight before she hit the sack every night. The bigger question? If someone had to break in to find out what happened to JoJo, how would a killer have gotten inside and out? Was I wasting my time? Everyone knew psychics were crackpots.

I tapped floors and walls in the tidy home, listening for a hollow echo, which could indicate a hidden space. I checked windows for locks that didn't work and climbed into an attic looking for an exterior entry point. All I got were cobwebs in my hair and a snag in my sweatshirt.

JoJo's jewelry sat inside a pillowcase on the top shelf of her linen closet. I counted a ruby ring and matching bracelet, and an assortment of old coins. A stash of Benjamins lay hidden in the inside pocket of a quilted winter coat in the hall closet. Why would someone break in, do away with her, and leave valuables? I needed more background information on JoJo. And not the kind provided by a psychic.

I opened the door of a large pantry in the kitchen and jumped to the side, gun drawn, as something swished past me. A mop had tumbled to the floor. My hammering heartbeat filled my ears as I pushed the mop back in place. Before I closed the door, a floorboard creaked again, louder this time, near the entry, followed by another creak, and another. That was no four-legged creature trekking across the front porch. I strained my ears, listening for the slightest sound. As soon as quiet was restored, I tiptoed to the living room, penlight off.

Scooting beside a brick fireplace, I planted myself on the edge of the hearth and inched away the curtain. The fabric felt coarse and rough, like a burlap sack. Had someone seen me sneaking up the driveway and followed? My BMW was parked a few hundred yards away to avoid any connection to this property. I'd left it near residences on smaller plots of land along the narrow road leading to Means Well Ranch.

A pale sliver of a moon gleamed behind drifting clouds, providing about as much light as a birthday candle. I listened hard, but only the gentle, low hoot of an owl ruffled the stillness.

I turned on the penlight. Before I could rise, something glinted near my boot. Something small and round. I flashed my thin beam on an oval brooch made of gold-tone metal.

"Who do you belong to?" I squeezed the pin-backed brooch between my thumb and index finger. A little bigger than a coat button, a worn carving of deer appeared on the front side; a stag with branching antlers, and a smaller doe behind him. I read the front, "Conservationist, Empire State." Tiny letters on the back were so faded I couldn't make them out. The pin couldn't have been lying there too long. JoJo had kept the place spic-and-span.

I'd barely shoved it into my pocket when the front door swung open, banging against the wall.

A broad-shouldered, gray-bearded man stormed inside. The beam of his flashlight danced a frantic waltz around the floors and walls. His other hand gripped a handgun. My heart beat double-time as I crouched behind a large woven basket brimming with logs. He stepped into the living room. Now what?

I dove behind the sofa, then shot off and tumbled into a bedroom, thumping footsteps in my wake. His strides were longer than mine, but I topped him in speed. He wouldn't fire a shot inside the house, would he?

I unlocked a single hung window and shoved it upward. A breeze whisked back the sheer curtains, scenting the room with rosemary. I rolled beneath the four-poster bed, willing my panting to slow.

The bearded man thundered inside. His beam of light roamed until it landed on the open window. There was just enough light for me to spy a small white envelope tucked beneath a metal bar of the bed frame. As the guy took off, I gently tugged the envelope free, running my fingers against something odd-shaped inside that weighed the paper down. I stuffed the envelope inside my purse, waited a decent interval, and blew out a sigh. All clear, for now.

Chapter Two

I tiptoed across the floorboards, taking note of a flashing red light on an old-school answering machine in the living room. JoJo used a landline, which made sense since cell reception was sketchy around here. I quick-stepped forward and flew out the back door into the creeping darkness. I debated hightailing it down the driveway and back to my car, but I opted for sticking around. My night had barely started, and the intruder might know something. What made me think I could overpower a man the size of a grizzly bear? I was better at asking myself questions than I was at answering them.

Bypassing the driveway, I dashed off to the side and onto soft, sandy ground toward a large wooden barn with a gabled roof. A cool, steady breeze nipped my cheeks, and a dog barked in the distance. No sign of the bearded fellow.

I'd barely reached the rear of the barn when steps pounded close by. The earth around me glowed. The man must be a human bloodhound. I grabbed a rock and tossed it far to one side while I edged away. The beam of light switched direction, and I jetted off.

Hustling around the corner, I collided with something short, rough, and tough. I stumbled, tripping along to regain my footing.

"Maaaa!"

A barrage of rapid tap, tap, taps, like a muffled drum roll, shook the night. The clouds parted, and moonlight exposed a herd of small livestock about ten yards ahead.

Hurrying forward, I listened for steps and watched for the light. Just as

I rounded another corner, the big guy barreled toward me. He sure had plenty of energy for an older gent. I spun around and hung a right, aiming toward the road. So much for an uninterrupted job preview.

I glanced over my shoulder. The man slow-jogged in my direction. I picked up speed and ran at full throttle. As I cut a left, a large bulky creature blocked my path.

Turning sharply to avoid another collision, the toe of my boot stuck in a squirrel hole. I stumbled forward, arms flailing, and landed with a thud. My head knocked against something rigid, and my world shut down.

* * *

Tiny beads of pain crashed together in my head like bumper cars made of steel. It felt like I'd emerged from a deep slumber. A wave of nausea passed through me. As I blew out a long breath, sparkling starlight blurred above, pixie dust in the black sky. I lifted my leaden head. I lay sprawled in the middle of a field. Did I lose consciousness?

My fingers crept to my belt buckle, and I slipped the Japanese throwing star into my palm, relishing the shuriken's cold metal and sharp points. I caught my breath. A flashlight illuminated the night. A dozen goats huddled together a good thirty feet away, their backs to me. A deep voice stirred the air. I couldn't make out the words. Who was talking?

A large man stood near the goats, light beam in one hand, while the other dangled a pistol. As he shooed away the livestock, I lowered my head and stiffened. What was it Dad used to say?

A problem presents an opportunity to turn things around.

The guy trekked closer, stopping a few feet short of me. He smelled faintly of tobacco and beer. Shoving aside the pain, I jumped to my feet, only it was more like I heaved myself to a crouching position, shuriken ready. I sucked in a breath and sprang forward, straightening up enough to press my throwing star against his thick neck. Meanwhile, he stuck the muzzle of his gun to my side.

"Steady now, young lady." His voice was a baritone growl that rustled the weeds. His crinkly blue gaze lit up like sparklers. "I'm going to lower my gun the same time you lower that sharp pointy thing. I know you broke inside the house tonight, but I'm willing to give you a chance to explain before I call the police."

"Before you what?" I pressed the star deeper, a whisker away from drawing blood. "Who are you?"

"Friend of the Means family. Hank Ramos. I live nearby. You?"

"Corrie Locke, private eye with Nightingale Investigations. I'm looking over the place to decide whether or not to investigate the death of JoJo Means." Did those words actually come out of my mouth? Since when was I so forthcoming? A quick head shake shifted the gears in my brain. "That is…" I wanted to say that he should be more concerned about my slitting his throat, which I'd never do, but he didn't know that. "…I'm here on behalf of a prospective client." What was wrong with me? The truth rolled off my tongue like melted butter. I was, by nature, a highly skilled liar with little room for the truth, especially in questionable situations.

"You're investigating JoJo?" He gingerly placed the gun back in its holster. "I thought she had a heart attack."

I kept my shuriken steady. For all I knew, he had another weapon on him.

"I'm gonna need to see some identification." His gaze stuck to mine like gum on a rubber sole.

Keeping the star in my hand and my stare firmly in place, I reached for my crossbody bag. I unzipped an outside pocket and pulled out a business card.

"How's your head?" He took the card without breaking eye contact. "You fell kinda hard. You nearly crashed into the steer. Poncho can be ornery."

"So can I." I self-checked my vitals—no lingering nausea, no memory issues, no loss of balance meant I was good to go. My run-in was more of a scrape. I touched my head and winced at the nasty pain. "Crashed against…who?"

He pointed his flashlight off to one side. A bull the size of a dune buggy watched us. His horns shot straight out from his head, like lightsabers, about four feet long on each side.

"Him?" My voice had a squeak to it.

"That's what you get, running willy-nilly on unfamiliar terrain at full speed.

You ought to exercise some caution. That's how you hit your noggin against that old wooden bucket. Any bumps on your head?"

"I doubt it." Not yet, anyway.

"No surprise there."

He wasn't the first to call me hard-headed. "Why were you sneaking around?"

"I don't sneak. I stopped by to look in on the place. That's what I do. Except... when I don't." He ran a hand through a fuzz of unkempt silvery hair while he examined my business card. "I walk on nights I can't get any shut-eye. This was one of those nights. Passed by and saw something movin' toward the house. Thought it was a bobcat or raccoon until I noticed boot prints in the dirt, headed up the porch."

I had to give him credit for being observant. I didn't see that coming. "You're the one who broke into the house and found JoJo." Hank likely knew things I needed to know.

He lowered his chin. "I didn't break in. I called a locksmith to get inside." He caught my gaze again. "Jo and I...we've been friendly a long while." His shoulders drooped, and his stare skidded away. "Maybe even more than friends in recent times, but we had a little tiff days before she..." Hank blew out a huff. "She didn't want anyone to know about us. JoJo was a woman of many secrets."

"What secrets was she keeping from you?" The side of my head throbbed like a woodpecker slammed its chisel-like beak against it. I massaged it with my fingers.

"Now, how would I know that?"

Good point.

"Better get you some ice. Follow me." Hank turned toward the house.

I lumbered after him. Hank was a hunky man who looked to be in his seventies with a strong jawline that could handle a fair amount of punches. His thick mane and dark brows reminded me of a border collie herding sheep to their pen, quick and smooth. No wonder I had trouble shaking him off. "Did JoJo have a lot of friends?"

"Not as many as some folks, but she had plenty of acquaintances."

He hung his head and paused so I could walk ahead of him up the porch stairs.

"JoJo spoke her mind, which made some people real mad." He climbed behind me.

"Mad enough to kill her?" I turned to face him.

"Why would you say that?" He strode across the porch. "She riled people, and maybe had things others wanted, which was worrisome."

"What things?" I matched his strides. What was he getting at?

"You're awfully young to take on a job like this with just that star for protection." Hank rubbed his fingers across his hairy chin.

He was so wrong. "It's a shuriken. A Japanese throwing star."

"Who hired you, anyway?" Hank asked and held the door open for me.

I wasn't going to spill any information before he did. "That's a private matter."

"I wouldn't believe anything Marti says. She doesn't just have a screw loose. She's got a mess of tools loose in her noggin, clangin' against each other." He pointed to his head.

I stepped inside. "What do you do for work around here?"

"I'm the proprietor of Hank's Place in town. Best burgers west of the Grand Canyon."

That didn't tell me much, other than I needed to try his burger. "Any idea of who'd like to make JoJo disappear?"

"That's crazy talk. JoJo died, plain and simple, like people do. I was the first one here. Nothing was out of the ordinary."

"Her valuables–"

"Weren't touched, far as I could tell. Only proves my point. Marti and I sorted through JoJo's stuff afterward. Everything seemed to be in its place."

Did he or Marti know the contents of the house well enough to spot any missing items? I doubted that.

Hank strode into the kitchen, opened the freezer, and pulled out a bag of frozen green beans. He held it out to me.

I grabbed the cold plastic and pressed it to my head. The icy surface numbed the lingering pain and pumped new energy through my veins.

"What if you're wrong, and someone killed JoJo and got away with it? How would you feel about that?"

He dropped his gaze. "I don't believe in hypotheticals."

I slapped a hand on the counter. "I've got nothing so far. Unless evidence turns up to prove an unnatural death, I'm declining the case." He knew more than he was saying, I was certain. "Anything you care to share?"

Hank regarded the business card in his hand again, turning it over, then stopped and fastened his crinkly blues on mine. "It started out as simple theft." His voice was a hoarse whisper. "Sticks of firewood went missing from JoJo's wood pile; apples were pilfered from her trees, even chicken feed was fair game."

"Neighborhood squirrels. They love fruit and chicken food. Plus, chewing wood keeps their teeth in shape." So much for evidence.

Hank pressed his lips together and rolled the tip of his tongue around the insides of his cheeks. "Told you there wasn't anything to go on."

I thought of the envelope taped beneath JoJo's bed. What was in it, and why hide it under there? I'd better play nicely if I wanted answers. "I appreciate any light you might shed. Did JoJo collect anything? Old books, pins, or vintage jewelry?" It was possible Hank played a hand in her demise. Assuming she was the victim of foul play. I reached into my pocket and opened my palm. The gold-tone, metal brooch sat in the center.

He bent forward, peering closer, and read the writing on the pin. "Conservationist, Empire State. What is this?"

"Did it belong to JoJo?" I asked.

"Doubt it." He picked up the brooch and turned it over before dropping it back in my palm. "She was no tree hugger or conservationist, far as I know." His fingers were calloused and coarse.

"Know anyone who is?"

"Not around here." He stood. "Where'd you find that?"

I tilted and tossed my head toward the house. "Living room, under a curtain."

He hissed air between his teeth. "Must've been left over from her parents' odds and ends. Or a neighbor or a family member could've dropped it during a visit. Heck, it could've been laying there for a while."

"Or it could've—"

"Means nothing."

"Really?" My gut told me this little nothing held the key to what happened to JoJo. What was Hank holding back? Had he given her the pin?

"It's time I escorted you out." Hank pressed his lips together. He'd clearly run out of words and patience. "You got a car parked around here?"

"I know where to find it, thanks." I took a few steps and flipped around. I stared at his craggy profile. "If I walk from this job, and a criminal played a hand in JoJo's passing, a killer could go scot-free. If you have something to say, my number's on the card."

He pressed his thin lips together. "I'll keep that in mind."

I turned on my heel. Condensation from the icy bag slid down my forehead. I wiped it with my sleeve.

"Wait a minute."

I spun around.

"There's something you should know. Caleb Means, JoJo's father, died about fifteen years ago. His wife passed shortly after. That's when the remaining Means family got to squabbling. Been going on for a while now." He took two large steps toward me. "I'd like to know why, wouldn't you?"

"What do you think it's about?" Was he on the verge of telling me something worthwhile?

Hank shook his head and toed the dirt. Minty greens scented the air while the chilly breeze slapped my cheeks, seeping through my clothes. Nearly a full minute passed without either of us speaking.

"You have anything to add?" I needed a crowbar to pry information out of this guy.

"Not a word."

"Okay, then." I headed for the road; the far-off whirr of car engines hummed on a nearby highway, but the area closest to me remained quiet. Did Hank have another reason for stopping by the place tonight? What secrets did JoJo keep? And what was the family squabbling about?

Chapter Three

As I motored away from JoJo's ranch, a realization hit me. I couldn't leave yet. I wasn't finished nosing around. After all, that old brooch didn't just lie there for ages. JoJo kept her place clean. Maybe there were more clues for the taking.

I hung a quick right onto a bumpy dirt road leading to a vacant lot and angled behind a tangle of leathery oaks. I cut the lights and the motor. There were no structures in sight, making the chances of discovery remote.

Minutes later, a flashlight flickered between the branches, and Hank weaved his way back home. As the light ebbed, I stepped onto a soft layer of oak leaf litter and retraced my steps. I'd nearly made it when headlights sliced through the darkness. I knelt behind a stately maple with a trunk the width of a wine barrel. Gravel crunched beneath fat tires as an SUV lumbered past and turned a corner. I flicked off leaves and twigs from my clothes, peeked around the trunk, and headed for my destination. This time there'd be no interruptions.

* * *

I crawled along the floors of JoJo's house on the hunt for anything to tip the scale in favor of criminal activity. The furnishings were in browns and taupes, just like the towels and sheets. Even the floral wallpaper was beige.

Rummaging through drawers and cabinets, I scoured shelves, shoeboxes, and… got nothing. No prescription meds, no hard liquor. JoJo was a beer and wine kind of gal. Nothing out of place. Was I missing something?

The red light on the answering machine relentlessly blinked. I pressed it and upped the volume.

"Your car warranty is about to expire," a robotic voice chanted.

"Next." I pushed a button.

"Sorry, I…um…missed you, Aunty Jo. Just got back…" The rest of the words were mumbled. "Um…call you tomorrow." His voice was low, slow, and uncertain.

Another message came from the lowly scam bot, but the rest were different.

"I'm not putting up with any more of your nonsense." This voice belonged to a surly man, growling into the receiver. The tone was different from Hank's assertive, hoarse voice. The next message was more of the same.

"You'll be sorry if you pull out. You know we need this to happen."

What was he talking about?

In the final two messages, a woman's agitated voice called JoJo names and accused her of breaking a promise. The voice was accented. British? Caribbean? I couldn't tell, but an angry tirade turned into a tearful plea in the second call.

Had anyone else heard these?

Three quick thumps shook the floorboards of the front porch, followed by a tapping on the entry door.

"I don't believe it," I whispered. This place saw more action than a lone gas station in the Mojave Desert. Hank again?

I slid to the hallway, shuriken in hand.

"Corrie? It's me. Are you in there?"

Didn't sound like Hank. Insistent raps beat against the door.

"Michael?" My sweetie was the only other person who knew I'd be here. He'd insisted on joining me, and I'd almost caved in, until I discovered he had a faculty meeting in San Francisco.

I yanked open the door. "What are you doing?"

In front of me stood six feet of handsome goofiness in one smart package. Part Saint Bernard, part Clark Kent, Michael Parris' smile lit up the porch. His dark hair was more tousled than ever, and his eyes the sweet hazel I loved. My bestie, my boyfriend, and now, my not-exactly-a-psychic.

"I was going out of my mind with worry. You have no phone reception, no one to watch your back, way out in the middle of nowhere–"

"I can practically hear the 101 freeway. Granted, reception's sketchy, but…what happened to your faculty meeting?"

"I left before dessert."

"You did?" That was no small sacrifice. Michael wore a gray quilted travel coat, a loosened tie, and a blue dress shirt; the first few buttons opened enough to display just the right amount of chest hair. Sexy. His low-top Chuck Taylor All-Stars came along for the ride. His favorite sneakers. I couldn't decide if he looked the part of a dashing hero…or of someone who couldn't remember if he'd left the stove on.

"Aren't you going to invite me inside?" he asked. "I should…get a vibe on whatever's going on, shouldn't I?"

Michael was the dean of the computer science department at L.A. Tech College when he wasn't doing double-duty on my cases. His in-depth research at our last P.I. gig earned him his psychic stripes, at least to the person who'd referred us to this job. Michael kept me on the straight and narrow just by being himself, although I veered off now and then, like passing him off as our agency psychic. I stepped back, sniffing sandalwood, new car leather, and something else as he swept past.

"Why do you smell like the inside of a movie theater?" That would explain my sudden hankering for red licorice.

"I stopped to get gas, and the station sold popcorn." He reached inside his jacket and pulled out a small red and white striped bag. The top was folded over to prevent spillage. He handed it to me. "Thought you could use a snack."

"Just what the doctor ordered." I popped a buttery kernel in my starving mouth. "Yummy, thank you. By the way, we'll have to confess to Marti Means that you're not really a psychic."

His head snapped in my direction, and his brows dipped. "Is there someone else here?" He stared down at me. "I heard a voice that sounded strangely like yours, but those words couldn't have come out of your mouth. You okay?"

"We shouldn't lie to her, that's all."

He pressed his lips to my forehead. "You're feverish."

I pulled back and clenched my teeth. "I am not."

"What happened here tonight?" He gently held my shoulders. "I should've come sooner."

"Almost nothing happened." I gave him the run-down on JoJo and Hank. Michael's gaze drifted to my hair. He pulled something out from behind my ear.

"Straw. You were inside that big barn, weren't you?" He snapped his fingers. "You got into a tussle with some livestock. I knew it."

And this is why he made a great semi-psychic. His powers of deduction rivaled that of Sherlock Holmes. "I tripped over a goat in the pasture, but I'm fine."

"Something else happened. What?"

My hand shot to my head. The throbbing had lessened, but it still hurt to the touch.

"You were hit in the head!" He flashed a light and pointed to my crown. "There's a cut…" His fingers gently touched the spot.

I winced and slapped away his hand. "It's nothing."

"I'll patch you up in no time."

He cleaned my head with a damp paper towel and alcohol wipes he found under the sink. "The whole drive, I kept asking myself, why would Marti's psychic bring up foul play with no evidence whatsoever?"

"Because psychic predictions are generalizations, which means Heidi said something that led Marti to believe in the possibility of foul play."

"I can make generalizations."

I squeezed his hand. "We need to be better than Heidi." I moved into the living room, Michael close behind. "I'll text you a list of names connected to JoJo. Can you look up the backgrounds, so we can figure out how they fit in?"

"My favorite part of the investigation," Michael said and examined the knick-knacks on the fireplace mantel. "I'll dive into their history and find things they don't even know about themselves."

I linked my fingers with Michael's. "Nothing would make me more excited."

Michael flipped around. "Nothing?"

We kissed our way over to the opposite side of the room.

"How about we go on a date after all this is over?" I mumbled between kisses. "A long one."

"Like a four-hour date or forty-eight hours?"

"I was thinking seventy-two." We'd taken turns lately canceling our dates. Michael was a sight for my sore and tired eyes. "If JoJo had something someone wanted, it was more valuable than jewelry, cash, or antiques." I took his hand. The warmth of his skin soothed any lingering pain. "I'm glad you're here."

He kissed the back of my hand. "I'm gladder."

"Wait." I pulled out the small white envelope from my handbag. "I found this under JoJo's bed, stuck beneath the bed frame."

He pressed his thumb against the paper. "Feels like a key. An old school one."

I ran my fingers along the shape. "Right." I examined the envelope. A seal secured the flap. If I opened it, I couldn't seal it to make it look unopened. "I'll hold on to it, for now." I stuffed it in my purse and headed out. "There's one place I haven't checked yet." I really wanted to call it quits, but I had to be thorough, or I'd be up all night thinking about it. "I could use your expertise."

"Computer-related?"

I shook my head.

He pointed a finger at me. "Kitchen related?"

"Sort of." Michael's culinary skills would have made Julia Child blush. He knew his way around every kitchen nook and cranny, whereas yours truly believed fast food belonged at home.

He pulled out a pair of vinyl gloves. "I came prepared."

We walked into a square-shaped kitchen with white tiled walls and pale green cabinets. Everything was old-timey, from the drop-in farm sink to the checkerboard floor. The only modern piece, a three-door fridge, was a stainless-steel number with an ice maker in the door. The kitchen extended into a family room with a large round dining table and chairs.

Michael shuffled through the drawers. "I don't need to be a psychic to know that JoJo baked from scratch. She's got wooden spoons and a box of hand-written recipes with notes about who likes what." Michael lifted a small tin box. He knelt and peered into a cabinet. "See-through bins, vertical storage of coffee cups, stacked by shape. It's clear JoJo graduated with honors from the Martha Stewart College for Home Organizers."

I stared into the cool, bluish glare inside the refrigerator. Leftover meatloaf in a plastic container, a jar of pickles, eggs, and half a loaf of bread sat on the top two shelves. Was the meatloaf all for herself? Or had she entertained before dying?

"Nothing here to make even the back-page news of the morning paper. Wait." Michael slid next to me and eyeballed the wall next to the fridge. "A schedule for marketing, laundering, watering the garden, houseplants, vacuuming…" He pointed to a plaque hanging above the list. "An organized home is a happy home."

I turned toward the back of the house. I had a hunch buried in the pain pinballing inside my head. "Do you mind stepping outside?"

"Because we should get some air?"

"Because we need to check the trash receptacles, see if they're still full."

Michael's lips parted sweetly. "A smart and beautiful P.I. once told me garbage cans aren't just messy, foul smelling containers. They're treasure troves of secrets." He headed for the back door and flipped toward me. "Which is why I never ever throw out anything incriminating."

"What do you have that could be incriminating?" He was always on the up and up. Except when he helped on my cases. "Never mind. Let me know what you find. I'll poke around in here some more."

Michael took a big step backward. "On my way." He leaned forward and kissed me on my lips. "If I don't come back in ten minutes, send in the cavalry." He raced outside.

The screen door slammed shut, and I wound my way slowly through the house. What was out of place?

I puttered along to a small room, eyeing a hope chest, a bookcase overflowing with cookbooks, and a mahogany sewing table that looked like it belonged to Martha Washington. A framed photo of a smiling JoJo and a toothy shepherd sat on top. The small closet held clothes, all in beiges and grays. Another bedroom housed a roll-top writing desk, a modern recliner, and a linen-colored divan resembling a recovery couch in a doctor's office. JoJo used this room as her office.

A door creaked shut, and I headed for the kitchen. Michael stared at me, eyes rounded.

"You found something," I said.

"Not what I expected. Two receptacles filled with bagged trash and tightly knotted twisty ties."

"That's not unusual. I was hoping—"

"—for a little something pushed deep inside between the bags?" He held out an older model cell phone. "Someone threw this away. But get this: the cans didn't smell like garbage at all. They smell clean. Who does that?"

"You and my mom."

"And that's how I know that JoJo kept her trash under control with disinfectant and baking soda. It made trash diving so much easier."

We exchanged a high five. Was the old phone a clue? "Maybe JoJo got a new phone and tossed away the previous model." I examined it.

"No SIM card." He planted his hands on his hips. "Someone deliberately removed it."

"What's a SIM card again?" I should know this.

"A teensy memory chip inserted in a smartphone that stores information and helps activate the cell."

"Does that seem suspicious to you? That it's missing?" Bad reception meant there wasn't much use for a cell. I scratched my throbbing head.

"Everything is suspicious at a potential crime scene."

An idea glowed above my head. "Put the phone back in the garbage just the way you found it."

"Why?"

"Because, my dear home-grown psychic, tomorrow, you will use your not-quite-telepathic powers to lead us to the phone, and we'll watch how Marti reacts." Finally, we'd turned the corner into interesting territory.

Michael wiped away lingering bits and pieces of garbage from his sleeves and stopped. "But if JoJo bought a new cell phone, it makes sense to insert the old card from her previous phone into the new one."

"If it was her phone. Can you figure out who it belongs to without the SIM card?"

"Did a T-Rex have scary-sharp teeth the size of bananas?"

* * *

After rummaging around some more, we headed for a detached garage. Garages are notoriously messy, but this garage was different. It would make my mother swoon, then weep with joy. No clutter, no overstuffed boxes, or crowded spaces. A wall-mounted tool rack held everything from a ladder to an apron. Cleaning products were organized in plastic bins, and baskets strategically organized smaller items from paint brushes to rags. Center stage was an old, dark red, two-door Ford. A thin layer of dust sprinkled the car.

Michael barely noticed the tidy garage once he laid eyes on the car. His hands grazed the hood, and he softly sighed. "Dear Lord. So pristine. A 1969, unrestored Ford Galaxie 500."

I wasn't a fan of old cars…until now. Cushy bench seating with plenty of leg and body room. A trunk that would fit my weaponry, my bed, the clothes in my closet, plus a few watermelons. The Galaxie was a luxury land yacht. What was there not to like?

Michael peered into the open window with a low whistle. "Seventy-four thousand miles. If they sell this baby, I'll mow lawns, sweep porches, cat-sit…whatever it takes to buy it, just like I did for my Mustang in—"

"Junior high." That's when we first met.

The inside of the Galaxie was empty, but the trunk held a box of emergency food items, a folded sweater, shoes, flashlight, water bottles, and a long metal pipe perfect for conking someone over the head. There was even some cash hidden in a false bottom of a toolbox. JoJo was a woman prepared for anything.

I continued my garage search while Michael ogled the car. He gently rubbed a spot on the trunk with his sleeve.

"This car…" Michael appeared beside me, "… it's more than just a slice of history. It's a time capsule. I'd love to get my hands dirty on that engine."

I turned to face him. "We've got a pin-backed brooch, an old cell phone, and threatening voicemails for clues so far."

"Puzzle pieces that don't fit." He bit his lower lip.

"They never do in the beginning." I looked up at him. "If a crime has been committed, we'll make them fit."

Michael's smile was back. "I love it when you talk tough."

Was I as tough as I sounded? Not at the moment. "Let's call it a night. Or a very early morning."

"What about Michael, the psychic? When will he make his appearance?" he asked.

We headed for the entry. Lying was not part of Michael's repertoire. It chipped away at the perfectly polished block of sincerity he carried around. "Don't worry. I'll let Marti know exactly what our roles are."

A small high note escaped his lips. "That's a relief."

I opened the front door. "There isn't much crime in Los Ranchos from what I've heard. Would JoJo keep a spare key under the mat?" I squatted and lifted the thickly woven welcome mat. Nothing was hidden beneath.

"She lived alone and didn't want to chance leaving a key in an obvious place," Michael said.

"I think she would've hidden one somewhere." That's what a woman of many secrets would do, if Hank was right. If she locked up the home every night, she probably did the same when she left her house. What if she forgot her key?

The beam of my penlight ran across the front door. No door knocker, just an old-school doorbell. Michael's beam shone on a ceramic planter housing a red geranium. He checked under a metal rooster posted next to the pot. I strolled the porch while Michael headed down the stairs. I was about to join him when my beam lit up a plastic outdoor socket cover, resting near the geranium. I knelt closer and tilted my head. A slight gap existed between the cover and the wall. Was that usual? "Michael?" I flipped open the cover, and there it was.

Michael skipped up the steps. "Whoa, a key hideaway."

I removed the key with a gloved hand and placed it on the wooden floorboard. I took a couple of photos with my phone of the old, round-headed copper key, and replaced it. "What if someone else knew that JoJo hid her key here?" I straightened. "This is something a psychic might intuit, wouldn't you say?"

"With help from a smart P.I."

"Not smart. I'm trying to think like JoJo." A personality profile for her was formulating in my head with the word "secretive" at the top. I compared the picture of JoJo's key to the one Marti gave me. Marti's was a traditional, pyramid-shaped key with a flat top, made recently by the locksmith that helped Hank get in.

"You never told me how you hurt your head." Michael knelt close to me, warm breath on my cheek.

"I fell and hit it against a bucket. I might've briefly lost consciousness, but I'm fine."

Michael's easy smile fell a few notches as he moved a strand of hair from my face. "Corrie, I'm here for you. And tomorrow, I'm going to make you proud. But tonight, I may just take a dip into the sea of insecurities."

"Stick with me, kid. I'll toss you a life jacket, every time."

He squeezed my hand. His smile was back.

Chapter Four

Just before noon the next day, I exited the 101 freeway and motored onto Las Virgenes Road, a scenic, mostly one-lane connector to Pacific Coast Highway. The wind whirled through my open window, whisking around my hair before wandering out through Veera's side. Her honey-colored waves were gathered in a classic high bun that no wind could touch. On our right, a casual shopping center fortified locals who lacked the motivation to drive to the city for grub. A few low-rise office buildings placated those who resented traveling to work. Signs of civilized life soon gave way to a laid-back vibe where Mother Nature's heartbeat was heard throughout the many hiking trails and pathways. The road gently wound past golden hills. No need to hurry or worry around these parts.

We cut a left onto Mulholland Parkway, cruising along until a sign invited us onto Old Canyon Road. A straight and narrow trek, dark green shrubs dotted the sun-kissed fields. Eucalyptus saluted us on either side with treetops that tickled the skyline.

"I'm kinda enjoying this peaceful nothingness," Veera said. "We're knee-deep in real nature."

"As seen from the inside of a car." I had to admit, her dusky complexion did have a healthy glow to it.

"I wouldn't mind stretching my legs."

I couldn't blame Veera for feeling cramped. Full-figured and topping at six feet, she'd folded herself into the passenger seat of my BMW 3-series by pushing it all the way back, which still didn't leave her much wiggle room. We'd started the drive over an hour ago, slinking along the clogged arteries of Southern California traffic at twenty miles per hour. Yet her sunny-side-up smile never faded. Veera was not only my legal assistant at the studio and P.I. colleague, she was my friend.

"I don't even have the urge to check our Instagram account. It's been nearly ten minutes," she said.

A yellow, diamond-shaped sign appeared on our left featuring silhouettes of three little birds following a parent bird wearing a fancy head plume.

"Aww, would you look at that? When was the last time you laid eyes on quail? Don't think I ever have."

"They're adorable." I filled my lungs with fresh, clean air.

Another mile and another sign appeared, showing the silhouette of a deer with antlers.

"Slow down, now," Veera said. "We don't want to hurt any of Bambi's relatives."

My lead foot turned into one made of cotton. There was really no reason to rush around.

The next sign featured a different kind of silhouette.

Veera squinted. "Is that what I think it is?" Her gaze remained pinned to the sign, as we motored by.

"It is, if you're thinking mountain lion."

She pulled out a bottle of pepper spray from her backpack. "I like cats, so long as they weigh under twenty-five pounds and keep their fangs and claws to themselves."

"We'll keep our distance. Isn't nature wonderful?"

"If you say so."

I hung a right onto a narrow dirt road, kicking up clouds of dust in my wake. By daylight, the road seemed friendly and inhabited. Last night, it was deserted and ghostly.

We arrived at Means Well Ranch with a few minutes to spare, but it didn't matter. Fifteen minutes later, and still no sign of Marti.

Veera slapped a hand to her neck. "Did you see the size of that thing? Must've been a horsefly."

The sky was a pure, clear blue with the type of sparkling sun that convinced

Southern California visitors to forsake their childhood homes for the endless summer, swaying palm trees, and all the avocados one could eat. I leaned against a gnarly old oak, its bark divided into valleys and ridges. Its roughness felt reassuring against my upper arm. Strong enough to outlast its neighbors and scatter away the elements.

Veera patted her chest. "Can you hear that? It's my heartbeat." Her gaze swept the surroundings, and she strolled up to a two-story high eucalyptus. "I could just hug this big old hunk of nature. I'm soaking in all the peace and harmony I can get." She wrapped her arms around part of the peeling trunk. "We should visit the country more often."

You'd think we'd traveled across a few states instead of a few towns. Dressed in jeans, tees, and suede boots, we fit right into the rural surroundings. Pale splashes of blue flowers dotted the chaparral-studded hills surrounding the ranch. A beefy longhorn stared at us from inside a fenced enclosure. His whitish horns jutted straight out, turning up slightly at the ends.

"Poncho." I couldn't believe I nearly ran into him last night. Creamy-colored freckles splattered across his milk chocolate hide. Reddish-brown ears swiveled while he chewed his cud. He watched us with doe-like eyes. I had to admit, he looked more like a Jersey milk cow today than a dirt-pawing steer.

"This place is one big petting zoo." Veera eyed a pair of pygmy goats. She swatted the air around her shoulders. "There's that super fly again."

"They're harmless gnats." A swarm of tiny black dots swirled above our heads.

"Well, this one must be oversized."

"Let's look around the back."

We strolled around small sheds dotting the property. But a short rock wall ran around a different kind of structure. Bell-shaped and made of glazed plastic, it was JoJo's greenhouse.

A steel frame held the glazed plastic together. The front door was tall, topped by a narrow sliding glass window. The glaze wasn't enough to hide the inhabitants. Succulents crowded together like refugees from a Siberian winter. The structure looked wind-resistant, snow-resistant, even tornado resistant.

"Kind of messy in there." Veera slowly circled the greenhouse.

Which told me someone other than JoJo was in charge of it. "There's barely room to walk around."

"Who would want to with all those spiny, prickly plants?" Veera stepped back.

Toward the rear, Christmas cacti sat on a gardening cart. On the same cart were Venus flytraps, pitcher plants, and bladderwort. Dad once had a client who was into carnivorous plants, so I knew all about them. In the very back, tall, purplish flowers bloomed. The front door was padlocked. "Who waters all these?"

"Maybe she does." Veera pointed behind me.

An ancient white pick-up truck ambled onto the dirt driveway, crunching and spitting up loose rocks beneath its tires. We quick-stepped toward the truck.

"What do we say if she asks about our psychic?" Veera whispered.

"We'll ask about hers."

"Maybe she'll be so impressed with the two of us, she'll forget the psychic."

"She won't forget. That's how we got this job."

Marti had wanted a second psychic opinion about her sister's passing. "Two seers are better than one," she'd said. "I always request a second opinion when dealing with professionals."

Since when were psychics professionals? My phone pinged as a text rolled in from Michael.

We can do this!

Maybe he *was* psychic.

Your PI skills will more than make up for my lack of seeing into the future, or the past, or whatever it is I'm supposed to see into. See you soon! XO

A small, compact woman hopped out of the driver's side with a nimbleness that belied her age. The wind pressed her green tunic against her roundish form. Faded jeans were tucked into worn leather boots, and turquoise jewelry adorned her hands. Marti Means may have been petite in stature, but she had the swagger of a woman who meant business.

"We're going to do right by her, like we always do." Veera beamed her brightest smile.

I didn't doubt it, but we had a tendency of taking quite a few left turns before going right.

Marti's wide-brimmed straw hat and oversized black sunglasses shielded the upper half of her face. Dark blonde curls flared away from her prominent cheekbones. I reached out to shake her hand.

"Corrie Locke," I said. Prior to this point, our business had been conducted over the phone. This was our first in-person meeting, and we needed to make a good impression.

Her gaze flicked toward my hand. "I'm a bumper." Her low voice crackled. She held out a small fist, and I obliged. "Are you the psychic?" She pointed her finger toward Veera.

"I'm the assistant investigator at the Nightingale Agency." Veera stepped up for a fist bump. "And a student of the law. You're getting the best of both worlds."

By day, we worked as legal eagles in a production office at Ameripictures. Veera attended law school at night, when we weren't case-cracking. "Michael, the…" I couldn't bring myself to lie to this woman, which was another first for me. "…one with the special talents, isn't here yet."

"Why is that?" Marti fixed her questioning gaze on me and lowered her shades slightly to peer at me.

Could I keep my honest Abe streak going? "He's a man whose skills are in big demand, which is why he's running late." Apparently, I could. Michael *was* a man of many talents. Time to switch topics. "I paid a visit here last night." I might as well get that out of the way. "To look around."

Marti leaned into me. "What'd you find?"

"A large guy with a gun."

"A good-looking, cowboy type with a manly beard?" She wiggled her fingers beneath her chin.

"That's right."

"Oh my. Hank's gone all Lone Ranger on us. When he's not flipping burgers, he's keeping an eye out for lawbreakers and up-to-no-gooders. He's a volunteer police officer. He'd never hurt you, though. He'll just haul your butt into the law when you least expect it." Marti narrowed her stare. "Folks thought he and JoJo would get hitched, but it never worked out, I guess. Come on, let's get this over with." She marched her way to the house, mumbling under her breath. "There's a dark cloud hanging over our ranch."

Veera and I swapped a glance.

"Why do you say that?" I asked.

Marti tapped her chin with her index finger. "It was JoJo's doing. Always running over people who tried to reason with her. My sister was a human cannon, firing off iron balls to break us down. A bully, that's what she was. Plain and simple. Why, she kept the family heirlooms and furnishings for herself and didn't share any with the rest of us." Marti clenched her fists. "Worst of all, JoJo refused to sell this property even though she promised she would at the hundred-year mark. That anniversary passed six years ago. She gave Means Well Ranch a bad name."

Sounded like JoJo angered at least one person. "You said there was no sign of a break-in?"

"Nada. But it's what Heidi said that matters."

"Who phoned Hank to come over and check on JoJo?" Veera flanked Marti on the other side.

"Gifty Carmichael. She lives in a small house on this property, a quarter mile down. Said she hadn't seen JoJo feed the animals in days. Hank called us and offered to look in on things."

"Who's 'us'?" Veera asked.

Marti loped up a dirt path to the porch. We shadowed her.

"Me and Red, my brother. We've been after JoJo to sell this place since Mama passed. It was Mama's will that put JoJo in charge of the ranch. JoJo moved right in and took over.

"Then there's our nephew, Bart, the son of our late sister." Marti shook her head and stared at the ground. "He's been all torn up since JoJo died. Bart might be the only person on earth she cared about. I'm all that's left of us girls. We're a tight-knit family, you'll see. You'll meet everyone tonight at my house. I'm having a small party."

Seemed like a strange time to throw a party. "What happened when Hank arrived here, after he got the call?"

"Couldn't get in, so he called a locksmith."

"A big, burly guy like Hank couldn't get in without a locksmith?" Seemed to me he'd find a way to break in if he was worried about her.

"You don't know what it was like when JoJo got mad." Marti reached for the doorknob. "No one wanted to get on her bad side. Besides, she was always gallivanting around on trips without telling anybody. That's why no one was too concerned." She shoved a key into the lock and pushed open the door. "All yours, ladies." She pressed her lips together and stepped back.

Veera and I didn't budge.

Marti shrugged a shoulder. "I'm not going inside. I've seen it all. And, there're a slew of critters waiting on me to say hello. They're lonely these days." She stomped down the porch stairs and aimed for the barn.

Veera hurried after her, pulling out a folder from her oversized handbag. "If you'll sign on the dotted line, we'll officially get started." She handed Marti the folder and a pen.

Marti took her time to review the one-page contract. "Don't think I won't keep track of the time." She signed and stormed away.

Veera returned to me and lowered her voice, "Just how close a family was this if it took days before anyone noticed JoJo had passed? If she'd gone on a trip, wouldn't she have told one of them? What's Marti not saying?"

My thoughts exactly. Did she hire us to throw the scent off of her own dirty deed?

"And why invite us to her party?" Veera asked. "Not that I'm complaining."

"Marti has her own spin on what happened, thanks to the psychic. We're invited so she can watch how we do with our hair down on her turf. Let's be sure to wear our hair up tonight."

"You know we will."

"Take a look around, Veera, while I find out what Marti's up to. I might've missed something last night."

Veera headed for the house, while I joined Marti. She kicked back on a knotty wooden bench near the barn, a fluffy gray chicken nestled on her lap. I'd never seen a hen like that before. The size and shape of a feathery basketball, her abundant plumage ran down her legs like fluffy petticoats.

"She's pretty," I said.

"Coco is one of my favorites. Sweet and kind, she looks after everyone's chicks when they're hatched. Too bad JoJo didn't learn a thing or two from her."

"Will there be a memorial service for JoJo?"

"She didn't want one." Marti stroked the hen's plushness.

"You're throwing a party instead?"

"I'm not throwing anything. It'll be a small gathering. You'll be there to learn about our family." Her knee bounced up and down enough times to make the chicken cluck and hop to the ground with a thud.

"I need to ask—"

"Enough with the questions already."

Wow. How was I supposed to collect information without asking questions?

Marti slowly rose. "What's that?" She pointed over my shoulder.

I gazed out over a fenced-in pasture. Trees shook their leafy heads, and goats lounged in the shade. "You see something?"

She gave a slow nod. "Thought I saw someone running around." She squinted and stretched out her neck. "I'm not sure of anything anymore."

No matter what she said about JoJo, she'd still lost her sister. Maybe some kind of guilt was fueling her need to delve into JoJo's death. "You two were close as kids."

"How would you know?"

"I don't believe you're the type of person to put all your eggs in a mystical basket. Heidi's not the only reason you think there was more to your sister's passing." How was that for not asking her a question?

Marti glared up at me. "Not the only reason, you say?" She lowered her glare and adjusted her belt. "If you knew JoJo, you'd know she made plenty of folks mad." Marti kicked a piece of sod with her toe.

"Doesn't mean anyone did her in."

"Gifty's been livin' on the ranch for decades. She's a tenant who doesn't pay rent. Sometimes she worked for JoJo, and everything was hunky dory. Until three weeks ago, when JoJo gave her notice to vacate."

Why would JoJo let a tenant stay on for free? "Gifty was mad because…"

"The property's in escrow."

That brought my stagecoach to a screeching halt. Why didn't Marti share that small detail before? "Which is what the family wanted. To sell the ranch, I mean."

I waited for Marti to confirm or deny, but she stayed silent.

"Gifty speaks with an accent. A light, pretty accent. Maybe Caribbean." The voice messages made sense, finally. Gifty made the calls about JoJo breaking a promise. Why would JoJo let her stay without paying as a tenant?

"All I know is Gifty was spitfire mad. She refused to leave." Marti threw up her hands and stared up at me. "I'm surprised she didn't set fire to the place."

There were some complicated dynamics at work. How to sort through it all? Why did JoJo finally decide to sell the ranch? "JoJo put the ranch up for sale. That must have made the family happy." I tried again.

"Maybe Red had something to do with that. He can be pretty persuasive. JoJo had planned on moving into a property next door that she owns, but I don't even know if that's true."

"You're thinking Gifty killed JoJo because she didn't want to leave the ranch."

"That's what deranged criminals do." She wiped her hands together. "Gifty has a criminal record. Petty theft. Even a murder charge back in the day."

I stared at a pygmy goat standing a few feet away, pointy-tipped goatee waving in the breeze. She stared back with dark, oblong-shaped eyes and short, curvy horns. Baby horns compared to the horns on Poncho. Was the goat a witness to all the goings on?

"Maaaa."

I took that as a yes.

The proof in favor of a homicide was still wobbly. "You gotta give me something concrete to back up the psychic visions."

"That's what you're here for. It would help if your psychic was here, too."

A loud whirr shoved the quiet aside as a motorcycle raced up the driveway. The rider eased to a stop, boot pounding the dirt, as a whirlwind of dust and dry leaves swarmed around him. He swung his leg over the back of the bike and pulled off his helmet. Tall and lean with dark wavy hair, he was muscular in all the right places. The sun stretched its rays above him; jeans and a black leather jacket completed the calm, cool, and cute look that I loved. Michael jogged over.

"Who's that?" Marti stepped forward.

"The team member you've been waiting for."

Michael strolled up and threw me a quick grin. "Ms. Locke." He turned a somber face to Marti. "There's something you should know, Ms. Means."

Her hand fingered her throat as her eyes rolled over Michael. "You're the psychic. Call me Marti."

"The contents of the trash bins on this property need to be examined."

She sucked in a breath. "You had a vision?"

"More than a vision." His laughing eyes turned serious. "There's reason to believe the garbage on this property holds valuable information concerning your sister."

Marti's hand shot to her mouth.

"We need to see her trash." I hurried toward the back of the property, Marti at my heels, with Michael bringing up the rear.

Marti turned to him. "Spirits tell you anything else, Psychic?"

"Call me Michael." He took the lead. "You should know that my other world communications are mixed with everyday logic. Lots of logic and rational thought. I don't see visions like regular seers. I operate using science and math skills." He turned to Marti. "The garbage is calling us."

Moments later, we stood near an open trash receptacle. Michael dug around inside and fished out the cell phone. He showed it to Marti. "Have you seen this before?"

Marti took a step back. "How did you do that? That's JoJo's old phone." She turned to me. "He's amazing." She faced Michael again. "I don't know why she held onto that old thing. Reception's not great around here."

"Bad reception made her throw it out?" I asked.

"No. She got a new phone."

Michael stepped forward. "This should be recycled."

"Golly! Is that what the spirits say we should do?"

"No one wants hazardous metals seeping into the environment," he said.

I turned to Michael. "See anything else?"

He closed his eyes a few moments and flicked them open. "I see a way into the house. An easy way in for a stranger."

"What stranger?" Marti wrinkled her nose at him.

"It's not clear, but I see something near a door, but not on the door." He stared down at her and gestured with his hands as we walked toward the front of the home. "Something to help JoJo when she was forgetful."

I climbed up the porch stairs, Marti and Michael close behind me. I pretended to look around, then pointed to the electric socket cover. "This is near the door." I flipped it open, and there it was.

Marti sucked in a breath. "Is that how the killer got inside?" She turned to Michael.

His eyes opened wide, brows riding high a few moments before his face relaxed. "I'm feeling pulled in different directions. Which means I've got another appointment to run to."

Marti looked at me. "He just got here."

"He works for us freelance."

Michael waved and jogged toward his bike.

"We were just getting warmed up!" Marti said.

"Let's finish our chat." I motioned for her to follow me toward the house. "About the antiques..."

"That's a sore subject among us remaining Means family members. Makes me go ballistic thinking about the...heirlooms...my parents left us. JoJo got rid of stuff without ever talking to Red or me. She took over Papa's coin collection, his stocks and bonds, and Mama's jewelry. JoJo had the nerve to say the hired hands must've stolen some furnishings and that Papa liquidated the stocks. Know what I think?" She jabbed her chest with her thumb. "She sold a bunch of it off and pocketed the cash."

"You and JoJo argued."

"You think?" She blew a curl out of her face and switched direction, marching toward the barn. "Once Mama got sick, JoJo moved in to help, temporarily, she said. Instead, she took over, never left, and convinced Mama to leave everything to her. It wasn't fair."

"Who paid for the upkeep of the ranch?"

"I'm done talking. Stresses me out."

I was willing to bet that JoJo paid the taxes and ranch expenses.

Marti picked up speed, then stopped to face me. "JoJo hardly ever invited us over. Heck, I hadn't been inside the place for nearly two years, until last week." She sniffled and wiped her nose with the back of a hand. "We always met at Hank's Place or had a picnic by the pond."

Marti paused near the barn and scooped up the little gray hen before heading toward her truck. "Coco's coming home with me." She stroked the feathers gently. "She's not happy here. Don't need a psychic to see that."

"That's a nice greenhouse out back. Somebody likes cacti." How was that for a safe topic?

She gathered her lips in a straight line. "They're euphorbia, not cacti. There's even an African milk tree in there. Watch out for those. They're dense and thorny."

"The greenhouse is locked."

"And now you know why."

I followed Marti to her truck. "JoJo must have loved visits from her nephew."

"Bart spent hours here with JoJo the past year. But there was a time he hardly came over." Marti opened the car door and inserted the hen in a small animal carrier on the passenger seat. "I'll text directions to my home. Seven sharp. Don't be late." She motored off and yelled out the window, "You might miss something important."

That was the most unhelpful potential client meeting I'd ever had. I had a mind to walk away right now. Except I had a party to attend, family members to meet, and a decision to make. We'd either take the case or walk away tonight.

Chapter Five

I heard Veera grumbling from the opposite end of the house. She sat cross-legged on white hexagonal tiles in JoJo's bathroom, eyeing toiletries inside a metal cabinet beneath the sink. I crouched next to her. "Find anything?"

"I'm creating a personality profile on JoJo. Besides being a perfectionist, an animal lover, and a boss of everyone, she was a compulsive labeler. Everything's labeled, with its own special location." Veera picked up a bottle of hand cream and sniffed it. "I'd never lose a thing if my bathroom looked like this."

"Who has the time to be so organized?" Besides my mom, that is. "Where's the challenge in that? We sharpen our investigative skills every time we hunt down that missing hairbrush or lipstick. It's an important life skill."

"Never looked at it that way." She put the lotion back on a tray. "Did Marti seem on edge to you?"

I headed into the bedroom. "She's got anger issues." Which made me wonder why it was so important for Marti to prove that JoJo's death wasn't natural? Could the psychic be the only reason? I opened the dresser drawers in the bedroom. Everything was neatly folded. Socks were clipped together; undergarments, pajamas, all in earthy tones. JoJo wasn't a fan of color.

"Her sister dies, she thinks somebody killed her, and she throws a party?" Veera joined me. "Who does that?"

I thought of the guilt trip again. "Maybe Marti's trying to make up for something. Or maybe she dotes on her psychic." I closed the drawers. "That's who's fueling this investigation. Unless there's a motive we're missing. Who inherits everything now that JoJo's gone?"

"That answer could land us right on the killer's doorstep," Veera said.

"If there's a killer." I took a spin around a small walk-in closet. Clothes were neatly hung and folded on a top shelf. Shoes rested in labeled plastic bins. A wicker hamper fit snugly in a corner, half filled with towels in hues of beige and brown.

Veera peered under the bed. "I don't like saying this only because it means we'll be out of work, but I don't smell foul play."

I told her about the cell phone and held out my palm. "There's this." The small brooch pin lay in the center.

"An old pin?" Veera peered closer.

"Found it in the living room last night." I turned it over with my fingers. "It's a conservationist pin from New York. I saw some like it on the Internet. Circa 1920."

"JoJo could've been an environmentalist, living on a ranch and all. I'll add nature lover to her personality profile."

"How do you know this belongs to JoJo?"

Veera sucked in a breath. "Does it belong to her killer?"

"Neatnik that she was, the odds favor this ending up on the floor after she was gone."

Veera's body quivered. "It's starting to smell foul in here." She ran her hands up her arms. Something knocked against the wall, and she stiffened. "You hear that?"

"Just an old pipe. Or it could be the house settling. This place is ancient." By Southern California standards, anyway.

"I've been hearing things."

"Like voices or things that creak?"

Veera tiptoed to the doorway and peered out. "Like bubbling and gurgling in the bathroom…"

"Air pressure in the pipes." I channeled Michael, who fixed up his parents' old home plenty of times.

"What about hissing noises from a faucet when the water's not on?"

"Leaky hose bib or the toilet needs fixing." I felt knowledgeable enough to be a guest on *This Old House*.

"Don't laugh, but there's something creepy about this house."

"Relax. It's because you know someone died just a few feet away, not necessarily from natural causes."

She stiffened. "I guess that could—"

A clanging interrupted our chat. Veera was on her feet and out of the room before I could point my finger. I reached the living room in time to see her rocket out the front door. I headed toward the kitchen. The noise came from the back of the house.

I flew outside and landed on the gravel. Not a two-legged creature in sight. I sprinted toward the front and froze midway. Metal pipes rose up from the ground, close to the side of the house. I knelt next to them. There was no sound coming from the pipes. I straightened and ran down the driveway. Veera waited near the road, doubled over and panting.

"Did you see anything?" Not that she could, running off like that.

Veera shook her head. "That wasn't no house settling. Sounded like an evil spirit dragging a chain around."

I had to agree. But there had to be some logical explanation. Was someone trying to spook us?

Chapter Six

It took more convincing than I'd thought to get Veera to venture back. "No one's inside the house, I promise. That knock came from outside and whoever it was didn't stick around. Follow me." The front door stood wide open. Veera had been in such a hurry to leave she hadn't bothered shutting it. "Probably kids or a neighbor." I told her about Gifty.

"An irate neighbor, I can accept. And bored teenagers get into all sorts of trouble. But if there's any ectoplasm—" She gripped her can of police-grade pepper spray. The kind that shoots out twelve feet and will burn the eyes out of the sockets. Not really, but it burned pretty badly.

"It's your brain misreading sensory cues, like bumps and knocks, and thinking it's a ghost."

"You're right. Sorry, C., for runnin' off like that. I don't usually scare so easily."

I patted her shoulder and waited outside while Veera walked in the door. "It's okay to be scared. It's not okay to stay scared." I sucked in a breath. "Wait a minute."

"Science and common sense are the real ghostbusters. I'm gonna fill up on those."

"Veera, go inside and close the door."

"By myself?"

"You'll have to trust me on this. You'll hear some noises like the ones you heard before. When you do, come join me on the side of the house." I tapped my finger in the air toward the side closest to the front door. "I'll be waiting with the ghost."

Veera's brows shot up, and her brown eyes widened.

I ran off to where I'd seen the exposed pipes and pulled a small wrench out of my purse. I banged against the metal. A loud clanging broke the quiet apart. Ten seconds later, Veera flew around the corner. I held up the wrench.

Her fingers pressed against her lips. "You mean someone hit the pipes with that thing?"

"Or something like it. Did it sound like your evil spirit?"

She nodded and pointed to the pipes. "Look at all those dents and scratches."

My gaze scanned our surroundings. "Plenty of hiding places to run away to."

Veera knelt next to me. "Maybe they're hiding out right now. Watching us."

We locked gazes.

"Someone's trying to spook us," I said. "Let's get back inside. I think I missed something." Something that didn't fit in.

We wound our way back as my insides tingled with anticipation. I headed for the hamper in the laundry room. It was full of clothes. "What's off in here?"

"There's no dirty laundry smell. Should be stinky by now."

"That's not where I was going, but you can add that to JoJo's personality profile." JoJo made Felix Unger look like a slob. I stuck in my gloved hand and pushed aside the laundry. I pointed to a small potpourri bag at the bottom filled with white powder. "Baking soda."

Veera leaned downward and squinted into the hamper. She pulled out a face towel stuffed midway. "Yellow? This towel is suspicious. Doesn't fit in with her neutral color scheme."

I gently removed the intruder. Every single piece of laundry was beige, brown, or white except for this one. "JoJo has a hamper just for towels in her bedroom closet. Why would this end up here?"

"It's not hers, which means she had a visitor," Veera said.

I headed toward the pantry near the back door. Veera joined me as I peered inside.

"Did you see a broom? It's missing." I pointed to the empty spot beneath the labels. "Wasn't in the trash. What do a yellow towel, a missing broom, and an old conservationist pin have in common?"

She snapped her fingers. "At least one should be a clue." Veera lifted her nose. "My logic-loving nose smells something."

I sniffed. "A barbecue." I opened the back door, and a frenzied barking sliced through the quiet. I hot-footed outside and around the corner of the house. Thick coils of black smoke puffed upwards, about 100 yards away. Veera trekked after me.

"Fire!" I jetted past her, back into the kitchen, and grabbed an extinguisher hanging in the pantry.

We raced toward the smoke. Flames shot out of a hefty woodpile burning in the pasture beyond the barn.

"Lord, I need reception!" Veera ran frantically around the pasture, cell phone in the air above her head.

A loud jangling drowned out the barking. When I reached the burn, I aimed the extinguisher nozzle low and squeezed. Thick whiteness spewed out, and a siren wailed. Within minutes, two fire officers had arrived and had everything under control.

"You okay?" Veera handed me an alcohol wipe.

I cleaned my face and hands. "Fine and dandy." Except that I smelled like I lived inside a chimney. A tiny price to pay to help put out the fire. I circled the scorched pile, eyeing the remains, and stopped halfway.

"Shouldn't get any closer, Miss," a fire officer said. "You've inhaled enough fumes for today."

"How'd you get here so fast?" Veera panted.

"A neighbor reported smoke. And our station doesn't see much action."

I pointed to a metal object in the pile. "What's that?"

He stepped closer and bent forward to examine the debris with a gloved hand. "Two wire rings and matching metal bands. Looks like copper rings from the neck of a broom. There are some bristles barely hanging on."

The hair rose along my arms. "JoJo's broom."

"Why's there a pile of branches and tree trimmings all stacked up?" Veera asked. "Is that what people do around here?"

"It's the beavers. Ever since this drought made the dam run dry, they've been making these piles."

Veera stared at him. "Did you say beavers?"

He snickered and stepped around the smoldering remains. "I'm joking. Residents make piles to burn. They get a permit, and they're good to go. It's cheaper than having the stuff hauled away."

"Was a permit pulled for this?" I knew the answer.

"Not yet."

"Are brooms often included in these piles?"

"Almost never." The officer removed his helmet and ran a hand along his crew cut. "Don't recall Ms. Means throwing one in before."

"What do you think started this fire?" Veera knelt by the edge of the burn.

"That'd be a question for a private arson investigator. Since there's no real damage, this won't be investigated. Excuse me, ladies." He walked back to the fire truck.

I pulled on a glove and zipped to the nearest tree. Veera appeared behind me.

"Are we looking for something?"

"A branch long and sturdy enough to lift the metal rings and bands out."

Within minutes, I'd fished out a piece of metal that belonged to a broom. The fire officer returned just as I'd dropped it on a pile of rocks to cool off. He pointed to the pile.

"Are you taking that?"

"It has sentimental value. It's all that's left of JoJo Means' favorite broom. Her family members would want this. Is that okay, Officer?"

"Totally." He turned back to the pile. "Hold on." He had his own tool for poking around the smoldering ashes: a steel fire hook. He picked out some more metal pieces and dropped them onto my pile. "These came from a special broom."

"They did?" Veera was as surprised as I was.

He nodded. "A handmade Japanese broom. The regional fire chief has one. Made of organic materials so it doesn't scratch any surface. New, it costs about two hundred bucks."

Veera and I traded glances.

"Any idea of where we could buy one around here?" I asked.

"You can't. Check online." He stomped off.

Veera turned to me. "You think there'll be some kind of DNA on the broom's metal parts?"

"Not likely. But this broom has a background we might use." I didn't know how yet, but I was positive the remains could help us clear some mental cobwebs.

We waited a while for the metal to cool and dropped the pieces in a cloth bag Veera kept rolled up into her purse. We turned toward the ranch.

"We should go door-to-door and ask neighbors questions the police would ask if this was an active murder or arson case," Veera said.

"Brilliant."

We hit the road leading to JoJo's house. The first two homes showed no signs of life, but the next one seemed inviting. A guy in the driveway whistled a cheery tune while washing his Range Rover. He was dressed in shorts and a collared polo shirt. His baseball cap was pushed back to reveal an aggressive tan line. His forehead was pale, while a deep tan covered the rest of his face.

I marched up with a smile. "Aren't you that professional athlete?" It was a wild guess on my part, but a tan like that doesn't happen to an average Joe.

He grinned and tossed his towel onto the hood. "Patrick Moon. Just won the Toyota Tournament of Champions. I'm ranked fifty-seventh in the world." His brow arched, and his eyes darted between us, awaiting our reactions. "That's big, in case you don't know."

Veera and I oohed and awed over that worthy achievement. Now, if we only knew what sport? I cut a glance inside his garage. It overflowed with golf clubs and wire buckets brimming with small white balls. A tricked-out golf cart in spiffy blue parked in its own space.

"Do you have a minute to chat about the fire today? We're friends of the Means family."

"Called the fire department as soon as I saw the smoke." His smile shrunk. "Sorry about JoJo. I feel really sad about her." He pulled off his cap and hung his head for a moment before slowly lifting his chin back up. "What do you want to talk about?"

"Do you know how the fire started?" Veera asked.

"Why do you ask?"

"Since the fire was on the Means Well Ranch property, we're trying to figure that out," I replied.

"Okay. Not sure, though." He scratched his cheek. "I was on my putting green."

"Did you hear any unusual noises a little earlier today?" Veera flicked a look at me.

"Can't say that I did." He replaced his cap and retrieved his towel. "I will say that I've seen people on the road lately that don't look familiar. I know the faces that live here."

Veera and I perked up.

"How long have you been seeing these…strangers?" I crossed my fingers that his observation skills were as sharp as Hank's.

"Over the past month, maybe longer. Started when I picked up the mail one day. A guy walked up the street. Thought it was a tourist checking out the homes. A lot of people from L.A. want to move here, you know." He pulled his cap lower. "Saw him twice since then."

"The same person?" Veera asked.

He stared at her a few beats before nodding. "It was his hat. That's something I notice."

"What kind and what color?" Time to put Patrick Moon to the test.

"Black baseball cap. Golf caps usually have fewer ventilation holes." He grinned. "Hey, you two play golf?"

Veera stared at me.

"I've golfed." In high school for a full semester. I wasn't half bad. "It's a mental game."

He nodded in understanding. "Attitude is everything."

"It always is."

We bumped fists, and I handed him a business card. We hurried toward the ranch.

"Hold it!" He jogged toward us.

Veera and I put on the brakes. Did he remember something significant?

"Yes?" I prompted him.

He slapped my card against his palm. "Since you're a P.I., I should give you a better description."

I liked the sound of that. "We're listening."

"The man's skin looked kind of tanned, brownish, and his nose was large, Jimmy Durante style. His brows were really bushy. He was a funny-looking dude."

"Did you ask the neighbors about him?" Sounded like a unique fellow. One that would be hard to forget.

"Nah. We usually talk golf."

"Thanks." I turned to walk away and paused, facing him again. "Do you have a Japanese broom? It's handmade with soft bristles."

"No, but it sounds sweet."

I gave him a small wave and walked away. "Call if you recall anything else."

Veera and I didn't talk till we reached the road.

"The yellow towel, the conservationist pin…how do we find out if these are real clues?" Veera asked. "And is the guy in the black cap related to what happened at Means Well?"

"Maybe."

We made it back to JoJo's, and I stepped into the kitchen, Veera close behind.

"We've got to make tonight's shindig count," I said.

"If we go around asking too many questions, people might clam up."

"Not if our resident seer Michael asks." I texted Michael about the broom and the fire.

"He'll ask, while we can watch their reactions."

Too many things didn't add up, even if there was a perfectly logical explanation. "We'll make this gig work for us, even if no crime was committed."

"How's that gonna happen?"

"We prove to Marti her psychic is taking advantage of her."

"Which'll either make her happy or real mad."

"Let's focus on the happy."

Chapter Seven

I stabbed the accelerator and zipped past walled-in estates lit up just enough to allow glimpses of massive homes hidden behind shields of well-tended shrubbery. Draping branches from feathery pepper trees hung over the edges of the road, creating a second shield. Darkness tucked itself between the glimmering homes. Marti lived near Westlake Village, fifteen minutes south of Los Ranchos. A smallish city, Westlake had its own championship golf course, luxury hotels, and big box retail stores.

"Destination coming up on the right." Veera stared down at the map on her phone screen. "We'll be right on time."

I eased my foot off the pedal.

"Still can't figure out what kind of party Marti has in mind." Veera fidgeted in her seat and perked up. "Hope they pass around hors d'oeuvres. If you notice me and an appetizer tray missing, that won't be a coincidence." She applied peach-tinted lip gloss and smacked her lips while staring in the small mirror of my car's sun visor. The mirror light still worked despite the grumbles of my twelve-year-old BMW.

"Don't you dare go MIA without me. Especially if food's involved." Mom snapped on the backseat light and pulled out a compact. She'd insisted on joining us tonight to watch our backs. She was all decked out in photo-shoot-ready makeup and a dress that would cause a stampede of shoppers if it went on sale: a black, knee-length number paired with a shawl made of gold chains and rings. Her feisty red lipstick was applied with the precision of a diamond cutter. She'd learned the tricks of the fashion trade when she worked as a buyer in a high-end department store.

I caught her gaze in the rear-view mirror. "You're supposed to disappear in the background tonight, remember?" Why did I think that bringing her along spelled trouble? After all, as part of our PI staff…correction, the only member of our support staff…she added legitimacy to our fledgling operation. At fifty-five, she was close to Marti's age group, making us twenty-somethings more relatable and trustworthy. Plus, Mom proved herself useful on our last gig.

"Fading in the background doesn't come easily to me, honey," Mom said.

"You know that's true." Veera beamed back at Mom. "She's got getting-people-to-talk skills."

"Aw, thank you, sweetie." She patted Veera on the shoulder. "I can spot a phony a mile away. I'll let you know if the psychic is the real deal."

"There's no such thing as psychics." How many times did I have to remind her? "They make vague predictions about subjects people like to talk about, like money, romance, and work. Give a psychic enough detail, and they'll pull something together that sounds legit, but isn't."

Mom leaned toward Veera. "She's always been a skeptic. Got that from her father. She never believed in Santa or fairy tales, either. Not even unicorns, which were real, by the way."

"No, they weren't." Veera cranked her neck toward Mom.

"They lived in Siberia and ate tons of grass. Which explains why they went extinct during the Ice Age. Michael told me all about them."

Michael's trivia expertise was well known, but why did he have to share that tidbit with Mom? "When we agreed that you'd play a part in our new agency, remember what we put in your contract?"

"Of course I do. My job is to provide support as needed."

"What else does it say?"

"My personal memories of little Corrie won't be shared unless they are relevant to the case, which this is."

I wasn't even going to ask.

"You shouldn't be so skeptical before dipping your big toe in mystical waters."

"She's right about that." Veera beamed even more brightly. "We're all about opening minds and encouraging loose lips."

"The contract said no personal stuff. Period." I'd gone from simmer to boiling.

Veera pointed. "There. Marti's crib."

I screeched to a halt by a stone pillar and eyed a ranch-style home. More modest than the surrounding estates, it lacked the high hedges, walls, and wrought iron entry gate, which made easing onto the circular driveway a cinch. I cut the engine. "Why's the house so dark?" Where was the party?

Only two nondescript cars were parked in front.

"Maybe everyone's out in the yard." Veera straightened the skirt of her sapphire blue cocktail dress. "Could be a barbecue. Are those ribs I smell?"

"The quiet reflects the somber occasion. They're calling it a party, but it's really about remembering a loved one." Mom stuck her head between us.

"As long as they serve alcohol, we're fine," Veera said. "We've got a whole lotta questions that need answering."

We stepped into the lavender-scented night. A light mist moistened my cheeks from sprinklers whirling on all sides, spreading the velvety scent of freshly mowed lawn.

"Are you sure we're not early?" Mom's shoes matched her crimson lips, adding more pizzazz to her black ensemble.

There was an unsettling quiet that even the roar of traffic from the 101 freeway couldn't quell. Why did I have the feeling that something fishy was going on inside the house? "I'm having second thoughts." I stepped toward the car.

"What do you mean?" Veera backtracked with me.

"If we start out by taking hocus pocus cases, what's that going to do for our reputation?" We had a backer to consider. We'd impressed a VIP enough during our last investigation to convince her to invest in our fledgling agency. Now, all we had to do was keep on convincing her with our stellar work. "We don't want our investor to withdraw her support."

"You've got a point, but look at this place." Veera's hands swept upward. "If we get this job, our client can afford our services, which means we'll get paid. Besides, there could be more to JoJo's death. You said it yourself."

"That was before I realized no other P.I. would bother with an investigation involving the spirit world. We need a real case." I sniffed… had Veera imagined the food smells? "Marti's up to something."

Mom took my arm. "Isn't that what you love about investigating? Uncovering the truth? One way or another, you're going to discover what's going on. You always do."

"We'll connect the dots until it turns into a shape we recognize." Veera moved in closer. "There could be criminals in this house."

"All right." I hustled to the trunk of my car and popped it open. "What kind of P.I.s would we be if we didn't at least take a look around?" I rummaged around a cardboard box, extra shoes, sweaters…

"That's my girl." Mom squeezed my arm. "I'm sensing a low-key event, with just a few people, all somehow related to the murder victim."

"We don't know if there was a murder." No matter how many times I explained something to Mom, she always came up with her own set of facts.

"Maybe you could be the assistant to the staff psychic," Veera told Mom. "You'd be good at it."

I cut Veera a glance so hard it nicked her gold hoops.

Veera turned serious. "On second thought, we need you more as the voice of maturity."

Mom waved a hand at Veera and giggled. "I'll just be my usual sensible self."

When I agreed to hire my mother as the agency receptionist-slash-assistant, I didn't expect her to have such high ambitions like joining our investigations. But I had to admit, she had a spring in her step these days.

I finished rummaging around the trunk and pulled out a small cloth bag. "Focus and follow me."

"What's in the bag?" Veera asked.

"A little something for the psychic."

Chapter Eight

We crouched behind hydrangea bushes as we inched closer to Marti's house. Large, glossy leaves and blue floral balls gathered together to give us cover. Still no sign of a party, but a dim light glowed from within the house. The oversized glass entry door made it easy to spot the silhouette of a woman peering out from the foyer.

I marched up and knocked, Veera and Mom at my heels.

"Even if there isn't a party, I'll pass out some of our P.I. business cards to whoever shows up." Veera whipped out a small leather cardcase.

She and Mom shared a high-five.

The door opened just enough for a slice of a face with a round blue eye to peer through. Marti widened the gap and stepped back. "Come in, already."

A polka dot hair wrap restrained her blonde curls. The wide-legged pants of a white suit practically swallowed her pumps. Somewhere between fifty and seventy, she seemed like the type of woman without a shelf life. She rolled her gaze over me.

"You don't look like you've had enough experience investigating suspicious deaths."

Veera stepped forward. "Have you seen her resume? Have you read the headlines about what she did for that major Hollywood actress at Ameripictures Film Studios? And what about the Lakers player? He had a murder charge hanging over his head."

"I didn't mean—"

"Just so we're clear." Veera turned to me and spoke out of the side of her mouth. "We should include that information on our brochures."

"What I'm trying to say is…" Marti gave Veera a sideways frown and took a step closer to me. "Tonight's important. It could change the course of my life."

Botox had already changed the course of her life by playing a heavy hand in her looks, as did other beauty secrets that were beyond my reach and not needed in my still youthful twenty-six years. "I'm here to determine if there's a crime to solve."

"That's what I'm saying." Marti cocked her head. "The last P.I. didn't get that at all."

Her sister died less than a week ago. How many P.I.s had Marti been talking to?

"We're not like other investigators," Veera said. "We know what we're doing."

Marti pointed to Veera and stared at me. "Who's she again?"

I didn't need to see Veera to know she was smiling. The warmth lit up my bare arms. "Veera Bankhead, my go-to associate P.I., and this is…" I gestured toward Mom. "…she's the…"

"Head of quality control." Mom put out a fist, which Marti bumped with her own. "Victoria."

How did Mom know Marti was a fist bumper?

Mom stepped past me into the wood-paneled foyer. "You have a lovely home."

Veera stuck her neck out and looked around. She whispered to me, "Think the party's underground?"

"Hate to break this to you, but it's not looking like a party." I followed Mom with Veera close behind.

"Where's your psychic?" Marti stared out the entry door.

"On his way…" Michael was running late.

"Part of my skill set is reading people and predicting behavior," Veera told Marti. "I can tell you're going to show us where the other guests are, so let's not waste any more time."

Marti scurried past to take the lead, frowning some more. "This way."

The whole house was dimly lit and library-quiet. Double-height ceilings lifted and opened the dark wood foyer. Metal sculptures livened up the walls. As Marti swaggered past a white orchid arrangement sitting in a bed of moss, I darted closer to her.

"Did your sister have a special broom?"

She slowed and turned to look at me over her shoulder. "Is that a trick question? What makes a broom special?"

"Not all broom bristles are created equally." Mom widened her eyes at me and nodded before pushing past.

"How would I know that?" Marti picked up her pace. "My broom's from Home Depot."

As we trailed her along the wide corridor, I caught my reflection in a rustic wall mirror. Silver drop earrings glinted at my ears; my longish, dark hair fell in its usual casual mess around my shoulders, and my floral print dress held up pretty well. Not too shabby tonight. I hurried to catch up, but an open door made me pause. I wandered inside.

The paneled room was comfortably furnished and lit by a small antique lamp on a mahogany writing desk. Shelves along one wall housed gardening books. *The Expert Flower Gardener's Handbook, Flower Power from Seeds.* A silver-framed photograph on the top shelf displayed a smiling Marti, not the uptight, forced smile she'd flashed at me, but a genuine, full-blown one, like she was actually happy. She sat in a garden with blossoms of tall, purplish-blue flowers behind her.

"What do you think you're doing?" Marti stood behind me. Her brows fell so low they nearly crushed her eyelids.

"I can't resist a bookshelf." I shrugged and filed past her.

She shut the door and took the lead once more toward a spacious, step-down living room with high beamed ceilings. A used brick fireplace hosted candles in different shapes and sizes.

"How many people are you expecting tonight?" Where was everyone?

Marti drifted off to the right and skipped down a few more steps. "Enough for us to get somewhere."

What did that mean?

Veera tugged my sleeve and whispered, "We need to take control of whatever she has planned."

"You can count on that." I wasn't worried. It's the little surprises in investigations that sharpened our case-cracking skills.

The doorbell rang just as we entered a shadowy, octagonal-shaped room.

"Pick out a chair, and I'll be back straightaway." Marti jogged up the short staircase.

Three occupants lounged around a large, oval table in the sparsely furnished room. Curtains shut out stray moonbeams. Mom pushed past me with a grin that provided more lighting than the flickering candles on the hearth.

"Hello, I'm Victoria. How are you doing? Nice night, isn't it?" Mom made the rounds, shaking everyone's hand like a seasoned politician. If there was a baby present, she probably would have kissed it.

"This definitely is not a party," Veera whispered.

Veera was right. It looked gloomy. No flowers, no photos, just a few wooden chairs along mostly empty walls. This room was set off from the rest of the house like it had been an afterthought.

"What's that earthy smell?" Veera sniffed. "It's like sittin' in a forest."

"Cedarwood. It's the flooring." A bearish man stood, showcasing thick brows and a no-nonsense, eighties-style mustache that buried his upper lip. He wore the same frown as Marti. Must be a Means family trademark. "The scent reminds me of freshly sharpened pencils and woodworking. I taught shop in the local high schools. Redmond Means. Only brother of the deceased."

He had the voice of a surly cab driver who growled out of the corner of his mouth. His dour expression matched his tone. He'd left the messages on JoJo's answering machine telling JoJo she'd be sorry if she pulled out. Pulled out of what?

"Were you and JoJo close?" I asked.

"About as close as a wasp is to a honey bee. If there's enough food for both, they get along fine." Red sank into his chair, scraping the legs against the floor as he pulled it closer to the table. He cleared his throat and scrolled through his cell phone, helping himself to salted peanuts from a glass dish on the table. "Bart, you got anything to add?" Red lifted his chin toward a wiry, muscly guy. "Meet my nephew."

Bart's loose, tan T-shirt and khaki pants would easily camouflage him in a wheat field, as would his hair. His longish locks were the same shade as toasted oats. JoJo's color scheme had obviously rubbed off on him. Mid-thirties or so, his clean-shaven face was grainy and rough. He wore the telltale Means grimace.

"There's a lot riding on tonight." He twirled his index finger upward. "Watch out for all the emotional baggage floating around. If you're not careful, you'll get hit when one drops."

I should've worn a helmet. "Good to know." Bart had also left a message on JoJo's answering machine about calling her soon. Were they here to read JoJo's will tonight? Maybe Marti wanted us close by, in case things went south.

My mother approached a woman not much older than me and extended a hand. They shook briefly. Cinnamon-hued hair was pulled back in a loose, low bun. A daisy was tucked behind her ear. The sleeves of her white, billowy shirt were rolled up to her elbows like she was ready to get down to business. A snake tattoo slithered up her arm as she slouched low in a velvet armchair.

"You work in the fashion industry," she told Mom.

"Oh, brother," I whispered to Veera. It wasn't hard to figure out who the supernatural poser was at the table. "And she calls herself a psychic." Mom's bio was on the Nightingale Investigations website.

Heidi's gaze never left Mom's face. "Correction. You *worked* in the fashion industry."

Mom's smile broadened, and she tapped her finger in the air as she spoke each word, "You are good."

Heidi's stare flicked to me. "I'm Heidi Honeyman."

I pushed my way forward. "I'm skeptical."

"Nice to meet you, Detective Corrie Locke." Her thin brow arched, and her lips curled into a grin.

"I'm a private investigator," Let's see if she'd caught on to the fact that I wasn't even official yet, "not a police detective."

"Same difference."

Silence stretched between us as we sized each other up.

"You're going to believe in my abilities by the time you solve the case," Heidi said.

"You're going to need a new job description by the time I'm done with you."

"We're gonna help Marti, one way or another." Veera sat and pulled out a chair next to hers. I claimed it, and Mom took the seat on my other side.

"Where's your medium?" Heidi asked.

"Our man's handling another assignment at a prestigious college. He'll be here." Veera pulled out a pen and small notepad. "I'm Corrie's associate, Veera Bankhead. I'll take detailed notes until he arrives."

Heidi chuckled. "Why would a medium worth his chops need anyone to take notes?"

"They're not for him. They're for me to analyze your every word to make sure you're on the up and up. I'm like a human lie detector."

"I'll be sure to throw in a lie or two and see if you catch on."

"Are you saying psychics don't lie?" I asked.

"I'm a medium, not a psychic." Heidi draped a leg over the arm of her chair. "A clairvoyant, you might say."

"What's the difference?" Veera asked.

"I'm a channel to help connect people with lost, loved ones."

"She's a psychic," I told Veera.

"I don't predict or see into the future. I tune into frequencies and pass on messages."

"Heidi is like a ham radio operator." Red jumped into the conversation.

I tapped my fingers along the tabletop.

"It's not a hobby. It's a calling." Heidi's gaze turned into slits.

Veera and I exchanged eye-rolls on the sly.

"You should know, being clairvoyant and all, that Corrie is the best P.I. in all of Southern California, and she's a pretty good lawyer, too." Veera switched on a smile. "She doesn't need to tune into frequencies to get answers."

"Think of me as a wellness coach, okay? Not as a connection to the supernatural." Heidi leaned back in her chair. "All I did was help Marti tune into her intuition." She turned toward me. "That's when it hit her that there was more to JoJo's death. You need to prove that so the police get involved."

"How did you and Marti meet?" Mom asked.

"The spirit world led me to her," Heidi replied as if it was a common occurrence in her life.

"As next of kin, Marti can request an autopsy," I said. Why hadn't she done that already?

"She can't." Red's bloodshot eyes swung between us. "Our dear departed sister signed a certificate of religious objection prior to checking out. Who knew?"

"Aunty Jo couldn't stand the thought of being cut up in some lab," Bart said. "She said she was no lab rat."

"Rats have no conscience, no compassion, no consideration for others. They exist for themselves. In that sense, JoJo was like a lab rat." Red's grim expression never once shifted.

"That's cruel, Uncle Red." A deeper frown spread across Bart's features. "You may not have gotten along, but she loved you. All of you." He looked around the room.

"I doubt she loved us," Veera muttered. "Seeing as we'd never met."

Bart buried his face in his hands and let out a sob.

"No disrespect intended." Veera got up and patted him gently on the back, like she was trying to lull a baby to sleep.

"Sorry, I'm late." Michael hovered in the doorway. "I wanted to be sure I made an entrance." He flipped his hands out in a ta-da! flourish. His boyish grin made the rounds, but only his team members responded. The rest of the audience remained stone-faced. "I'll just…" he pulled out a chair, "sit over here." His navy and white bandana print shirt over jeans practically made him a psychic hipster.

He caught my stare, and his eyebrows jumped up and down. The brow thing was his way of telling me he was wearing his psychic hat.

Marti swept into the room, loose curls covering half her face. "Is everybody ready?"

"For what?" I asked.

Marti huffed. "For the séance, of course."

Veera jerked upright. "Séance? Didn't you say this was a party?"

"That's not till after we contact JoJo's spirit. There'll be time to socialize later."

This was not what I'd signed up for. I stood. "I'd love to stay and chat with the spirits, but I just remembered another appointment, with the living."

Mom grabbed my arm. "Hold on. I've got something to say."

Chapter Nine

"I 've always wanted to attend a séance." Mom placed a hand over her chest like she was about to recite the Pledge of Allegiance. "Ever since that *I Love Lucy* episode where Ethel poses as a fortune teller to contact a cocker spaniel. Did you see that one?" She gazed around.

Red nodded.

Mom turned to Heidi. "Are you psychopathic?" Mom's chuckles filled every corner of the room. She slapped my arm. "That's what Lucy called Ethel. Funny, huh?" Her laughter shriveled as she shifted under Marti's scathing stare. "A little levity never hurts. What I really want to say is that we're an open-minded investigative agency that provides exceptional services to our clients by employing the most innovative methods available. Investigating the spirit world and attending séances fall right under 'innovative'." She ended with a big nod.

Red's grumpy giggles stole the attention away from my mother. Meanwhile, I contemplated running out the door non-stop until I got to the nearest ice cream shop so I could banana split and chocolate sundae my way to sweet oblivion. I talked myself out of it when I realized I'd miss a chance to unmask the phony occult-world operator. As much as Marti caught me off guard with the séance, it would be the perfect opportunity to show Heidi what I carried in the bag I'd brought tonight. "Let's proceed."

Veera raised her brows, but flashed a nod.

Heidi cleared her throat. "Here are the ground rules in order to speak to the spirit world." A bossier, sterner, Heidi took turns giving each of us the stink eye. "No shouting, no yelling, no rudeness, no applause until afterward, understand? Watch what you say. We don't want angry spirits, trust me."

"What are they going to do, make our heads spin?" A corner of Red's lip tugged upward.

Like Mom, he regarded the séance as a comedy show, where jokes and peanuts flowed freely. He scooped up a bunch more and tossed them into his mouth.

"Spirits are not playthings, brother. Take this seriously, or leave my house." Marti's stare was so sharp it nearly sliced Red in two.

"I want to talk to JoJo just like you do, Marti." He spoke between chewing. "See how she's doing, find out if she needs anything, and ask where Daddy stashed his LeMat revolvers. Those babies can fetch twenty-K these days."

Marti tossed a beige and white shawl on the table, which fell in line with JoJo's favorite color scheme. "This will help bring JoJo here tonight."

"Will there be any table-tilting?" Bart asked. "I hear that's what happens at séances."

Was he serious?

Marti shot him a killer look. She got up, blew out all the candles, and took her seat.

"Cell phones off." Heidi nestled deeper into her chair and extended her hands onto the table, palms downward.

"Shouldn't we be holding hands?" Mom asked.

"We can raise energy without hand-holding," Michael replied. "Positive attitudes are all that's needed." He closed his eyes and settled into mystical mode.

"That's the spirit." Marti slapped her palms on the table. "Let's get down to business." As she lifted her chin, her eyes rolled back so that only the whites showed.

"That's what I call spooky." Veera stared at Marti.

"Quiet. Let your hands rest lightly on the tabletop. No finger or foot tapping. Deep breaths." Heidi's posture was relaxed, but her fox-like gaze rested on Michael. She didn't want anyone stealing her thunder. "Let's close our eyes and free our minds of mental noise. Focus on JoJo Means. Beautiful, loving, kind JoJo. Beloved sister and aunt to family present tonight. Family that deeply misses her."

Someone snorted. I didn't need to sneak a peek to know the snort belonged to Red.

"JoJo Means, won't you join us?" Heidi murmured in a low drawl like she'd had one too many mint juleps. "You left this earthly plane far too soon. By whose hand? We want to right that terrible wrong. We have professionals here who can help us find out what really happened."

"You know that's right," Veera whispered.

"JoJo, are you with us?"

Silence filled the stuffy room. I opened my eyes. The darkness was so complete I couldn't even see the tabletop. It was like sitting in a cave.

Minutes ticked by, and the table started to shake. Someone's knee was bouncing up and down. The thump of a slap sounded, and the shaking stopped.

"Who's there? I feel a presence." Heidi blew out a slow breath. "A strong female presence. I see short, gingery hair. But why are there tears?" A few beats of quiet passed. "What's that? She's…talking a mile a minute." Heidi paused a few beats. "She says she's sorry."

"Sounds like JoJo," Red muttered. "Except for that last part. Never heard her apologize before."

"Shh!" Marti said.

"There's something in the ranch house," Heidi spoke up, "something she wants you to find."

"Wants who to find?" Mom asked.

"Her!" A loud, breathy voice whooshed through the room. "Her!"

Veera jumped in her seat. So did Mom.

I flashed my penlight. A light scent of garlic pricked the air.

"Who was that?" Mom asked. "Why does it smell like a pizza parlor?"

Everyone spoke at once, and I shined my light around the room. Heidi's shaking hands gripped the table, and she panted. Her billowy sleeves were no longer rolled up.

"Where's Michael?" He wasn't in his seat.

"Over here." He popped up from behind his chair. "I was so blown away by the ghostly voice, I fell out of my seat. What just happened?"

Heidi stared out into space. "Spirits work in mysterious ways."

What was Michael up to?

"Are we done?" Red's frown upped a few notches.

Marti was re-lighting the candles. "Not nearly." She turned to Heidi. "Can you pull yourself together? What needs to be found, and who does JoJo want to find it?"

"Well, it's obvious who JoJo meant," my mother said.

"It is?" Marti and Veera asked simultaneously.

"Oh no," I mumbled. "Mom…"

Mom pointed to me. "She's 'her.'"

"Mother!" It was all I could do to keep from grabbing her hand and pulling her out of the house.

"Corrie will find out what really happened to your sister faster than you can say—"

"Heidi needs a drink," Marti said.

* * *

It took some air freshener, a glass of water, and a jigger of tequila, which I discovered is equal to about five ounces of the gold liquid, to revive Heidi out of her stupor. She hiccupped and swayed. A dim light glowed from a brass lamp.

"This is good stuff," she said with a goofy smile.

Marti started to pour another half-jigger.

Michael slid his hand between the glass and the bottle. "That's best sipped while admiring a backyard sunset, not while conducting a séance. Let's handle business while we've got the spirit world on the line." He closed his eyes and threw out a question, "JoJo, what happened to your favorite broom?"

"What's with the broom?" Marti muttered as she took her seat and closed her eyes.

"I'm getting something," Michael said.

Heidi's wide-open gaze was on him.

"I sense frustration combined with sadness and a hint of regret. The broom was destroyed in a fire. Recently."

"Is that true?" Marti's mumbling rose.

Heidi scrolled through her phone while Michael spoke. So much for her psychic abilities.

"Wait!" She jumped in, tucking her phone away and closing her eyes. "I see flames at Means Well Ranch. The fire was no accident. Brave firefighters extinguished it this afternoon. JoJo's sadness is because she watched her special broom burn. Someone deliberately set it on fire."

"What could possibly make a broom special?" Red asked.

"It traveled a long distance to reach her," Michael said.

"Possibly from the Orient," Heidi added.

Veera clicked her tongue. We both knew that Heidi had read about the fire on the Internet. She must've heard about the broom from someone in the family.

"I have two questions for Heidi." I moved closer to her. "Did JoJo get a new cell phone recently?"

Bart raised his hand. "She did. We bought the phone together three weeks ago."

I slipped back to my seat. "Where is it?"

Bart shrugged. "In her purse, maybe."

"Heidi, where's her purse?" The only handbags in the ranch house were in JoJo's closet, empty.

Heidi's shoulders sagged slightly, and her lips bunched. "No one in the spirit world is responding."

I leaned across the table and pushed the bag I'd brought toward her. "What does JoJo have to say about what's in this bag?"

Heidi hiccupped and removed a cream-colored half apron. She held it up by the edges. Small blue flowers were embroidered along the hem. Something Mrs. Cleaver might have donned when baking brownies for Beaver. "Strange looking skirt."

"It's an apron." I'd borrowed it from the props department at Ameripictures just for tonight.

"It's darling. Looks like it's straight from the fifties." Mom examined the sheer organza baking apron.

One look at Heidi told me she was done for the night. To make it easy on her, I helped her out. "I found it in Grandma's attic and felt an instant connection. Can you give me a reading on it?" A section of the film studio props department was called Granny's Attic, so it wasn't really a lie. It's where all vintage movie items were stored.

Heidi stared up at me. "Like I said, I don't do readings…"

"I'll do it." Michael reached out a hand.

"…but I'll try to connect to a spirit." Just like I'd thought. Heidi wasn't keen on competition. She pulled the apron closer and gently rubbed the fabric against her chin. She closed her eyes and sighed, blowing out a deep breath. "Yes, yes. I see. Makes perfect sense." She gazed at me. "You are connected to this piece. It represents who you were, in a former life." Her gaze swept the room before landing on me. "A scullery maid."

Oh, brother. Although it would explain why I loathed cleaning up after myself.

"*What* kind of maid?" Veera asked.

"The lowest female worker in old English manor homes," Bart replied. "The one who did the grunt work and kept out of sight of the nobility." He gazed around the table. "What? I watched *Downton Abbey*."

Heidi handed the apron back to me. "You should know that you were skilled at your job, which brought you immense joy."

"Sounds just like me," I said.

"What about the message from JoJo?" Marti asked Heidi. "What does she want our P.I. to do?"

Heidi rubbed her temples like she was warding off a tension headache. "That's all, folks. The connection's gone."

"You can't just stop like that," Veera said.

"I stop when the spirits do, and they called it a night."

Inwardly, I shook my head at breakneck speed. Someone was putting on a cheap show for a gullible audience. "With so many spirits around, you'd think one would be willing to put in some overtime."

Heidi slowly turned my way. She gave me a sad smile. "Messages from the other side don't work that way. They come in bits and pieces and… tender morsels. I don't think you understand what a major effort it is to communicate such a long distance." She turned to Michael. "Tell her."

He put a finger to his temple and shut his eyes. "I'm seeing the main house at Means Well Ranch. It needs to be searched more thoroughly by everyone present tonight at the same time."

"I'm not going inside that house." Marti crossed her arms.

"We'll come with you," Veera said. "We'll form a human shield against any loud, creaky noises or big old spiders. Plenty of those in there."

Marti looked alarmed about the prospect. "You don't understand." She chewed on a nail. "That place is haunted."

"Looks like we'll need an exorcist." Red gobbled up more peanuts.

Chapter Ten

"I need a drink. A whole pitcher of drinks." Marti headed for the exit. "Follow me, everyone."

I didn't budge while the rest of the gang made their exit. Everyone except Heidi, that is. She hovered by the doorway and regarded me like I was a hamster trying to escape its cage. When we were the only ones left, she plodded over and spoke through clenched teeth,

"Asking about the apron skirt from your granny wasn't funny."

"It wasn't?"

"You're playing games when you should be finding JoJo's killer. You don't have to believe in me to investigate her murder."

"Where did that voice come from?"

"The spirit world."

"Come on." I admired how her hair stayed put together, every loose strand in place. Wish I could get my hair to behave that way.

"You have to teach it to obey," Heidi said.

"What?"

"Your hair." Her light stare mocked me. "It's plentiful and thick, but it won't cooperate with you, am I right?"

If she was trying to impress me, it wasn't working. She obviously noticed my gaze on her hair. My stare flicked to her hands. "You should practice playing the guitar more often."

She waved her fingers. "Big wow. You saw the calluses on my fingertips." She stepped closer. "You're not afraid of a little friendly competition, are you?"

"As long as it doesn't involve people trying to best each other."

"I'm trying to help you."

Why was she so eager to help? I opened the curtain facing the yard. Mom, Red, and Michael mingled around a brick patio overlooking a circular pool. A yellow and white awning hung over an outdoor bar. I dug into my purse and pulled out my cell phone. I turned to Heidi.

"Let me see your driver's license."

"What for?"

"To see if you're who you say you are."

She reached into the pocket of her jeans and pulled out a slender bag, just wide enough to hold business cards and loose change. She flashed me her license. "Don't feel bad. Even my own parents don't believe in me."

"Smart parents."

"Are we done?"

I took a photo of her license with my phone. "Why did you become a psychic?"

"Because," she said, "I simply couldn't be anything else." She grabbed a slouchy velvet bag from a chair and headed for the door. "Even the police use clairvoyants."

"There's not a single documented case of a missing person ever found by a psychic, dead or alive."

"You can try to shake me up all you want, but you'll discover I'm a medium, not a can of soda."

Dad had used psychics on occasion, but only because they'd approached him with clues that never panned out.

"We're more alike than you think." Heidi relaxed her shoulders. "This is where I pass the baton to you, daughter of famous private investigator Monty Locke."

I clicked my tongue. She sure spent a lot of time on the Internet.

Heidi walked to the door and whirled around to face me. "I'm a Bogart fan myself."

My favorite movie, *The Maltese Falcon*, was listed on my Instagram account. "Is that the best you can do?"

"I haven't even started." She turned on her high-heeled wedges and left the room.

What was up with Heidi? Had Marti paid her a tidy sum to find out what happened to JoJo? It was just a matter of time before I exposed her carnival sideshow act. Meanwhile, I needed to tone down my cynicism. It clouded my mind.

I mulled over my next move. I was itching to question someone. Marti? Red? Or Bart? Where was Michael?

"Corrie?" Michael filled the doorway. "You'd better let me iron that apron before you return it to the props department."

"What?" I'd twisted the organza so tightly in my hands, I could have threaded it through a needle. I shook it out. "Heidi says she knew I was conning her about finding this in Granny's attic."

He threw his hands up. "Of course she did. With your background working at a movie studio and your obvious suspicion of her powers, she knew you'd toy with her."

"And she toyed with me right back." I should've anticipated that. "Next time, I'll hit her from left field."

"I can help with that." He moved in and whispered so close, his lips brushed mine, his breath was sweet and saucy. "During the séance, I kind of took a detour."

"Like you mentally checked out?"

"Like I crawled under the table with a tiny flashlight in my mouth."

"How much crawling?" I did feel something brush against my leg.

"Very little, actually." He flashed a picture-perfect grin. "I lay on my back, mostly watching Heidi's knees."

"Really?" I wasn't sure I liked that.

"Taped above her right knee was a small remote-control button."

I sucked in a breath. "Of course." Why didn't I think of that? I linked my hand with his. "The voice. She pressed a button and had a speaker nearby with a recording."

He gave a slow nod and took over the chair where Heidi had been sitting. "I'd say she used a USB mic, EQ, compression, and some light RXing."

"I love it when you talk nerdy to me." I moved closer to him.

"Did I tell you that you look especially pretty tonight?" He kissed me and reached under the table. He pulled back and patted his hand beneath the table. "It's gone." He stuck his head underneath.

"What?"

"The remote control that turned on the otherworldly voice. Heidi must've removed it."

"She's slick." Slicker than an asphalt highway after an oil spill. I should take her more seriously.

Michael skimmed around the room. "What about the speaker? Maybe it's still here."

We circled the area, peeking into lampshades and behind bookshelves. We met up halfway.

"Marti used to date Hank, but they broke up when she found out he was two-timing her," Michael whispered.

"With JoJo?"

"They wouldn't say. I talked to two older ladies at the gas station in downtown Los Ranchos. I checked their oil and pumped their gas while we chatted."

I held out my hand. Three cloves of crushed garlic lay on my palm on a plastic bag. "Found these near Heidi's chair."

"Garlic keeps evil spirits away. Those innocent-looking bulbs make a big impact." Michael's megawatt smile brightened the gloomy room.

"Is that your professional opinion?" I asked.

"Sure, if I believed in werewolves and vampires." His brows dropped, but his grin didn't waver.

We circled some more.

"Anything left of the missing broom?" Michael stopped to look at me.

I showed him a photo on my phone. "Someone really took a torch to it. I need to figure out why." I shifted my attention to the ceiling. A black, 4-blade fan sat perfectly still. I stood on a chair and peered over the top of the fan. "What does a speaker look like?"

"It's going to be portable, compact enough to fit on your palm, and round with holes all over it." He stopped to sniff a candle. "Vanilla with a hint of bourbon." He spun around toward me. "Maybe she stuck it on top of the fan, using a magnet or duct tape."

I flashed my penlight and looked all around. "Nothing here."

"She might've kept it close and took it with her when she left the room."

"Or maybe it's not portable." I stared up at the middle of the fan. Stuck on the bottom was a round piece filled with holes like a mini speaker. I hopped down. "Take a look." I shined my light on the fan.

Michael took my spot and squinted. "That's a speaker, which means, Marti might've known about this. They must think we're suckers." He hopped down and fixed his hazel gaze on me. "Even though I'm not a psychic, I feel pretty good about our chances of solving this case."

"Maybe." I texted him the photo of Heidi's driver's license. "For starters, will you look into Heidi's background?"

"If there's dirt, I'll find it." He struck a Superman pose so realistic, I leaned a little sideways looking for his red cape.

I grabbed Michael's hand and pulled him out the door. "Come on."

"Where are we going?"

"I just thought of a way to ruffle Heidi's imitation feathers."

* * *

Everyone milled about in the spacious living room that opened to the patio. Glen Campbell crooned in the background about a rhinestone cowboy as I moseyed up to Heidi. She slid a gooey slice of pepperoni pizza onto her paper plate and took a bite, slurping a long thread of cheese.

"Can we talk privately?" I asked.

She licked her fingers. "You have a question." Strolling over to the French doors, Heidi eased outside, gulping a mouth full of pizza. "You're not sure if your dad's part of the spirit world or part of our mortal world."

That one sentence managed to raise every hair on my arms. I inhaled slowly. Be cool. Act like a believer. I widened my gaze and opened my mouth slightly. "How...how did you know?" A few months ago, a rumor circulated claiming that Monty Locke had faked his death. I'd started the rumor after a forensics lab tech claimed she'd spotted Dad. I wanted to see if anything came of it. Nothing did. Where did Heidi get that intel?

"That message arrived in the inbox of my mind the moment we stepped outside." She turned to stare at the moonlit pool as she gobbled up the rest of her pizza. Dropping her plate onto a nearby table, she closed her eyes, as though pondering something. "Do you know someone named Pamela? Or Paula?"

Did she run my family tree? "In the spirit world? Dad had an Aunt Pauline. She was known for her penchant for lies and exaggeration." My gene for lying, when necessary, came from Dad's side of the family.

"Yeah, her. She says your father was a master of disguise." Heidi flicked open her eyes. "He's not where you think he is."

Aunt Pauline's lying streak was still thriving in the spirit world. Heidi must've gotten that information from Mom, or she'd unearthed information about Dad. "Maybe I was wrong about you," I said. Her head was too large to doubt my sincerity.

"Told ya. I'm going to grab another slice. Want one?"

"I'm good." Heidi was a hindrance to this investigation. Of that, I was certain.

* * *

I perched on a dark leather couch in Marti's living room. Veera made herself comfortable on a recliner next to me.

"This chair has serious lower back support." Veera nestled deep into the smooth cushioned upholstery.

"And massaging, heating, and rocking elements," Marti said.

"Why the séance?" I asked.

"Like Victoria, I've always wanted to experience the supernatural, and when Heidi said JoJo didn't die a natural death, I felt responsible for finding out what happened. A séance seemed like the logical answer."

More like an illogical answer. "How did you meet Heidi?"

"She sort of drifted into the ranch right after my sister passed." Marti turned to me, head slightly tilted. "The spirits probably gave her directions."

Yeah right. I'd get to the bottom of how Heidi fit in, sooner or later.

"Did the police look into the matter at all?" Veera asked.

"They're still investigating, but I don't want evidence to grow cold. That's what happens, right?" Marti switched her worried stare over to me.

"It could. If a crime is involved."

"We need to speed things up," Marti said. "It's not cheap keeping JoJo on ice."

JoJo's burial was on hold because of Heidi? "Does Heidi come from a family of seers?"

"Her mother's in plumbing, and her father's an LAPD detective." Marti straightened a cheese tray.

That hit a little too close to home. When Dad was around, he helped the LAPD, sometimes with yours truly, to crack cases. The answer of how Heidi knew stuff about Dad just dropped into my lap. And plumbers also had a way of finding out things. They got around.

"Heidi's mom can replace a water heater in less than forty-five minutes."

"She's done work for you?" Veera asked.

"She plumbed here last week." Marti munched on a cracker.

"Did Heidi arrive early tonight?" I was still trying to figure out how she rigged the scary voice.

"She arrived in time for breakfast this morning," Marti said, "She had to get the séance room in order to entice the spirits to come, she said."

Marti just explained how the mic and speaker got in the ceiling fan. Heidi had time to fiddle with the fan. I debated telling Marti. But what if she was the one who'd planted them? "Is that usually a party room?"

"Do I look like a person who likes to party?" Marti regarded me as if I'd swallowed her prize parrot. "It's my yoga and meditation room. That's how I stay so centered and calm. My therapist recommended it. We moved out my stuff for tonight."

Heidi showed up behind Marti holding a citrusy cocktail topped with crushed ice.

"Where's JoJo's phone?" I gave Heidi another chance.

"My spirit source says it's near the ranch."

"JoJo isn't your spiritual informant?" How I'd love to pull her outside, shine a spotlight on her, and threaten to hang her by her thumbs until she came clean.

Heidi squeezed her eyes shut. "Someone else has joined in. Someone with the initial T."

Marti's eyes rounded. "Must be Cousin Thelma, on Mama's side. She was our second cousin, who passed away three years ago when her house caught on fire. She liked to smoke in bed. Thelma lived up north."

News that could make the local paper. Easy for Heidi to look up. "Where up north?" I needed to look it up, too.

Bart and Red joined us. Michael stood behind me.

"A town named Weed." Red stroked his thick mustache. "Thelma and JoJo were close. Birds of a crooked feather, you might say."

"Red thinks they cheated at card games," Marti added.

Time to introduce the conservationist pin. Heidi couldn't possibly know about that. Or could she? "What does Thelma have to say about a certain vintage piece found at Means Well Ranch?"

Heidi slowly rubbed her hands together and went silent. Her eyeballs rolled behind her closed lids. "I'm creating an energy force to attract the answer."

I bit my tongue to keep my verbal energy from spilling out.

A few beats passed before she spoke again. "I'm getting a message about a carving. Faded and worn, but meaningful to the wearer."

Veera clicked her tongue again and wore a rare frown. "What's going on?"

"I see brass. Maybe gold. No, another kind of metal, not valuable."

"Who does it belong to?" I stood. She'd seen the brooch before.

Everyone leaned toward Heidi.

"I...oh." Her eyes opened. "The connection broke off."

"Convenient," I muttered.

Heidi focused on me. "You have the piece?"

Good guess. Might as well show it to her. "I found this on the floor inside the house." I reached into my purse.

Heidi held up a hand and stared up at the ceiling. "Wait." A beat passed. "I see wilderness. And something going in different directions." She rested an index finger on either side of her head. "Is it branches from a tree? No, wait. Antlers."

Veera stiffened. A chill trickled down my spine, even though Heidi had likely known about the brooch already. In fact, she might've been the one who'd dropped it at the ranch. I placed it on my palm, deer side up.

Marti gasped. "That's amazing."

Mom slapped a hand to her chest and turned to Heidi. "I can't believe it. Honey, you've got a gift."

"Thank you, Victoria." Heidi gave Mom a small smile and sucked in a breath. "You're going to have a life-changing experience."

My mother waved a hand. "Oh, I have those all the time. Like I always say, sailboats are meant for sailing, not mooring to some dock."

I'd never heard her say anything close to that.

"I see a partnership." Heidi was still in mystical mode.

"You do?" Mom's smile broadened, and she winked at me. "Is he tall, dark, and owns a fine jewelry store?"

"He's tall, broad-shouldered with silvery hair. Wears square-rimmed glasses. A strapping fellow, some would say. Handsome for a man his age."

"Sounds vaguely familiar," Mom said.

I slapped my palm to my head. How dumb does Heidi think we are? Dad's photos were all over the Internet.

"He loves you." Heidi's eyes closed. "And he says, 'Don't be afraid.'"

"Says?" Mom's cheeks puffed out. "Like in the present tense?" She spoke out of the side of her mouth. "Who does she think she's kidding?"

"What's Victoria got to be afraid of?" Veera asked Heidi.

"Loneliness." Heidi's gaze was pinned to Mom. "A deep, heartfelt loneliness."

I grabbed Mom's hand. "It's okay. I'm here."

She yanked her hand away. "What a crack—"

"You will soon meet a special person. Then the urgency to be in a relationship will go away."

"Now, listen here…" Mom started.

I stared hard at Mom. Don't blow up. Keep your cool. I suddenly realized I wanted this job. Something was going on, and I needed to find out what. I caught Mom's glare, and her expression softened. She turned toward Heidi and held up her index finger.

"Why is it that the spirits can send you a message from my late husband, but can't tell you who killed JoJo?"

Little threads of conversation halted as though they'd been snipped by a pair of invisible scissors. Even the music stopped playing.

Heidi closed her eyes and gently swayed from side to side. "Because… JoJo…she never saw her killer coming."

Good one. "You're saying JoJo didn't know who finished her off?"

"If she was attacked, there'd be marks on her body," Michael said.

"The lady from the mortuary didn't see any," Marti said. "Her death was called heart failure. But that's wrong. Heidi said so."

"Why can't you all just let Aunty Jo be?" Bart said. Tears ran down his grainy cheeks.

"I went to all this trouble for a reason, Barton." Marti stroked his hair. "You'll thank me later."

He put his arms around her and sobbed.

Michael stepped up to Heidi. "Have you been inside the house since JoJo's passing?"

She shrugged her shoulders. "Once, briefly. I met with Marti about contacting JoJo, but I haven't been back."

That explained how she knew about the brooch.

"I have the spirit world at my disposal. I don't need to visit. You should know that." Heidi gazed up at Michael.

"I'll get a better reading if you and Marti are there." Michael held his palms out to her.

"I'm not going." Heidi folded her arms over her chest. Her lower lip stuck out.

"Yes, you are. You two need to work together." Marti pushed Bart aside.

"Michael has a very unusual process."

Michael's high energy, close-mouthed grin, and the tiny head shake told me he couldn't believe how he got himself into this.

"He's mathematical and scientific about his visions. You'll be there, and so will I," Marti said.

Michael nodded. "There's something wrong about JoJo's passing. We should hear the spirit world more loudly from inside the house. That'll be very helpful."

I was all for it. "Tomorrow afternoon. Three p.m."

Chapter Eleven

The sun's first glow was faint when we arrived at Ameripictures Film Studios the next day. Since we planned on calling it quits in the early afternoon, a bright-eyed and bushy-tailed start was a must. Our boss, legendary film star Lacy Halloway, didn't usually stroll in until three or four. Jet lag had held her hostage ever since her return from India six days ago. So far, we hadn't bumped into each other.

"As long as you get the work done," Lacy had said, "I don't need to see you. There's no one I enjoy talking to more than myself, anyway."

Lacy was a fiery-haired hand grenade who lived to watch people squirm under her spit and spunk. Like an old car radiator, she spent a lot of time overheating.

Veera and I were reviewing last night's séance as we labored in our office, sipping on steamy hot chocolates from the studio's Starstruck Cafe. Mini marshmallows were our own addition.

"Are you saying you believe that phony psychic clairvoyant or whatever she calls herself?" Veera sat behind her computer. She was typing out a production schedule for Lacy.

"I'm saying Heidi's a sly operator who knows what resonates with who. She's also a liar." I was putting all my money behind Heidi having seen the pin-backed brooch inside Means Well Ranch after JoJo's death. Either that or she'd placed it there.

Veera printed out the schedule and handed it to me. "Last night, I almost believed in Heidi a few times until she showed her true colors. She's preying on that grieving family."

A soft humming sound came from somewhere in the office. "What's that noise?"

Veera spun around in her desk chair. "It's coming from somewhere close."

"Your purse."

Veera caught her breath. "It's the Nightingale Agency phone." She fumbled with her zipper and dug a hand into a purse the size of Dodger Stadium. "Here it is." She pulled out a sunglass case. "Wait." A few more tries and out came the phone. She sank into her chair. "Nightingale Investigations. How can we help?"

I stood over her.

"You do?"

I put up my hands and mouthed, "Who is it?"

"Let me see if she's available." Veera pressed the mute button and turned to me. "It's that gun-totin' cowboy you met at the ranch the other night. Hank Ramos."

I grabbed the phone and put him on speaker. "This is Corrie."

"Thought you'd want to know. I was up at sunrise this morning, walking to the diner like I usually do. When I got close to Means Well Ranch, something strange was happening. And then it wasn't."

I gazed at Veera. Her dark eyes rounded into perfect circles. Despite the hot chocolate and the comfortable temperature in the office, a cold chill trickled down my spine. "What do you mean?"

"Music was playing from inside the main house. By the time I got there, it had stopped."

"What kind of music?"

"Piano."

"It's a player-piano. Maybe it malfunctioned." Was that possible?

"A guy drove up from Orange County annually to tune that thing. The piano man came to the ranch last month."

Did he have a key to JoJo's place?

"All I know is that it shouldn't have been playing. Someone's foolin' around."

I heartily agreed and told him about the meeting we'd planned for this afternoon. "I'll check out the piano." I disconnected.

"You suppose somebody who knows we'll be there today is trying to spook us from going to the ranch again?" Veera asked.

"Not a smart move if they are. That only makes our going inside a sure thing. You know what this means?" There was only one way to find out what was really going on.

"We'll need a proton pack to capture a ghost?"

"Slumber party at the Means Well Ranch. Pack up your jammies and toothbrush, Veera. We're spending the night." We weren't leaving till we had some answers.

* * *

We skipped lunch, finished our work in record time, and navigated freeway gridlock to motor up to Los Ranchos. I'd called Marti and let her know we'd be sleeping over.

"We expect the family to do the same," I'd said.

"What for?" she asked.

"The more time we invest in the ranch, the more likely we'll determine what happened to your sister." Someone could slip, or we'd find incriminating evidence, or…we might find nothing at all. "Tell Red and Bart."

"I suppose I can do that."

"See you soon."

We pulled up to Los Ranchos just before two o'clock. First stop: Hank's Place. Loading up on carbs would be just the thing to ease our traffic blues. Plus, I wanted to talk to Hank.

Downtown Los Ranchos spanned two short blocks that resembled a preserved Hollywood film set from *High Noon*, complete with a saloon, general store, and a livery stable with a blacksmith. Wild West relics scattered up and down Main Street. Horses were tied to hitching posts near water troughs to keep the livestock hydrated. You could tell the visitors from the locals right off the bat. They held up their phones in a fruitless search for Wi-Fi. I fought an impulse to run into the general store to buy a two-cent stick of candy from a glass jar next to the brass cash register. A real cowpoke town…at least that's the way I saw it, being a big fan of classic Hollywood movies.

I parked my car in front of a gas station with modern-day, sky-high pricing, and we ambled on up to Hank's.

"I'm ordering a quarter pounder with onion rings," Veera said. "And a chocolate shake."

"Make that two." A small post office two doors down beckoned me inside. "I'm going to rustle up some information from the townsfolk."

"That'll give me a chance to soak up some local color."

She headed into Hank's while I sidled up to a compact post office.

An older patron chatted away with a big guy behind the counter, mid-forties or so, with bushy brows, a neatly trimmed beard, and black-rimmed glasses. A thin silver chain glinted along his neck, which made me wonder how his big fingers worked the clasp. The badge over his breast pocket read: Darin. The men zipped up their lips the moment I walked in, eyes all over me like it had been eons since they'd seen a female. It was all I could do to keep from knocking their heads together, Three Stooges style.

"Howdy." I walked up to them. "I didn't see a pharmacy around here. Any idea where I could buy some aspirin?"

"We have a traveling medicine show comes through every Monday. Can you wait till then?" The older man squinted at me through wire-rimmed spectacles. A slight, clean-shaven fellow, he had a high forehead, a patrician nose, and silvery hair cropped in a military crew cut that showed off his tan. He chewed a piece of gum with a spin motion, kind of like a washing machine.

"Seriously?"

They burst out laughing.

"The general store has aspirin." Darin reached into a drawer and slapped a small bottle on the counter. "You can have this. There are four left."

"Oh, thanks." I rubbed my temples. "I just heard about the passing of a longtime resident." I managed that without lying outright. It's like I'd turned a new leaf without even trying. "I understand her family founded this town."

"Are you referring to JoJo Means?" The older man put out a hand, and I shook it. "Alistair Wallaby. That news came as a shocker." His gum chewing continued.

"It did for a lot of folks," Darin added. "Really sad to hear."

"She invited some of us over last Friday for a meeting." The older man dropped his chin. "We didn't expect her to…well, kick the bucket like that."

Why hadn't Marti mentioned the meeting? Did she know about it? "What kind of meeting?"

"Didn't say. Wasn't often we got an invite to Means Well Ranch." Alistair ran a hand along his cropped hair. "JoJo promised a home-cooked meal. That was all the enticing I needed."

"Were you a close friend?"

"Close enough, isn't that so?" He slapped Darin's shoulder and laughed. "You might say that between JoJo and me, we owned most of the land and businesses in town."

"Who else was invited to JoJo's house for the meeting?"

"Not me," Darin said.

Alistair put a hand on his shoulder. "I'd have brought you back a piece of pie." He turned to me. "I assumed she'd enlighten me once I got there. Sounded like a hush-hush thing. Jo said we'd talk details later." He stuck his hands in his pockets and rocked back on his heels. "Who'd have thought she'd die so sudden-like?"

My insides tingled. I was getting close to something, but what? "If you remember anything that might explain why she'd invited you over, please contact me." I handed them each my card.

Alistair looked it over. "You didn't mention you were a private investigator."

"My line of work requires confidentiality. I was hired to make sure everything's accounted for." That was the best I could do.

"Got nothing else to say."

"JoJo sure had a nice broom." That was off the wall, but maybe Alistair knew something. "Had you seen it?"

Darin didn't blink, but Alistair's brows took a dip.

"Why would I care about her broom?" Alistair folded his arms across his chest.

He turned his back to me, so I left. JoJo and Alistair were power players in this town. JoJo had invited him over, but for what kind of meeting? Were there other power players?

* * *

Veera sat at the end of a shiny counter in Hank's busy diner. The décor was all cowboys and sports. The first time I'd laid eyes on a Texas longhorn steer was a few nights ago when I had that near run-in with Poncho, the steer outside of JoJo's house. Even so, I was glad Poncho wasn't here to witness the four sets of longhorns decorating the walls. Cowboy art and rodeo posters took up the remaining wall space. Metal siding covered the ceiling. T-shirts, jeans, and baseball caps mingled with cowboy hats and boots at the tables. Half the patrons seemed to be Angelenos passing through Los Ranchos on the way to a mountain hike or the surf at Malibu.

"I met up with Hank and introduced myself. Told him I worked with you," Veera whispered. "Seems he's a bigwig around these parts. He's board president of the Los Ranchos Cemetery. They're planning a burial for JoJo as soon as the family's ready." She slid a folded newspaper toward me. "There's a story in there about Hank and JoJo, and the committees they sat on together."

The whole paper ran six pages. I skimmed through it. "Lots of committees for a small town. The theater group, senior center, historical society, the backlash committee?" I looked up at Veera.

"It's a committee to anticipate and deactivate any possible backlash stemming out of stuff the other committees might do. The cook told me all about it. Tucker grew up in this town. He said JoJo and Hank sat on a lot of committees together."

I stuffed the paper into my handbag. "Where's Hank?" I craned my neck to peer over the heads in the dining room.

"He skedaddled before you arrived." She pointed outside. "Didn't have a chance to ask where he was off to."

"Did he say anything else about the piano playing?"

"No, but he mentioned the fire. He said it's strange how it started like that, with no one around." Veera eyed a plate of burgers passing by. "He didn't need much encouragement to admit that strange things were happening in a town where nothing much had happened for decades."

A server scurried toward us, balancing a large tray on one hand.

The world came to a halt once lunch was served. We bit into onion rings, large, fluffy, and crunchy with a soft, creamy center. I was surprised we didn't break out into a fistfight over the remaining one. That was because we ordered another basket. The burgers were juicy, the buns freshly toasted. And the shakes? Well, with every sip of the sweet, smooth liquid, my taste buds hummed in delight. To top it off, they brought us a plate of chocolate chip cookies, soft and gooey, just the way I liked them.

"I saw a couple of hammocks with our names on them near the senior center." Veera licked the chocolate off her finger. "Think they'll let us use them for a spell?"

"Remember that scene in *The Wizard of Oz* where Dorothy and her pals got sleepy in the poppy field?"

Veera shot up. "You think there was opium in this food?"

"I'm just saying we can't fall asleep on the job." I paid the bill. "We'll walk our delirium off at the ranch."

* * *

By the time we arrived, Marti was already there. She swayed on a porch swing with Heidi. My mother sat nearby, which took me a little by surprise since I'd told her we didn't need her today.

"Hi!" Mom waved the moment we stepped out of my car. She wore a brown and orange, suede diamond pattern dress with a brown leather belt and matching booties. Her version of cowgirl country fashion. "I was just telling the girls that I'll whip up a little supper for us tonight. I brought the fixings." Her high-wattage smile nearly drained all the power from neighboring homes.

"Supper? Who says that?" I asked.

"If I wasn't so full, I'd be jumping for joy!" Veera gave Mom a big hug.

Mom whispered to me over Veera's shoulder, "I'll keep everyone occupied so you can do your snooping. It'll be just like *Mission Impossible*, except you won't need to peel a mask off your face." She winked and gave me a thumbs-up.

I really didn't know where my mother was coming from with her fuzzy logic, but I had to hand it to her. She found a way to make herself useful, so her presence didn't need to be explained. I turned to Marti.

"I got a call from Hank. He said the piano was playing early this morning. On its own."

"What?" Marti shot up. "How can that be?" She tapped Heidi on the shoulder. "What do you know about this?"

Heidi gingerly stood and wiped the dust off the seat of her pants. "You said it yourself. The place is haunted. What did you expect?"

Marti did a little hair flip. "Heidi assured me there'd be no shenanigans tonight from the other world."

Heidi's stare fixed on me. "You're going to find something this evening that'll make all the difference."

What was she setting me up for? Now, all eyes were on me. I rubbed my hands together. "Goody! Let's go inside."

Marti unlocked the front door and hung back while everyone stepped in the house. I hung back, too.

"Is Michael coming? There's something so reassuring about his presence," she said. "He's like a bucket of fried chicken at a Fourth of July picnic."

That was the strangest compliment I'd ever heard. I must've looked puzzled because she said,

"He's like comfort food."

I couldn't disagree with that. "He'll be here a little later. Let's you and me walk and talk out here a bit. Tell me about the recent squabbling among the Means family."

Marti went quiet for a minute, then spoke in a low tone, "It was about selling the property. Like I said, we all wanted to. JoJo was the holdout."

"Even Bart?"

"Of course Bart. He's barely making a living. He could use the money."

"What does he do?"

"He's a mechanic at a car repair shop." She lumbered down the steps and aimed for the barn. "Or is he in sales at the Buy More?"

Mechanics had analytical minds. I didn't see that kind of mind in Bart. He didn't fit in sales either. "I met Alistair today. JoJo had invited him and maybe a few others to her house last Friday for a dinner meeting. She died before the meeting happened."

Surprise registered on Marti's face. "What was the meeting about?"

"Alistair didn't know much. Any ideas?"

"JoJo supported the town's local causes. Maybe she wanted to fortify the saloon building or hang more hammocks at the senior center. Who knows?" Marti stared at the ground.

"Did JoJo leave a will?" I asked.

"She did. But…" She bit her lip and lowered her voice. "It's not the one we expected. Mama put JoJo in charge of the ranch, like I said. JoJo could live here as long as she wanted, but once it was sold, it would be divided up equally, except for ten acres, which Mama bequeathed solely to JoJo for whatever she thought JoJo did for her. The ten acres come with a house and a pond. Didn't go over well when we first heard about it." She threw up her hands. "What did JoJo do exactly? We were never clear on that. She already owned her own home and had plenty of money, but she stayed in the main house after Mama died. She wanted to be in control." Marti plodded along, me at her side. "That ten acres should've been split among us."

"Do you have a copy of JoJo's will?"

"I do. Everything was split between Red and Bart and me, but JoJo left her ten acres to Bart." Marti stomped a boot. "That was wrong, too."

Had Marti been angry enough to harm her sister? Maybe Red was even angrier. I blew a strand of hair out of my eyes. "Does Bart know about his inheritance?"

"I suppose. We haven't talked about it. It's just… she should have told us."

"I heard JoJo was secretive." I didn't want to bombard her with questions again. I needed Marti to keep talking.

She stepped onto a gravel path. "JoJo had her secrets, but she was forthright about family holdings. She didn't care a fig if she hurt anybody's feelings. She would've said something."

"I'd like to see a copy of the will."

"I'll show you."

Gravel switched to a wide dirt path as we neared the barn. "Was Red mad about the ten acres?"

"He felt the same as me. Everything should be divided fairly between the siblings and Bart, since he's stepped into his mother's shoes."

"Right. His mother was your late sister." For a minute, I forgot how Bart fit in.

Marti turned to face me. "I apologize for stonewalling you when we first met." She squinted off into the hills. "I'm having trouble processing all that's happened."

A sour-faced guy exited the barn and headed toward us.

"Red's here." I pitched my chin his way.

Marti flipped around. "That man is infuriating." She yelled out to him, "Why didn't you tell me you were already here?"

"Charlotte needed my attention." His gaze shifted to me. "My '62 Lincoln convertible. I'm restoring her to her original condition. I'm much less depressed when I have a project."

"He says manual labor is an immediate pick-me-upper," Marti told me.

He flipped his thumb toward the barn. "That's where I parked my cars in the olden days."

"He means when Mama and Papa lived here."

I turned to Red again. "Did you visit JoJo very often?"

"About as often as I needed an oil change. The barn has a little car shop Dad and I set up."

"What do you know about JoJo's broom?" He didn't seem surprised about the broom at the seance.

He nodded. "Choosing the right one is important. JoJo's had wavy tips that caught dust in rugs. She even used it on her cashmere sweaters."

"Why would it be in her burn pile?" Marti asked him.

"Must have gotten damaged. Our sister was an enthusiastic cleaner."

I pulled out my cell phone as I started to back away. "Will you excuse me? There's something I need to do." I reversed my steps. "Be back soon."

"There's a bathroom in the barn!" Marti shouted after me.

I gave her a backward wave and hurried off. It wasn't a bathroom break I needed. I had a sudden urge to visit JoJo's tenant. The one who'd called Hank when JoJo hadn't been seen in a few days. I poked my head into the house and called for Veera. Heidi showed up.

"They're in JoJo's closet." She stared at me. "Don't worry, you won't be late."

"Just because I'm panting a little doesn't mean I'm in a rush to get anywhere. I'm getting some exercise in."

"To work off the lunch that's weighing you down?"

"Wow, you really do know everything." Heidi tried so hard to be psychic.

Veera showed up behind her. "You called?"

"Time for our appointment."

Veera's brows shot up. Heidi turned to face her.

"I almost forgot about the appointment," Veera said, taming her brows.

"I told Corrie not to worry," Heidi said. "It'll go fine."

"Oh, I know it will." Veera's smile nearly stretched across the street.

Once we got past earshot, Veera spoke, "Should I know where we're going?"

"To meet Gifty Carmichael. She lives next door. She's the one who called Hank after she hadn't seen JoJo around. According to the local paper, she hosts a knitting circle weekly." Knitters knew things.

Chapter Twelve

Three houses sat on the twenty-nine acres of Means Well Ranch. The main house, a smaller cottage, and the home on the ten acres left to JoJo by her parents. Gifty Carmichael was the tenant in the single-story, craftsman-style cottage in front of us. Just a short walk from JoJo's place, the structure sat at a slight angle, as if refusing to meet the road head-on. Overgrown shrubs and trees guarded all sides of Gifty's house. The top of a metal windmill stuck out in the back, spinning and clanging at the wind's bidding. We padded up the dirt driveway and onto a flagstone path leading to a front door, painted dark red.

"How do we get her to talk to us?" Veera asked.

"We'll tell her members of the Means family are staying at the main house," I said. "And that we're representing the family."

"But we won't tell her our exact role?"

I stopped by the entry. "Not right away." I knew almost nothing about Gifty. I pictured her as a cranky old lady. Lonely and reclusive, I could almost see her spying on us from the peephole. "We should admire her knitting."

Veera whipped out her P.I. notebook and jotted down notes. "When covertly interrogating a suspect, throw her off guard with flattery." She looked up at me. "That could loosen her lips. And if she clams up, we'll tell her you're a lawyer, and I'm almost one, seeing that I'll eventually graduate from night law school." Veera's smile grew broader. "We could make her think we've got something to do with JoJo's will."

"We shouldn't lead her on like that."

Veera's jaw dropped, and her hand shot out to my forehead. "You feelin' okay? You don't sound like yourself."

I pushed her hand away. "I'm fine."

Her face lit up. "Then this is the real you shining through. Not that I have a problem with your sly investigating self because that plays an important role in our being successful P.I.s. But I'm good with you being on the up and up. We can still get answers that way."

I rapped on the door and leaned my shoulder against the stucco wall. "This could take a little time." I could practically hear her shuffling slippers inching toward the entry.

I straightened in a hurry when the door opened. The woman facing us was nothing like the one I'd pictured. Instead of a low, slow-flying pelican, I faced a hawk poised to swoop down, talons ready. A side-parted bob packed with tight curls trembled around her fierce expression. Her skin was tawny, her lipstick bronze; she looked ready to land a punch with one hand and conk us over the head with the other, which gripped a stainless-steel frying pan. I was betting she could take us both at once.

"What do you want?" Her eyes bulged. Her voice rocked a thick accent, not quite British, but with a pronounced lilt. She was like a dragon guarding her lair.

"Gifty Carmichael?" I pushed my shoulders back and lifted my chin, making me a tad taller than her.

"What if it is me?"

"We're here to let you know that members of the Means family are staying at the main house, and would like to invite you to dinner." That not only took Gifty by surprise, it was news to Veera and me, too. "Seven tonight."

It took a moment, but Gifty slowly lowered the pan and her annoyance. Gray-green eyes darted from Veera to me.

"I'm Corrie Locke. This is Veera Bankhead, my associate. We're working with the Means family to look into JoJo's death."

"Am I being accused of something?" Her pan lifted again.

"We're not police." I debated bringing up the messages she'd left for JoJo. "No one is accusing anyone of anything, for now." I glanced at Veera. She stared at me round-eyed. I flashed her a grin.

"Pleased to meet you." Veera shifted her gaze to Gifty. "We heard you were a good friend to JoJo, and the first person to notice when she wasn't around."

"That was me." Gifty opened her door wider. "Come in now."

Sometimes, it's better to ditch the business plan for a looser version. Gifty seemed ever ready to put up her dukes. We didn't want to promote the prizefighter in her. We wanted to promote her friendly, gentler side to disarm her from the get-go.

"Thank you." I walked in, and Veera followed.

"What kind of name is Gifty?" Veera asked. "I like it."

"In Ghana, Gifty means tall, beautiful girl. That's where my ma was born."

She led us to a snug living room with a beamed ceiling and richly upholstered furniture. Vases on every tabletop bloomed with roses that scented the house. A glass-fronted cabinet brimmed with colorful china and vases. Color was everywhere. Quite the contrast to JoJo's neutral tones.

"Ma moved to Los Angeles, opened her own business, gave birth to me, and moved back to Ghana in less than a decade. She went to Heaven when I turned twenty-three. Then I moved here, on the ranch. This is where I belong."

I could almost see the anchor tied around her ankle. There were a few gaps in that timeline and a ton of questions. "That's what I'd call a round trip."

"Full circle," Veera said.

"Get comfortable." Gifty motioned for us to sit and aimed toward the hallway. "I'll get us lemonade."

Around forty or so, Gifty was like a succulent whose spear-shaped leaves had teeth along the edges and spiny tips that could poke a hole through your finger. A person could get all cut up if they didn't play her right.

Veera and I sat on the couch and studied our surroundings, trying to get a grip on Gifty's role in JoJo's life. Veera leaned toward me.

"She wasn't what I was expecting."

"I think we're in for more surprises." Anyone poised to do battle like she was didn't retreat quietly.

Gifty appeared in the doorway holding a rifle, pointed our way.

Veera's eyes flashed with surprise. "Is that any way to serve lemonade?"

I leaned forward and dropped my arm near my ankle. I raised my foot. A pistol was strapped into a holster beneath my pant leg. A large, chest-like table came between Gifty's line of sight and my pistol.

"Is there a problem?" I had a feeling she was acting on a suspicion that we were after something else. But what? Veera turned to me and dropped her gaze to my crawling fingers. She knew what I had in mind.

"I know what's going on." Veera flipped her eyes toward Gifty. "You don't believe we're who we say we are."

My fingers crept lower.

"I don't believe the Means family would invite me to dinner," Gifty said.

"Wait a minute. Are you saying you've never been invited to have dinner with them?" Veera was on a roll.

I slowly lifted my pant leg and gripped the pistol.

"JoJo used to invite me. Sometimes. But the rest never did." She waved a hand and lowered the muzzle so it pointed to Veera's boots.

I pulled my pistol out of its holster.

"Tell me why you are really here," Gifty said.

"Not until you lower that thing all the way down." Veera's brows dipped into a frown. "How's a girl of my sensitive nature supposed to hold down a conversation with a gun pointing at her?"

A bowl full of walnuts sat on the table in front of us.

Veera slowly rose and held her heart. "I'm feeling funky." She blinked and fanned her face with her hand. "I get fainting spells when I'm jittery, and right now, I'm a nervous wreck. This is not going well. Shame on you!"

Just as Gifty lowered the barrel, I flicked a bunch of walnuts across the room. Gifty turned her head, Veera plopped back on the couch, and I dove for Gifty. Knocking the rifle from her loose grip, I pointed my pistol a foot away from her chest.

"See? I was right." Gifty balled her fist. "You came to get me."

"What did you expect us to do when you threatened us with a firearm?

You let us into your home." I slowly walked around her. "Which means you had some faith in us being good people, which we are."

"You are pointing a gun at me now. Good people don't do that."

"You started it." Veera was on her feet again. "We're defending ourselves. You were assaulting guests."

I picked up the vintage rifle with my free hand. Its shiny walnut finish and intricate carvings came from an older era. I leaned it against the opposite corner of the room, far from her reach.

"I had to be sure you weren't sent to force me to get out. God is good, but some of his children have a long way to go. Maybe someone from the family wanted you to rough me up."

Veera clicked her tongue. "We could've taken you at the door if we'd wanted to. We gotta whole set of skills you don't know anything about."

I shot Veera a "tone it down" look and lowered my pistol. "We came in peace. The family wants you to come to dinner." They would if I told them why. "We're here to ask questions, that's all."

Gifty's stare swung between Veera and me. "Truce then?"

"Truce," I said.

"I'll get the lemonade." Gifty started to turn.

My pistol rose.

"Hold up," Veera said. "Why should we trust you?"

"I'll wait here. You get the tray. It's sitting on the counter."

Veera shot me a glance. I nodded my okay. Gifty sat on an armchair, and I perched on the sofa's armrest, pistol on my lap.

"That's a beautiful afghan." My pistol pointed toward a multi-colored blanket folded over a chair.

"I designed it myself."

"You're very talented." She knew her way around knitting needles and rifles. What else did she know?

Veera returned with a tray of three glasses, each with a lemon slice wedged onto the rim. Gifty parted a few vases so Veera could set the tray down on the pine chest.

Veera handed me a glass and passed one to Gifty, who regarded me with a steady gaze.

"The money JoJo collected over the years, it didn't belong to her. Any money she made from this ranch belongs to the family." Gifty spit out the last word, in case we were hard of hearing. "All the family."

"They agree with you." Why was she bringing up family money?

She shrugged a burly shoulder and sipped her lemonade, eyes flicking from Veera to me.

Veera sipped the lemonade and made a gurgling noise. "Wow! This is spicy."

Gifty stared at Veera. "It's good for you."

"Cleared up my sinuses real fast," Veera quickly said.

"Lamugin. Ghana-style lemonade made with ginger and cloves." She sipped her drink and regarded me with a squinty eye. "You have questions?"

"We're looking into JoJo's death. Did you notice any unusual activity or people around in the past week or two before she died?" Gifty seemed like she paid attention, being suspicious by nature.

She paused a few beats. "You know about the thefts?"

Veera and I swapped glances.

"Hank mentioned missing wood, apples, and chicken feed."

"There's more. A robber is stealing from homes on this road. At one place, thieves broke a window, climbed inside, and stole a laptop and money. They even took a toaster oven while the owner was in the intensive care unit."

Someone who knew the owner wasn't home. I needed to check out the local police report. Hank had mentioned smaller thefts. "You think it's a local behind the robberies?"

"Oh yes. If I catch that burglar, I'm going to use my gun."

Her gaze flew to the rifle in the corner.

"Where did you get that rifle?"

"My daddy gave it to me," she said.

I jerked my head toward Gifty. "Your daddy?"

"Caleb Wiseblood Means."

Veera caught her breath and muttered, "That's an unexpected plot twist."

Chapter Thirteen

"You didn't know Caleb Means was my daddy?" Gifty asked.

"Not exactly," I said.

"I am the half-sister of JoJo, Marti, and Red. I am Bart's half-aunty. We haven't gotten along very well, my sister and brother and I. But I have to admit, it was well-mannered of the family to invite me for dinner."

I stiffened, and Veera circled her eyes before flicking a speck from her shirt.

"Didn't you go to the house when JoJo was around?" I crossed my legs, but kept one hand on my pistol.

"Yes. Even after she tried to move me out, I went over." She gulped down the rest of the lemonade. "It was difficult because I was angry."

"Do you know why she wanted you out?" The bigger question was why no one had told me that Gifty was one of the Means clan.

"JoJo said she sold the ranch, and I could not stay." She slammed her glass down and scooted forward in her chair. "But this is my home. I am a tenant for life. Daddy wanted it that way."

"We'll look into this, and when we do, watch out, 'cause all sorts of things are going to hit a whole bunch of fans." Veera eyed Gifty like she was under a microscope. "Did you see anyone at JoJo's house the day she died?" She flipped her notebook open.

"Yes. Me. In the past month, I was there many times. On that last day, we cleaned the barn together."

"Did you help with the laundry?" I asked.

"We folded it together."

Veera and I both sat up.

"Did you set eyes on a small yellow face towel in JoJo's house?" Veera asked.

Gifty leaned back. "She would never allow anything yellow in her home. She had no use for things that attracted attention."

Veera cleared her throat and gazed around the room. "Know anyone who's a fan of yellow?"

Gifty had yellow throw pillows, yellow napkins, and a sun hat with a yellow ribbon hanging on a hat rack.

"If you are thinking I did something to JoJo, you are wrong." She sat back in her chair and stared off. "Besides being my half-sister, she was a second Mama to me. Lately. Now and then, anyhow."

Over the next thirty minutes, we covered enough ground to wear out a few pairs of sneakers. Gifty's mother, Juba "Junebug" Carmichael, met Caleb Wiseblood Means at an Inglewood dance club she managed, back in the day. Next thing you know, Juba was pregnant. She sold the club and moved back to Ghana. She and Caleb continued their relationship by mail.

When Juba departed the earthly plane, she left Gifty a box of letters between the long-distance lovers, including one from Caleb telling his daughter who he was, along with money and instructions on where to find him. Once she arrived, he embraced Gifty and expected the rest of the family to follow his example. They didn't.

Caleb moved Gifty into the guest house and had each child sign a notarized document promising Gifty could stay for as long as she wanted. He also bequeathed a tidy sum to her after he died.

"I have no enemies, except in my own family," Gifty said.

"If what you're saying is true, we'll fix that," Veera told her.

Veera set the bar high. And me? Things always turned out right in the end. But keeping Gifty in the cottage might be more of a challenge.

"Know anything about JoJo's favorite broom?" I couldn't get that sweeper out of my head.

"She never let me use it. That's all I know."

"That's not all." I could tell by the way she avoided eye contact that there was more to it. "What happened to the broom?"

She turned her head away. "I borrowed it once and returned it, without her knowledge."

"JoJo was very attached to that broom." It seemed that way to me.

Beads of sweat formed along Gifty's hairline.

Veera gave me a sidelong stare that said, *What's up with her?* "How long did you keep the broom?"

"Two hours, maybe. It was very soft and cleaned well. I put it back inside her broom closet."

"By the kitchen?" I asked.

"Yes, but after that, JoJo kept it in her bedroom closet. Did she suspect I took it?" Gifty lifted her chin. "Are you going to turn me in?"

I stood and held the pistol in my hand. "Show me where you kept the broom." It was a good excuse to take a closer look around.

We followed Gifty into her kitchen. She led us to a door that opened to a deep pantry. She pointed to the back. "It was a handsome broom with wide, thick bristles held together with copper wiring. The bristles were so close together, even the tiniest dust particle couldn't escape its clutches." Gifty stepped back. "I only borrowed it."

"How long ago?"

"Three weeks. Maybe more."

"Did you have something to do with—"

She shook her head wildly. "I did not."

What did she think I was going to ask? "We'll see you tonight."

Before Veera and I could budge, three insistent knocks rattled the front door.

"The family is here to throw me out." Gifty stepped back. "I knew it."

Somehow, I didn't think so. Marti didn't even acknowledge Gifty as a family member. We followed her to the entry.

"When was the last time you saw Marti or Red?" Veera asked.

"Last Christmas, at Hank's burger place." She yanked open the door. Veera and I peered over her shoulder.

"Hi. I'm looking for…" Michael's hazel eyes landed on me. "Corrie."

"Who is he?" Gifty asked.

"We work together," he told Gifty and turned to me. "We need to review the zip line pulley system."

Gifty turned to me. "What's he saying?"

"I'll find out."

We thanked her for the lemonade and joined Michael outside. Gifty kept eyes on us until we trekked out of sight.

"What's with the pulley talk?" Sometimes, Michael got carried away.

"It's code for deep background search completed on the surviving Means family members."

"What does a pulley have to do with that?" Veera asked.

"It's to throw outsiders off the track." He chuckled.

I patted Michael's back. "Pretty sure that worked. How did you know where to find us?"

"Heidi pointed me in the right direction."

She must have watched us leave, maybe even followed us, so she'd have something mystical to report later.

I briefed Michael on the events at Gifty's as we cut across a clover-scented field toward a large pond. The wind diminished to a mild breeze that barely ruffled my hair. Michael gave us the run-down during our hike.

"Martinique Means," Michael said, "sixty-three years old, divorced, no children, and has a sizable mortgage on her home. Almost went into foreclosure twice. Worked as a piano teacher and bank teller before becoming a real estate agent, which landed her in jail a few months ago."

"For fraud?" I wasn't surprised that Marti had a shady side.

"For assaulting a neighbor who didn't list a property with her. And for resisting arrest."

"Assault with a deadly weapon?" Veera asked.

Michael looked around before replying, "She threw an unopened plastic water bottle that landed on the neighbor's bare foot."

"Ouch." Veera scratched her head. "Maybe her temper got the best of her with JoJo, too."

"Who holds the mortgage on Marti's home?" I was back to figuring out the squabbling among the Means family. Squabbling nearly always meant money problems.

"Gee, I feel like a sheep dressed as a lion." Michael's closed-mouth grin said it all. "I'll find out."

"Who's next?" The skin on the back of my neck pricked like ants marched across, carrying heavy booty on their backs. I peered over my shoulder. A flock of doves fluttered skyward from the branches of a sycamore. Were we being followed?

"Redmond Means," Michael went on, "Sixty-nine years old. High school woodshop teacher until he was let go for harassment."

"What kind of harassment?" Veera asked.

"Mocking students and playing hooky."

"I can see that." Red was keen on doing as he pleased.

"He works for a cabinet maker. Currently divorced and living above a hardware store in Camarillo. Into muscle cars and horse racing. He's a gambling man."

Ten to one, he lost more than he won. That would be motivation if he stood to inherit a bundle. "Is he in debt?"

"Now I feel like a mouse in a lion suit," Michael said. "I'll find out. He also has a criminal record. Petty theft. Took school supplies home."

"Like paper clips and staples?" I asked.

"Like shovels, knee pads, and assorted tools."

"That's embarrassing," Veera said. "This family has issues."

"JoJo's record was clean. She's the upstanding citizen of the family." Michael's shoulders slumped. "And look what happened to her."

Had someone played a hand in her demise? It was beginning to feel that way. We needed to find that hand and cuff it.

We'd reached a large oval-shaped pond with murky green waters. Crooked branches from large oaks draped over the opposite end.

"Let's sit." I pointed to a picnic table. If someone was following us, I'd see them coming. "What about Bart?"

"Barton Means Lansing, thirty-two years old, former military, and nephew of Marti and Red. His parents divorced when he was four. Lost his mother in a car accident fifteen years ago. Plays the guitar. That's all I got from an old social media account of his. Wasn't much information about him on the Internet."

"Sounds sketchy to me." Veera reached into her purse and pulled out a pack of chocolate chip cookies. She ripped the plastic open.

A concrete lip defined the perimeter of the pond; dead branches were beached at the edges. Green guck floating on the surface didn't prevent ducks from paddling along in the shade. I turned to Michael. "Why do you think there's no info on Bart?"

"Maybe he doesn't have much going on. Or it's missing for the same reason information is scarce on us. Someone cleaned it up." He popped a cookie in his mouth.

"Did you do that for me?" Veera took a bite.

"For all of us." He talked between chews. "I removed private stuff, like your age, address, relatives. But any positive information on the Nightingale Agency is out there. Newspaper articles and Internet news that rave about cases you've solved. Bragworthy marketing items aren't going anywhere."

They did a fancy fist-bump handshake while I surveyed the trees and shrubs for movement. A scrap of a shadow darted between a clump of sycamores.

"You think it's possible that Bart removed background information about himself?" Veera asked.

"Web dwellers can become invisible online. I can't even find where he's working right now," Michael replied.

"That would mean he'd need to understand search engines." I broke off a piece of cookie. "Marti said he was a mechanic."

Michael snapped his fingers, and his smile came alive. "I'll ask him some pointed questions about cars when I see him today."

"Yes!" Veera did a fist pump.

A rabbit raced out of a bush across the field and dove between thick shrubbery to disappear. What had spooked it? "I think we're being followed." I wasn't entirely sure if that was true.

Veera stuffed the cookies back into her bag. "Should we divide up and look around?”

"Let's sit tight for a minute. I want to be certain." Was I being paranoid?

We waited and watched, but the scene before us was peaceful and quiet, like you'd expect in the countryside.

"Now might be a good time to bring up a…puzzling situation," Michael said to me. "You know I love puzzles." He gestured toward Veera. "Veera and I have been talking."

"Don't tell me you want a raise." Most of the money we'd made from the last few cases went into a savings account for the new business. Veera and I split the rest and left some for Michael and Mom to cover their expenses and a little bit more.

"No raise, although, if you want to throw a little something in the kitty…" He grinned and rubbed his fingers together before turning serious.

"It's about your accident the other night," Veera said.

"What accident?" Where was this going? I'd had plenty of accidents before and near misses, too.

"When you hit your head," Michael said, "you might have suffered a mild concussion."

"No biggie." I felt an eye-roll coming on.

"Even a small bump may lead to changes in personality."

"What?" That word came out so loudly that quail burst out of a bunch of shrubby honeysuckles. I turned to Michael. "What's wrong with my personality?" Suddenly, he'd turned into Sigmund Freud?

"Nothing. I love your personality! It's more about, well, you don't stretch the truth anymore."

"And that's a bad thing?" Michael was all about being sincere. Why couldn't I try sincerity on for size? "You, of all people, should embrace that change."

"I do. I mean, you were fine before, but maybe that knock on the head has something to do with how you are now."

"Tell you what. I'll donate my brain to science when I leave this planet. They're welcome to check it out. Meanwhile, my brain's telling me that we need to split up and scout around." I picked up my feet. "Just in case we're being tailed. We'll meet back at the ranch."

"Right." His knife appeared.

"I'll check the wooded area around that murky pond." Veera pointed. "Those trees make a sweet hideout."

"I'll patrol the side closest to the road." Michael pulled my arm. "Don't be mad at me. I love you whether you bend the truth in an investigation or not."

"We'll talk later." Truth was, I was annoyed. I lied more than some people, but never without good reason. And lately? There'd been no need to stretch the truth.

What I did know was that we were caught in a web that was getting stickier. Or making our imaginations work harder. Which was it? I promised myself I'd find out soon.

Chapter Fourteen

I aimed toward the hills surrounding Means Well Ranch, where knotty oaks stretched their branches to create shade for neighboring plants and wildlife. Wispy clouds weren't much help in cooling the warm afternoon. My every footstep crunched twigs, acorns, and tiny skulls and bones left over from feasting night owls. Birds tweeted, a plane rumbled, and…a soft padding glided along behind me. I flipped around. Who was there?

Pistol in hand, I marched forward, turning my head, so my peripheral vision could catch movement from different angles. The landscape grew wilder as I headed away from the ranch. Wildflower blooms fringed narrow, dusty paths. A wider dirt trail invited hikers up to the top of a hill, nearly hidden between scrubby bushes and leggy weeds. I kept an eye out for a pursuer, but my footsteps seemed to be the only ones. Cat and bird prints patterned the dirt, but not much else. Lack of litter meant the trail wasn't used much. Where did the sloped path lead?

I trekked up the twisty trail and paused for a minute before reaching the top. My clothes clung to my damp skin, and my heart beat double-time. I spun around.

No one was on the trail. But I was willing to bet plenty of critters were hiding nearby. My breathing normalized, and I wound my way back down. I paused. Near the start of the trail, a new set of prints joined mine before forging off into the brush. Work boots. A few sizes bigger than my sneakers, I pegged them as an eleven or twelve. The owner of the prints could be watching me right now. I crouched, pretending to tie my shoes. Looking off toward the pond, I gingerly pulled out a hairbrush from my purse…and my phone. I straightened and brushed my hair a few strokes before dropping the brush on the ground. I reached for it.

"Yuk." Burs and foxtails clung to the bristles. I sat and shook the brush out and photographed the boot print with my other hand. Reaching back inside my purse, I inserted the phone and brush inside. The boot had a horseshoe-shaped heel; a zig-zag pattern covered the sole. Had I seen that pattern before at the ranch? I continued my trek, keeping on softer, less rocky sections so I could hear nearby movement.

I'd nearly reached the pond's edge when a crackle of steps caught my attention. Reaching into my purse, I trudged toward the ranch, pistol pressed against my side. I hung a sharp left, barging into a thick stand of maple trees. Barreling through the dense foliage, I dove behind a wide trunk.

I waited a few moments to catch my breath, but before I could peer out, a groan sliced through the air, followed by a barrage of whisper-low swearing. Someone struggled on the ground, arms flailing beneath a large branch, legs kicking. The head was bare and hairless; the clothes were black sweats. Nearby lay a black baseball cap.

A dark scarf hid the lower half of the face. His shades were black, and his brows untamed. The bulbous nose was grossly large and exaggerated. Must be JoJo's golfer neighbor's guy. He fit the description. Then it dawned on me. He wore a mask.

My pursuer freed himself and rocketed off toward the clearing. Leaping over a tall stump, I reached the clearing at record speed, but the runner had given me the slip. I checked nearby hiding spots and came up empty-handed. Why did the most interesting things happen to me when I was alone?

I waited behind a thick tree trunk and rested my hands on my thighs. Black gloves hid the runner's hands. And the feet?

"Think!" I couldn't remember. What shoes was he wearing? More importantly, where were Veera and Michael? Were they okay?

I scuttled toward the ranch, unsettling a flock of geese resting in a cozy meadow. Their devil-may-care attitude told me the masked runner didn't go this way.

* * *

I took roll call once I arrived at the house. "Who's missing?"

"Everyone's here but you." Marti's deep blue tunic landed mid-thigh on her faded jeans. Her pointed-toe Western boots had been broken in long ago. "We were going through JoJo's drawers." Heidi appeared next to her.

I awaited Heidi's reaction, but she obviously didn't know what to make of my disheveled appearance. This morning, I'd pulled my hair back in a neat half ponytail, business-like and professional. Now, loose strands stuck out everywhere, like a dandelion gone to seed. On the upside, I really liked the speechless side of Heidi.

"We're having a taco bar for dinner," Mom yelled from the kitchen. She stuck her smiling face inside the room. "There'll be something to please everyone." She wiped off the grin when her gaze met mine. "What happened to you?"

My mother just proved you didn't need to be psychic to notice that something was off.

"I took the scenic route."

"On top of a train caboose during a windstorm?"

"Very funny. I took a self-guided tour of the ranch." I glanced around. "Where are…"

"In the barn with Bart and Red." Heidi found her voice. She'd gone all casual in a lavender cardigan over a white T-shirt and faded jeans. Her lavender Crocs had seen better days.

"You've been hanging out together? In this house?" Did any of them have the time to rush out, follow me, and get back here? Possibly, if there was a shortcut.

Marti's face looked like someone had pinched her arm, hard. "Isn't that what we were supposed to do? Heidi's not had much luck making contact. This is not going well at all."

"JoJo's not ready to chat," Heidi said. "But…" She placed her fingers against her temples. "I am hearing something. It's a word. Ho…ha… hell… hellraiser."

"Plenty of those around here," Marti said.

A perfect segue for my next comment. "I invited Gifty here for dinner."

"What?" Marti's brows dipped, and her lips formed a crooked line. "I don't want that woman in this house."

"Is she or is she not a Means?"

"Who knows?"

"Heidi, is it possible a member of the Means family took JoJo out?" I asked.

"Well, yeah…"

"That could include Gifty."

Marti's eyes rounded. "Oh, I see." She chewed on that for a few moments, probably finding the idea of fingering Gifty as JoJo's killer palatable. "You rounded up the suspects." Then she snapped to. "Hey, I'd better not be one."

"We're all suspects." Heidi plopped onto the sofa. "Even me. By association, since Marti hired me."

"Not me, I'm just cookin' up a storm." Mom twirled a kitchen towel. She looked as out of place as a crystal vase in a coal mine. Always a walking fashion statement, Mom's copper-colored apron matched her brown and orange suede outfit perfectly.

"I, for one, am glad Gifty's coming," Marti said. "I'd like to see the look on her face when you prove she did it."

"Here you are." Veera marched in. Bart arrived in her wake. "He was showing me around the picture-perfect barn." She gestured toward Bart. "There's a workshop for cars, a pottery wheel, and an artist's studio. I'm loving the little loft apartment. It has a sauna that looked inviting, if it wasn't nearly ninety degrees out. There's even a little library with a children's pop-up book section. Coolest barn I've ever seen."

Probably the only barn she'd seen. It didn't even sound like a real barn. "No animals?"

"Daddy kept his prized thoroughbreds there. There's an attached chicken coop with its own entry, but the livestock shelter is outside now." Marti looked like she was annoyed at having to explain to us city folk.

"Aunty Jo and I spent a lot of time in there." Bart's espresso-hued jacket matched his baggy pants. His shirt was a lighter shade of brown like his sneakers.

"Michael and Red are talking radiators and car engines," Veera said to me. "How was your walk?"

She could barely keep herself from winking.

"I ran into some…wildlife," I said. "Yours?"

"Peaceful like. I'm enjoyin' all that Mother Nature has to offer." Her smile beamed around the room.

"I don't know what you're talking about, seeing as we're here in a haunted house that doesn't seem haunted at all, and we've made no progress toward finding JoJo's killer, except that you invited her here tonight." Marti's hands hit her hips with that last part. She turned her blazing blue gaze toward me.

"The day is young, and the night hasn't even started. I suggest you practice staying calm for whatever's going to happen later," I said. Would something happen?

Marti threw up her hands. "I am calm!" Her voice rose an octave.

"Hold on." Heidi's fingers flew to her temples, and she closed her eyes. "I'm vibing like crazy." Her body shook like she was experiencing her own personal earthquake.

"Is it JoJo?" Marti leaned toward her. "Is she here?"

"When was the last time you ate something?" Mom looked at Heidi in concern.

My mother thought food was the cure for every ailment. "I hate to break it to you, but this is not about hunger," I whispered to her.

"Oh, right." Mom nodded. "She does look like she's possessed."

"It's Caleb," Heidi spit out.

"Papa's here?" Marti looked around.

"He says," Heidi's voice turned deeper, "'whatever it is you plan to do, you'd better start doing it.'"

"Sounds like he's talking to you," I told Heidi.

She shook off her trance and flipped toward me. "He's talking to you."

"Fine. Tell him to stop by after dinner, and we'll chat." I turned to Marti. "Is there a safe in this house?"

"In the floor under the coffee table." Marti stepped toward the spot and pointed downward. "We already checked. It's empty."

"Is there another safe?"

"Isn't one enough for you?" Marti picked up a framed family photo. "Why would there be another?"

"I've seen one." Bart stroked his stubbly chin. "In the barn."

"Well, why didn't you say so?" Marti aimed her scowl at him. "Didn't you think that could be of some importance?"

"Not really."

"Can you show us?" I focused on Bart. "Heidi can stay and listen for spirits and help Victoria with dinner." Mom was good at squeezing information out of people.

Midway to the barn, I pointed to the bell-shaped greenhouse. "Why is the greenhouse such a mess?"

"Aunty Jo never went in there," Bart said. "Grandpa put it up for Aunty Marti. She's the one with a green thumb."

"You flatter me, Bart." Marti blew a strand of hair out of her eyes. "I haven't been in that greenhouse for months. Got sick of getting thorns stuck in me, every which way I turned."

"Who waters the plants?" Veera asked.

"JoJo put Hank in charge. I heard Gifty looks in on them now and then, too." Marti snorted.

"And when she's busy?" Who else had access?

"Darin helps out."

Made sense. Reliable Darin probably knew everyone in town since he worked at the post office.

While Bart babbled about the joys of hanging out with Aunty Jo, I kept an eye out for a shadow. I slowed and touched Marti's arm. "Did Heidi stay in the house with you the whole time today?"

"Yes." Marti frowned in thought. "Except when she took a walk."

"A long walk?"

"Five minutes. Or was it fifteen? I didn't keep track."

"Is there a shortcut from the house to the trail near the pond?"

Marti pitched her pointy chin past the barn. "Used to be a little path up that hill that led straight to the main trail without going near the pond. Don't know if it's easy to find anymore. Haven't taken it in years."

"Heidi knows about the path, right?" Veera asked.

"Maybe. We met here at the ranch a few days after JoJo passed. I seem to recall seeing Heidi walking around."

We strolled into the two-story high structure. Veera was right. The inside was showstopping. A wide walkway led to clean stalls. A chandelier hung down the center of the aisle. The little library was something else, like a room out of a storybook with rocking horses and chairs with matching footstools. It was the sort of place where hours could instantly vanish, if one had hours to spend. On the opposite end, an auto shop appeared with everything from a car lift to old-school gasoline pumps. This was a car enthusiast's dream. Every tool imaginable lined a whole wall. A ladder on wheels waited nearby to put everything within easy reach. Natural lighting poured in through a row of pane windows along a top wall. Michael and Red were leaning in to peer inside the open hood of an old Ford pickup truck.

"You spent a lot of time here?" I asked Bart.

"Whenever I could." He started tearing up. "This was our special place. Aunty Jo and I were close."

Yet, JoJo kept a photo of her dog in her office, not Bart.

Marti patted his shoulder. "I know I can't replace Jo, but I'll always be here for you."

He flashed a tiny smile. "Thanks, Aunty M."

"Where's the safe?" She withdrew her hand.

"I'll show you." Bart led us to a corner of the barn, where a steep staircase led to the loft. He lifted a small woven rug at the foot of the stairs that fit JoJo's color scheme. Washed-out hues of blue and beige. Beneath the rug, embedded in concrete, a black safe with silver hinges waited to be opened.

"I don't see a combination lock." Veera bent slightly, peering at the safe.

"It's from the days when keys were enough," I said. "A combo lock would've rusted by now."

Red and Michael joined our little safecracking group.

"That old thing hasn't seen daylight in years. Probably rusted shut." Red's eyes were bloodshot as usual, his clothes wrinkled.

"I heard you're into horse racing. How often do you go to the track?" I ended my sentence by stepping closer to Red. I pretended to scratch my head while I stared at his boots.

"Used to go all the time till I realized my horse wasn't ever coming in. Walked away owing fifty grand and never looked back."

"That's a lot of money to owe." How could I see the bottom of his boots?

"Not compared to what I used to owe."

"How'd you dwindle it down?" Did JoJo help him pay the debt?

"I've got friends with money."

I couldn't see that happening, but maybe… "JoJo helped you pay some of it off, didn't she?"

"Ha!"

"Hand over the key, Bart," Marti said.

We all looked at Bart.

"I don't know where Aunty Jo kept it."

Michael and I locked gazes. He was thinking what I was thinking. The white envelope I'd found under JoJo's bed that first night held an old key. Was it the key to this safe?

"This is exasperating." Marti gave Bart the evil eye and scanned the group. "You think she would have told someone where the key is."

"She wore a chain around her neck," Bart said, "with keys on it."

"Now we're getting somewhere." Red looked around at everyone. "Where's the chain?"

"She wasn't wearing it when we found her." Marti fingered her own silver chain. "No keys in the house except for the front door and car." She stared at Michael. "Psychic number two. Where does your logical reasoning say the key is?"

"Close by." He shot me a glance before turning back to Marti. "It's going to pop up in the hands of the right person."

"When?" Bart asked.

"Sooner than you think, buddy." Michael patted his back.

"A word." Marti crooked her index finger toward me. I followed her to a corner of the barn.

"After Hank found JoJo, Gifty arrived before either me or Red got here." Marti slapped her hands together. "That woman spent a lot of time with JoJo recently. I say Gifty knew about this safe, which could mean she took the key off JoJo's neck. It was either her or Hank."

"What are the chances of JoJo sharing the key to the safe with anyone? Hank said she was good at keeping secrets." I couldn't get that thought out of my head.

Marti turned her lips inward before perking up. "If she had a mind to, JoJo would share a secret. To be certain Gifty wasn't involved, we'll need a search warrant to ransack her house."

I couldn't even begin to explain. "We need proof and a compelling reason to search."

"Hurry up and find a reason already."

"Heidi's not doing you any favors, you know." I had to get that off my chest.

Marti's mouth fell open like she'd realized I was the village idiot. "I know not everything she says is real, but it makes me feel good. And it costs a lot less than going to a shrink to figure things out. Shrinks aren't always right, either. Some of the stuff hits home, and some doesn't. That's the way it is."

Maybe Marti was smarter than I thought. "I might have a skeleton key in my car." I didn't know if the key I'd found would fit, but I needed to try. And, I had a hankering to get some fresh air. "I'll be back."

Walking backward out the barn door, I texted Michael, asking him to take a look at the boot pattern on Red's footwear. Then I whirled around and sprinted toward the small hill Marti had pointed out. Squirrel and gopher holes crisscrossed the pasture like little landmines, ready to trip me up. Plenty of opportunities to lose my footing in these fields.

Curly coated sheep froze mid-chew to fix unreadable stares my way. They'd eliminated all signs of plant life except for a few stubborn weeds and nubs. Hoof prints patterned the patches of dirt.

As I approached the small hillside, tufts of tall grass and mustard plants rose to border the narrow path that meandered upward between shrubs and trees. Parched plant life hung on for dear life. No sign of bootprints anywhere. I wandered up to the top of the hill where the trail and the view broadened over Means Well Ranch and neighboring homes. I even got a peek of downtown Los Ranchos's rooftops. But that's all I saw.

I wound my way to the other side and stopped. "Oh boy." A brown and white snake stretched across the path, like he was waiting to collect a crossing toll. I detoured off the trail and headed back toward the bottom. I'd only gone a few steps when I stopped again. A heel print stamped the dirt next to a scrap of weeds. It had the markings of the zig-zags and horseshoe heel-shaped print I'd seen earlier. The prints continued away from the trail, cutting another path. I didn't need to follow all the way down to know that he was headed for the ranch.

Chapter Fifteen

The prints stopped at the bottom of the hill. Had he changed shoes? Or direction? I walked in a wide circle before placing my hunt on hold. Maybe he'd dumped the boots and hidden them. I studied the surroundings. Wouldn't someone see him ditch the boots? I poked around some more, but finding nothing incriminating, I returned to the barn.

A small circle of people surrounded the in-ground safe. Red was on his knees, inserting a crowbar to pry open the door.

"This isn't working." He tossed it to one side. The crowbar scraped and clanged against the concrete floor. "Get me the sledgehammer."

Bart angled over to the wall of tools, grabbed an oversized hammer, and handed it to Red.

"If this doesn't work, the drill will." Red looked like he was chewing on the pieces of scrap metal that sat in a bin behind him.

"Explosives." Michael gazed at the round-eyed faces around him. "No, no, no! I don't mean we should use any. I'm saying some old safes contain vials of nitroglycerin, which could explode if not handled with care."

"Seriously?" Veera asked.

"In the 1920s and 30s, safes were booby-trapped with nitro or tear gas to keep burglars out. If this hasn't been opened for a long time—"

"—We'll get a real bang for our buck," Red said.

"Where's your skeleton key?" Marti asked me.

"Couldn't locate it." I itched my arm. Too many eyes made me break out into a rash. Or maybe I'd run across poison oak. The itch jumped to my neck.

Marti turned to Bart. "You sure you never saw JoJo open this safe?"

"No, ma'am. Not in front of me, she didn't. She said whatever was inside was of no value. That's why it's in the barn."

"Bull," Red said. "This would be the best place to bury treasure. No one would bother looking. Either here or bury the goods in the pasture."

"Maybe it's empty," Veera said.

"Then why would it be locked?" Bart asked.

"Probably where Papa's antique rodent traps ended up," Red said. "Or the pistols."

"Don't be ridiculous," Marti said. "There's cold, hard cash in there. Oodles of it. It'd be just like JoJo to lock it and take away the key. It's not empty, I promise you."

"Let's search the main house for the key before we destroy the safe." I suggested that for two reasons. One, I might have the only key sitting in my purse. Antique keys weren't easy to duplicate. Secondly, that house needed extensive searching. Why not get the whole gang to do it? Even if one of them was involved in JoJo's death, they might give themselves away.

"Maybe someone should talk to Gifty about the key." Veera sat cross-legged on the floor with a pop-up book in her lap. "Since she and JoJo were friendly, she might know something."

"Red, you got along with Gifty," Marti said. "Go find out."

"We bonded over a piece of rib-eye steak once." Red's red-rimmed eyes drifted around the group. "I'll go."

"The rest of us will rummage through the ranch house." Marti aimed for the door.

"Gotta find JoJo's cell phone, too," I added.

As everyone filed out, I hung back. "My team needs to regroup," I told Marti. "We'll join you in a few minutes."

As soon as the Means family left, we formed a huddle and spoke in fast whispers.

"Bart doesn't know much about fixing cars," Michael said. "He works at a tire place, not a mechanic shop, according to Red. Bart's been in and out of nine jobs in the past two years."

"Another Means family member strapped for cash." And with a motive to get rid of JoJo.

"Besides Red, you mean?" Michael glanced from me to Veera. "I asked Red how he plans to pay his way out of the gambling hole he's in. I suggested he pull the plug before he's fully electrocuted."

"What's that mean?" Veera said.

"It's gambling speak for 'quit while you're ahead.'"

"Did JoJo help him pay off his debt?" I was holding fast to that theory.

"He said he did fine without her moolah."

"Someone helped him pay." Red couldn't do it on his own. Unless he stole Means family antiques and sold them. Even then, it wouldn't be enough.

"And Marti's mortgage holder on her house? It was JoJo, according to Red," Michael said.

"That doesn't promote sisterly love." Veera shook her head.

"Heidi checks out. Her parents are who we know they are, and she lives at the address on her driver's license, but I'll look some more." Michael's eyes narrowed.

"Nice work." I turned to Veera. "What did you find?"

"When I had alone time, I hustled into JoJo's office." Veera's eyes shone with excitement. "She had four bank accounts with plenty of money. When I looked around the house to see what Marti was up to, I found her in JoJo's bedroom, taking out drawers and looking at the bottom of each one, like she expected something to be taped underneath."

"She was either looking for the key or watched one too many episodes of *Murder She Wrote*." I was betting on the key.

"She must not have found anything, judging by her mood." Michael rubbed his chin.

I regarded the double doors leading into the barn. "There are two entries into this place." I pointed to the big doors in the front and a smaller door at the back end. "Veera, the front's all yours. Make sure no one comes in. Michael—"

"You're not opening the safe without me."

"You don't think I can handle it?" There was no room for worry in an investigation.

"You're better off with me opening it. If there are vials of nitro in there and they topple over…"

"Trust me, there'll be no explosion." Famous last words uttered by some criminal mind before he was blown up. The good news? I wasn't a criminal. I dug into my purse and extracted the envelope. "Take a look at this key." I handed it to him. "The notches match the safe's keyhole. No vials will be shattered on my watch."

Michael examined the key and eyed the lock, while Veera stood watch at the main door.

"All clear," she said.

"Move it," I told Michael.

He squeezed my hand and hurried off.

I blew on the key for good luck and stuck the it into the lock. I turned it ever so slowly, trying not to break into a full-on sweat. Boy, could I use a shower. One small click, and I warily opened the thick door. My gaze wandered the interior. No sign of any vials.

"That's a relief!"

I jumped and slapped the muscular bicep behind me. "Michael!"

"I figured on the small chance it blew, we'd turn into smithereens together."

"That is so…not romantic." I said a little prayer of thanks that we were still intact.

Veera rushed over. "All this fuss and nothing to show for it?"

I told them about the boot prints on the hill.

"I tried, but I couldn't get Red to show me his soles." Michael looked up. "It's like his boots were glued to the floor."

"Maybe we should tie him up and yank them off his feet," Veera said.

"What's that?" Michael pointed inside the safe.

There were four compartments in the rectangular opening. Two tall slots in the bottom and two short ones on top. One of the top slots had a front entry with a place to insert a key.

"If the key fits." I stuck the old key inside and turned it.

Chapter Sixteen

We unlocked the compartment and stared at a legal-sized envelope. Nothing was written on the outside, but it had a seal like the one on the smaller envelope housing the key to the safe. I debated opening it.

"Don't we want to know what's inside?" Veera asked.

My fingers gave the envelope a squeeze. "Feels like a letter." I held it up to the light, but I couldn't see through. "We'll hand this over to Marti and let her open it. I'll tell her about the key, too."

Michael and Veera locked gazes.

"Okay, look, maybe something in me changed a little after I hit my head, or maybe I've wanted to change all along. How about that?" Did I just recently discover my conscience? I straightened and closed the safe. "We're starting a new agency, and I want our reputation to be solid, not just because we're good at what we do, but because we do the right thing."

My teammates gazed at me like I was wrapped in some sort of holy light. I looked around. Nope. Not a holy light in sight.

Veera turned to Michael. "Is it possible some kind of toxic fumes came out of that safe when she opened it?"

"No, she'd be clutching at her throat and wheezing."

"Stop being hilarious and start being the P.I. superstars we think we are," I said.

Both of them rolled back their shoulders and stood a little taller. Veera pulled out her P.I. notebook.

"Exactly what are the qualities of a P.I. superstar?"

"First off, you're never a superstar by yourself. We work together. Take care of your team. Keep an open mind. Do the right thing."

"Which may or may not include lying." Veera scribbled hard and fast.

"Lying should be kept to a minimum." I couldn't tell whether that statement made Michael nervous or elated. He looked slightly dazed. "Ask the right questions. Follow the evidence and check out all leads."

"That means you should open the letter," Michael said. "You're going to turn it over to Marti anyway, open or closed."

He made sense.

Veera's grin lit up the barn. "I'm liking the new you." Her grin faded. "But we're still not making much headway in this case. Of course, the contents of that envelope may prove me wrong."

I unsheathed the shuriken from my belt buckle. A sharp star point ripped open the envelope. Veera and Michael huddled closer to me, as I pulled out a folded paper.

"What's it say?" Veera shifted from one foot to another.

I unfolded the paper and read out loud, "Ha, ha. Foiled you again. Charlie Bucket knows."

They pulled back, and we shared the same surprised gaze.

"What does Charlie Bucket know?" Veera asked.

"This means..." Michael started, "...JoJo was a fan of *Charlie and the Chocolate Factory*."

"It means JoJo's playing games." I folded the letter back inside.

"With who?" Veera asked.

"Whoever expected the safe to hold valuables."

"That would be Marti," Veera said.

"How does Charlie Bucket fit in?" Michael asked.

"Must have something to do with candy, like in the book," Veera said. "She's handing us clues."

"Keep that last thought." I led the way outside. "Charlie had the golden ticket." That was my best guess. Golden ticket to what? Money? What was it Dad used to say?

Guesswork is an assumption that's all dressed up with nowhere to go. Use common sense to verify what you don't know.

My common sense told me someone close to JoJo wanted something from her that she wasn't willing to give. What was that something?

* * *

When I showed the letter to the Means family members, astonishment made the rounds. Bart located a notepad with JoJo's scribbles in her office, and I compared the handwriting in both. The same flourishes appeared in the cursive. JoJo was someone who took care to form her neat style. Could one have been a forgery? Not in my non-expert opinion.

"It's a joke." Marti looked skyward and hugged herself as if asking JoJo what was up?

"Aunty Jo liked games." Bart leaned against a wall. "She played with her students, to be sure they remembered the lesson."

"Why Charlie Bucket?" I asked.

"We had a cat named Charlie." Marti stared at Heidi. "You got something to add?"

"JoJo's still not talking," Heidi said.

Red shuffled into the room, and all went quiet. "Were you expecting someone else?"

"We're expecting answers we're not getting, even with two psychics in the house." Marti gave a little groan of disgust. She brought Red up to date and showed him the note.

"Would she use a word like 'foil'?" I asked. Was it possible someone else left this clue?

"She fancied herself a Henrietta Higgins, she did." Red's mock British accent sounded like he'd just regained consciousness after a dose of anesthesia.

"What about Charlie Cat, Red? Why'd she bring him up?" Marti asked.

Red's bug-eyed gaze swung from Marti to me. "She used to say Charlie had more integrity in his furry little paw than we did."

"Ridiculous." Marti jerked her head away from him.

"Did you talk to Gifty, Red?" He'd been gone long enough.

He sank onto a chair. "Nobody was home at the cottage."

"She's probably spying on us," Marti spoke through lips so tight that the words barely made it out.

"Did anyone find JoJo's cell phone?" Someone had to know where it was.

No one responded. The rest of the day was spent searching the house until a series of knocks rattled the front door. Gifty arrived just before sunset, and she wasn't alone. A large, rugged-looking fellow stood next to her.

"Hank," Marti said. "I wasn't expecting you."

"That's why I came. To heat up the pot and stir the kettle." In three long strides, Hank was in the living room. He wore a blue and red checked shirt over jeans. A brown leather jacket was slung over his arm.

Red stepped forward. "Glad I won't be the only one with machismo here tonight."

"Hey, now. Shedding a few tears is just as manly as chopping wood." Michael looked at me. "So I got a little excited over his pristine car engine and original upholstery. There's no shame in that."

I squeezed his hand. "I love sensitive men."

"I'm here." Gifty clutched a red handbag that matched her ruffled dress and low heels.

Marti's gaze collided with Gifty's. "Of course you are. It's time to bury the hatchet and act like we don't mind being around each other, even if we do." She stiffly embraced Gifty and pulled away.

"You arrived just in time for dinner." Mom put her arm around Gifty and led her inside. "No talking business until after we eat. We're going to be like one big family."

Red lumbered over to me and stuck his coarse mustache close to my ear. "Some might assert that Gifty didn't answer the door because she knew it was me. Or she was out and about, if you know what I'm getting at." He shuffled back to his chair and sat.

If Gifty truly wasn't at home, what had she been up to? She stood by the fireplace. I edged over to her side.

"Where were you before you arrived at the ranch?"

"Walking, until I ran into Hank. I asked him to accompany me here."

"How long was your alone time?"

"Long enough to put me in the frame of mind I needed to face the family."

That meant she had time on her hands, too.

* * *

It took less than twenty minutes to polish off every tasty morsel of Mom's dinner. And a fraction of that time to devour the chocolate layer cake. The delicious dessert loosened a lot of lips. They shared JoJo memories, from her fruit-picking parties to her barn sprucing. Her gatherings involved a lot of free labor.

"Hank heard the piano playing this morning." Surprise sprinkled with doubt registered on the faces. All faces except Marti's and Heidi's, that is. Clearly, Marti hadn't shared the news with the others. Heidi slumped low in her seat.

"That's what happens in a haunted house," Heidi said.

"Hank's imagining things." Bart tilted his chair back and clasped his hands together.

"He's been nipping at the moonshine." Red's mustache twitched.

"What song was playing, Hank?" Marti asked.

"*Let it Be.*"

"One of Papa's favorites," Marti said.

"Papa didn't play the piano," Gifty said.

"Mama did," Marti said. "Which is more than your mama could do."

"My mama ran businesses!"

"She ran a strip club."

Everyone spoke at once.

"Quiet!" I needed them to focus. "Why did you say this house is haunted?" I focused on Marti and Heidi.

"Because…sometimes…scary things happen." Marti gripped the arms of her chair.

"Like creepy sounds?" Veera was thinking about the noises she'd heard during our search.

"Every so often, a plane will fly overhead so low, it'll rattle the dishes. A cow will moo, and the meadowlark sings. Makes you wonder." Red's bland stare scraped across the room.

"I heard someone moaning once when I spent the night," Bart said. "Couldn't tell where it came from, but it was eerie. Didn't bother Aunty Jo, though."

"Marti, do you have more to share?" Why did I sound like a preschool teacher?

Her gaze flashed at each of us in turn. "It was four years ago. I sat in this same seat. Fog had rolled in, deep, thick, and soupy, like clam chowder. That's how it was in Istanbul."

"She went there on vacation in 1998, and now she's an expert," Red muttered.

I tried to fight back my eye-roll, but it was a losing battle.

"It was like being stuck in a cocoon. Just like tonight." She stared out the window. "The porch light was out." She slowly stood and pointed. "It's not working." Her hand shot to her mouth.

The porch was dark, but I couldn't recall seeing the light on.

"I'll take a look." Hank was on his feet, headed for the door.

In the next second, a snapping sound filled the room, and blackness permeated the house. Gasps and shrieks tore apart the silence. What were the chances of a power outage right now?

Chapter Seventeen

I pulled out my penlight, and within moments, Veera, Michael, and even Mom were shining thin beams around the living room. Where was Gifty?

"Has the electric bill been paid?" Veera asked.

"Aunty Jo always paid in advance," Bart said.

The front door opened and slammed shut.

"Where's Gifty going?" Mom asked.

"The guilty always run away," Marti said.

"Aw, shush, Marti." Hank walked in and waved a hand at her. "You're always pushing the blame on everyone else."

She flipped around. "What are you insinuating?"

"I'm saying that if you're not treated the way you think you should be treated, it's your own doing." He stepped onto the porch.

"When you talk sense, I'll listen." Marti jerked her chin up and turned her back to him.

Daytime soap operas had less drama.

"Porch light needs a new bulb, that's all." Hank stuffed his flashlight in his leather jacket.

Gifty raced back inside. "I called a couple of neighbors. This is the only house without power."

"Is there a generator?" Michael asked Red.

"Next to the garage. Follow me."

They'd taken only a few steps when the power flicked back on.

"What is happening?" Veera asked.

"It's showtime," Heidi whispered. "The spirits are at work."

"Did you know that fortune-telling is illegal in New York City?" Red asked Heidi.

"Well, we're not in New York, are we? And I'm no fortune teller. I'm a medium."

"Hooey." Red puffed out a short stream of air.

I was amazed at Heidi's lightning-speed turn from spirit communicator to grumpy guest. "Who would benefit by playing tricks on us?" I asked.

"Somebody that wants us out of here." Gifty's fists were balled.

It was my turn to head for the door. "Veera, let's take a walk. Michael, poke around inside." I turned to Mom.

"I'll maintain calm and order." She winked at me.

In minutes, Veera and I plodded around the property.

"What are we looking for?" she asked.

The lights at the ranch didn't shut off on their own. Someone was creating a distraction. Why? "Signs that someone's fooling around. Where's the fuse box or circuit breaker?"

"I'll hunt it down."

"Meet me back here in fifteen minutes." My legs were itching to run, and that's what I did. I flew toward the nearest hill with my penlight and gut instinct as my compass.

Take control of the things you can control in your life. It'll make dealing with the unexpected less of a challenge.

"I'm trying," I whispered. Advice from Dad trickled through my mind whenever I felt stress overload during investigations. But tonight, I felt something else. Unnerved.

I slowed when I reached the foot of the path. The reassuring medley of a cricket chorus, like tinkling bells playing soft and low, soothed the night's sharp edges. It was the only sound… except for padded steps behind me. I turned and circled the beam of light until its muted outer glow outlined a four-legged creature with ears pointing skyward. The coyote nearly blended into the night. I stomped forward, and the creature scurried off.

Partially crouching, I started the slow ascent up the narrow path. A high-pitched squeal scratched the surface of the stillness. "Nothing I can't handle."

Weeds grew hardier and thicker in my upward climb; the trees turned scragglier, and the path rockier. Even the scents shifted from floral and green to muskier, earthy smells. Halfway up, the odor of death washed over me, as I paused near the carcass of an opossum, fangs bared. I stifled a screech. The trail narrowed to a skinny ribbon. I pushed past overgrown shrubs to reach the top.

What happened to the choir of chirping crickets? All sound had deserted the night. There were plenty of hiding places for someone to wait and ambush me. A local who was familiar with the terrain would blend into the darkness as easily as a coyote. If someone wanted to take me down, wouldn't they have made a move already? And why was I up here, anyway? My hunches didn't always pan out.

A bush rustled ahead of me as a small burst of energy exploded from the undergrowth, flapping wings vanishing into the night. I jumped back, landing my heel in a small hole. My foot sunk deep enough for me to lose my balance and stumble backward across a jumble of shrubs that jabbed my arms. Tiny twigs pricked against the back of my neck like sharp fingernails.

"Argh!" I pounded my fist on the ground, and pain shot up my arm. My hand had slammed against an unexpected hardness. "That hurt." I rubbed my hand. The surface had some give, so it wasn't a tree branch unless it was covered by moss or some sponge-like covering. I untangled myself from the shrub and rose, aiming the light in the spot where I'd fallen. Needle-like greens poked out from woody stems, empty beer cans littered the ground, and…my face turned cold. My heart hammered in my chest. "Oh, no."

Chapter Eighteen

In a few dizzying seconds, I knelt beside a body and checked for a pulse. There was none. A man lay on his side, arms bent in front of him, fingers clasped together. He could've been sleeping except for the pistol near his bloody head. A small-caliber, semi-automatic handgun. A Ruger LCP. My insides felt like I'd been punched so hard that all air had left my body despite the fact that I'd visited enough crime scenes with my father to decipher the scene. A bullet had entered the right temple of a man with white hair cropped short, military style. Clean-shaven, his skin was tanned. For the second time today, I stared at Alistair Wallaby, the man I'd met at the post office, the other power player in town, besides JoJo. What was he doing here? Had he been following me today? The masked man I'd viewed looked bigger, bulkier.

I gingerly tipped the gun upward with gloved fingers. No serial number. I straightened and roved my beam around. Alistair's wire-rimmed glasses had fallen onto a pile of twigs and branches a few feet away. Was it a coincidence that he and JoJo died within a week of each other?

I took photos with my phone. With the weapon lying so close, it was easy to conclude this was a suicide. Too easy. I forced my eyes back to the body. The clasped hands looked like Alistair had begged for his life. Anger washed over me, and I turned away.

Since cell phone reception was scarce, I jogged down the hill, hopping over bushes and boulders, checking for cell bars every few seconds. Was Alistair right-handed? We shook hands when we met, my right to his right. Why come to this spot to pull the trigger? For one thing, there'd be no interruptions. Could be a while before the body was found. Was there enough time, over the last few hours, for someone staying at the ranch to meet Alistair, kill him, and return to business without anyone noticing? Oh yes. The whole scene could have unfolded in five minutes or less.

I put on the brakes when I reached the pasture. If this was a suicide, real or staged, there might be a note. With lead feet, I trudged back to the body, eyes searching the ground for bootprints. There were none. Thankfully, my pockets were stuffed with all the supplies I needed for a quick search. Pulling on the latex gloves, I reached inside Alistair's quilted coat, trying to ignore the blood splatter. I closed my eyes and held my breath, willing my heart to slow. I could do this.

The suede was soft; the lining satiny, as would be expected from a jacket belonging to a man of means. I patted and checked each of the six interior pockets. He'd carried a small wallet housing credit cards, cash, and his driver's license. Another pocket held a leather key fob with a silver ring holding three keys. Two *No Fresher* green chewing gum wrappers were stuffed in the same pocket. Where was his cell phone? Stuffed in an exterior pocket, I extracted a small, folded note on lined gray paper. Handwritten in black ink and block letters were these words:

I have found it unbearable to live without dear Josephine Joelle. I trust you will understand.

I took a picture of the note and returned it. The pockets of his jeans were empty. I regarded his boots. Square-toed with a leather sole, the circular pattern was not one I'd seen before. I studied the body from different angles before racing down the hill. Did the boot prints I'd seen earlier belong to the killer?

Wrapped in my thoughts, I hurried at such full speed, I whizzed past Veera as she waited near the barn.

"I was getting worried," she said. "Hey, where're you runnin' to?" She raced after me and caught up.

I slowed, leaning over, out of breath. Panting between my words, I gave her the abbreviated version of discovering Alistair.

"You think he killed JoJo?" Veera asked.

I paused near the garage. "That thought didn't cross my mind."

"You might've spooked Alistair today when you met him at the post office. Coming to terms with what he did was impossible, and that's what made him suicidal." Veera unrolled her theory as we passed the barn.

"Someone staged Alistair's suicide."

Veera's hand flew to her heart. "He was murdered?"

"I don't think it's possible to shoot yourself and hit the ground with fingers interlocked." I sidestepped around, holding my phone up till I had reception. I called 9-1-1 and reported the body.

"Oh, my Lord." Veera stared out. "Maybe he partnered up with someone to get rid of JoJo. Then, after meeting you, Alistair threatened to fess up, and the partner shot him down."

"Why kill JoJo?"

"A business deal went south 'cause of her, so he did her in, which would make him the town bigwig. Do we know who's buying Means Well Ranch? Maybe it's him. There's a motive right there."

Why didn't I think of that? "That's a little something Marti hasn't shared with us." Who exactly was buying the ranch? "But it could've been a different motive."

Footsteps crunched the gravel near the side of the house closest to us. I aimed my light and pulled out my gun.

A shadowy figure stopped about twenty feet away. I pointed my beam at his face.

"Michael!"

"I found something." Michael hustled over, carrying a large bag.

"You shouldn't startle us like that. You know how she gets." Veera pointed to the gun in my hand.

"She's been really good about not shooting people during our investigations," Michael said.

Although I was a crack shot, thanks to many hours at the shooting range with Dad, I'd done more damage by hitting people over the head with the butt of my gun than actually pulling the trigger. I planned to keep it that way.

"Before you go on," I didn't like being the bearer of terrible news, "I found something, too." I told Michael about Alistair.

"Horrible." He slapped his hand to his head.

Veera's fingers pressed to her cheeks. "Can't believe this tiny town had two murders in a week."

"They have to be related." I turned to Michael. "What do you have?"

He opened the top of a large plastic bag covered with bits of dirt. A pair of brown boots rested inside.

I grabbed one and stared at the sole. It was the same zig-zag pattern as the one on the trail. "Where'd you find them?"

"I checked each shed around the house and got nothing. Then that bull with the incredibly pointy horns started making moves toward me."

"Poncho," I whispered.

"I casually backed away and ducked behind a metal water trough."

"The ground's cracked and dry everywhere except around the trough." Of course. The attached drip line sometimes overfilled the trough, which made it easy to dig in that area. Made perfect sense.

"The dirt was turned over in this two-by-two-foot square and patted down," Michael's eyes were rounded.

"No animal can dig like that," Veera said.

"No animal could use a trowel, which he probably used. I took out my knife and started digging. Near the surface, I uncovered this bag."

Veera grinned. "You're like a human leather detector." She turned to me. "Hank or Red have feet big enough to fit those."

I stuck my hand inside a boot. Empty. "Size elevens. Maybe someone used larger-sized boots to throw the scent off. But whoever these belong to…"

"…is close by." Michael's eyes grew rounder. "Maybe inside the house right now."

I jumped up and dashed toward the house. Mom was in there.

"The circuit breaker is an updated version." Veera ran by my side.

"I noticed that, too." Michael raced past and turned to face us, still running. "It means the lights could've gone out using a digital app."

"Remote operated?" I knew that answer.

"Uh-huh. Somebody in the house is a tech nerd."

"Any guesses?" I asked. We stopped by the porch.

Michael landed in front of me. "Could be anyone. If Heidi rigged the speaker in the fan inside the séance room, I'd vote for her."

I was willing to bet Heidi worked the fan, but tonight's events were a little more sophisticated. "Did Red leave your sight today when you were in the barn together?" Did he kill Alistair?

Michael stared at the ground, brows dipping. "When we were working on the car, he left to go ask a neighbor about borrowing a tiny screwdriver. Took him like twenty minutes."

"Did he come back with the screwdriver?" I asked.

He shook his head. "Said the neighbor didn't have one small enough. Is Red our guy?"

"Not sure yet." I turned to Veera. "And Bart?"

"He didn't go anywhere. But I did. I was checking out the pop-up kids' books in the library, and I might've lost track of time, and him." She shook her head. "Pitcher takes her eye off the ball one minute, and it slams her in the face."

"It's okay." I patted her shoulder. "He would've found another way to slip out."

"If we're dealing with savvy criminals…" Michael ran a hand through his wavy hair, "…it's good if they think we're clueless."

"Come to think of it, after I came down from my library high, I set out to locate Bart. I thought he was with you…" she flicked her gaze toward Michael, "…but then there he was, coming in through the back door. Said he was checking the water troughs to make sure they were filled." She grabbed Michael's arm. "His hands were all wet."

"Because he just got finished burying the boots." Michael's eyes opened wide.

Or washing the blood off. Either Red or Bart could've gotten rid of Alistair.

"Marti's still in the running." How close a watch did Mom keep on Heidi and Marti? I raced up the porch steps.

"Gifty had an ax to grind, too. And what about Hank? Gifty found him out and about. He's a prime suspect, being the first to find JoJo's body and all. Should we frisk everyone?" Veera asked.

"I'll vote for that," Michael said.

"No frisking. We don't want them to know that we know anything, remember? Murder's never perfect. Sooner or later, it comes apart at the seams."

"I'll have my knife ready to encourage seam splitting," Michael said.

I squeezed his hand. "We might have to rile them up to get them to cooperate." Being a fan of classic Hollywood films, I loved talking tough. "Hold on to the boots, for now. Meanwhile, I'll tell them about the body and provide some bonus material, and watch how they react." An idea bubbled to the surface of my brain. "We'll throw in a little something that should pique the killer's interest."

Chapter Nineteen

When we stepped into the living room of JoJo's house, it was like someone had pushed the mute button. Everyone seemed to be holding their breath. If I closed my eyes, I'd think I was alone.

"You were gone a while." Marti broke the silence. "Find anything?"

"I did. Alistair Wallaby. Know him?" My gaze scoured the room.

"Sure. Most of us do." Marti got to her feet. "What about him?"

Was it my imagination, or did she perk up at my easy question? What was she expecting?

"He's a longtime family friend," she added.

"Used to give me piggyback rides to church." Bart grinned at the memory. "He's cool."

"Eats at my place for breakfast nearly every day," Hank said.

"And lives to talk about it." One side of Red's mouth turned up.

"What's going on?" Mom asked me.

She knew me well enough to recognize that there was more to my question.

"Bart took it upon himself to step outside right after Michael left." Red put the spotlight on his nephew.

"What does that mean?" Marti asked.

"It means I needed some air." Bart pulled at the collar of his crewneck tee. "It's hard sitting here with all that's going on and knowing Aunty Jo isn't…" He dropped his head and quietly moaned.

Marti rubbed his back. "Leave him alone, Red. You took your sweet time coming back to the house before dinner." She turned to Red. "Couldn't have taken you that long to find Gifty, especially since she wasn't home."

"I was out walking." Gifty's lower lip popped out.

Red stuck a hand in his pocket and took out a small plastic bag. It was mostly empty, except for some squishy stuff at the bottom. "I went to the pond, with grapes and apple bits. I like feeding the ducks. There's something so primeval about swallowing your food whole."

"Did anyone see you at the pond?" I straggled closer.

"Besides Daffy and Daisy Duck? No." He stretched his arms above his head and yawned. "I might've dozed off between feedings."

I turned to Marti. "Why didn't you tell me that Alistair and JoJo were an item?"

"That's not the way it is. Or was. They partnered up to get things done, but they weren't romantic." She turned to Hank. "You know something I don't?"

"I do not." Hank fixed his squinty stare on me. "Why are you asking?"

"Marti, who's buying this ranch?"

"JoJo never said, other than it was some L.A. investor. You can ask the realtor. Want me to find her number?"

"There's something more pressing." I turned to Hank. "I've called law enforcement. Alistair's body is near the top of the hill, above the sheep pasture."

"Body?" Marti shrieked as both hands flew to her mouth. Gifty rose unsteadily and Bart cried out.

"Can't be." Red frowned more than was humanly possible.

Despite his bulk, Hank rushed out the door like a deer fleeing a fire.

"Should I go after him?" Michael moved toward the door.

"Tail him," I said. "Make sure he's going toward the police, not running away from them."

Michael rushed out, and everyone spoke at once in a blur of shocked reactions. If one of them was acting, I couldn't tell. Mom passed a box of tissues around the room.

"Did Alistair just keel over and die?" Red asked.

"Yes," I said, "with a little help from a pistol lying next to him."

"Are you saying he killed himself?" Marti fingered the necklace at her throat.

"You're certain he's dead?" Gifty asked.

"As certain as I am that someone in this house killed Alistair." Was I certain of that? What if whoever did him in was off my radar?

Wide-eyed stares turned on each other with a healthy dose of suspicion. What was I hoping for? A confession, for starters.

"We have airtight alibis," Red said. "None of us had enough time to kill anyone since we arrived here."

Veera stepped up. "How do you know how much time it took to kill him? Kind of defensive for someone who doesn't have the details and who spent time alone at a duck pond."

"There's no such thing as an airtight alibi." Not for this group. I had to give enough information to alert the killer he'd be caught shortly, assuming the killer was present. "I studied the body."

"Are you saying someone wanted it to look like a suicide? Has to be the same person that wanted JoJo to look like she'd died in her sleep." Marti blew her nose and reached for another tissue. "I knew she didn't just up and die on us."

"How do you know it wasn't a suicide?" Gifty's gaze was glued to mine.

Was she trying to squeeze details out of me? Fat chance that would happen. "The police will confirm." Everyone here was a poser, showing sides they wanted us to see. Bart cradled his head in his hands. Red perched next to him, his frown as doleful as a basset hound's. Marti stared at the floor. And Gifty? She watched everything unfold while chewing on a knuckle.

"Who would want Alistair *and* JoJo dead?" Marti tilted her head toward me and sank onto a chair.

"I saw him today, in town." Gifty's lower lip quivered. "Alistair said he planned to come by so we could talk."

"What about?" Mom asked.

Gifty shook her head. "He didn't say."

"Why would he want to talk to you?" Marti rose and balled her hands. "You must have some idea."

"I have none."

"Doesn't anyone here know anything?" Marti's face flashed red.

"I met Alistair today," I said.

"When he was alive?" Mom asked.

"Yes, Mother. When he could walk and breathe and talk about who killed JoJo."

Marti gripped the armrest. "Who did it?"

Now what? "He didn't give a name, but I… found a note." If I didn't spill the beans now, the killer could come after me next, thinking I knew more than I was letting on. Was that such a bad thing? It could speed up the investigation. And remove me from it, permanently.

"Now, honey," Mom said. "Tell these nice people who did it so we can put him or her away and be done with this whole thing." She leaned closer to me. "This is getting dangerous, and I don't mean driving-on-L.A.-freeways dangerous, I mean great-white-shark-infested-waters dangerous." She swiveled back to everyone else. "Corrie has something to say."

The universe was practically pointing me in one direction. "Two notes were found on Alistair's body," I said. "Handwritten notes from Alistair. In one, he said he couldn't live without JoJo. I found that in a jacket pocket."

"Then it *was* a suicide," Gifty said.

"And the other…" I scoured the faces. All eyes were fastened on me. "…said to check his office desk drawer." Not too shabby. I needed to put something out there that was vague enough to keep them guessing. The killer would want that note. All I had to do was get to Alistair's office first.

"Where did you find this second note?" Red asked.

"Stuffed inside Alistair's shoe." After all, I forgot to check his shoes and socks. For all I knew, a note could be tucked in there.

"You've been awfully quiet. Aren't you getting any messages?" Marti turned toward Heidi. "Seems JoJo would have something to say about all this, opinionated as she was."

Heidi sat in a corner chair, stroking a velvety beige throw with a faint smile like she was detached from the whole scene. "I'm sensing that JoJo doesn't feel Alistair played a significant role in what happened to her. She has nothing to say."

"Hogwash." Red turned blazing eyes on Heidi.

Michael shot inside and skidded to a stop. He nodded my way. I took that to mean Hank was on the hill with law enforcement.

Red turned to Marti and pointed to Heidi. "It's demeaning to JoJo's memory to have her here. She's adding confusion to chaos. Or maybe it's the other way around."

Heidi pulled the throw closer to her chest. "JoJo warned me about you. That you wouldn't appreciate my highly developed sixth sense."

"You met JoJo?" I asked.

"I'm talking about her spirit. She spoke to me from the afterworld." Heidi rolled her eyes.

She was definitely toying with us.

"What I don't appreciate is your offering advice based on the insights of dead people, one of whom is my sister." Red stood.

"I don't have to sit here…" Heidi shot to her feet.

"The police will want to question you. Everyone's a suspect." Michael's index finger roamed the room for a few moments, then he dropped it. "Except us. The investigating team, I mean. I can't speak for the rest of you."

I turned to Marti. "Where's Alistair's office?"

"In the Community Services Building," Gifty replied. "On Saint Joseph Street, one block north of Hank's."

"Listen up, everyone." Michael was on a roll. He stood tall in the center of the room and walked a slow circle to view everyone. "Nobody leaves this room until after the police take statements."

"We didn't see the body," Red said.

"But you knew the body." Michael's gaze swung to mine.

"Since it happened on Means Well Ranch, they'll want to talk to everyone," I said. That sounded official, and it was the truth.

"I need to use the ladies' room." Marti dabbed at her eyes.

"I'll come with you," Veera said.

"I can do my business without your help."

"Then you better do it fast. I'll be listening. We need to make sure no one leaves our sight in case one of you was responsible." Veera put on her I-mean-business face. No one would dare cross her looking like that, especially while she held the can of industrial-strength pepper spray in one hand.

"I'm going to the crime scene to talk to the cops." I gave Michael and Veera my silent thanks for giving me a chance to hightail it to Alistair's office.

Gifty stood up. "Will you walk me to my home first? I need to get something."

What I needed was to get to Alistair's office and plant a note.

"You can't leave, Gifty!" Marti cocked her head as her face pinched with annoyance.

"I'll be responsible for her." I nodded, and Gifty followed me outside. Once we were on the driveway, I swiveled to face her. "What do you need to get?"

"Nothing. I want to talk."

Gifty picked at a broken nail. Her fingers were long and graceful; her nails painted a sparkly red. Except for the broken one. Did she break it in a skirmish with Alistair?

"I was not truthful about Alistair."

Confession time. The hillside was lit up with spotlights illuminating the crime scene.

"I want to talk about the night JoJo died." She let that sink in for a minute. "Yes?"

"I came to see her on that night." Gifty gulped. "She wasn't alone."

Chapter Twenty

"How do you know JoJo wasn't alone?" I strained to listen for movement in the darkness.

"I rode my bicycle to the house, expecting to see her, to return items I'd borrowed. A wrench to fix a broken drain pipe and a pie plate. I'd filled the plate with candied coconut balls. They were her favorite."

"Did you see her or not?"

Gifty's stare drifted toward the house. "I never went inside. I stopped over there." She pointed to an oversized maple with low-hanging branches. A perfect place to hide. "Someone waited on the porch. I couldn't see who, until he walked down the steps."

I knew who it was. "Alistair."

Gifty nodded. "JoJo opened the door and called him back. They talked for a while, but I couldn't hear the words." She gazed off into the darkness, withdrawing into the memory. "Then he walked to the end of the driveway."

"To his car?"

"To his horse."

So far, there was little to link Alistair to JoJo's death. "What happened next?"

Gifty shifted her gaze back to me. "I walked the bike toward the house and stopped. JoJo had turned off the porch light."

"So?"

"The light off means no more visitors. I turned the bicycle around."

"But you didn't go home." I had a hunch this was going somewhere important.

"I heard a crackling, like walking on dry leaves." Gifty sucked in a deep breath, dropping her chin to her chest. "I hid again and watched. Someone else had been watching too, from beneath that magnolia." She pointed to a smaller tree with leathery leaves, closer to the house. The lower branches swept the ground, creating a shadowy canopy. "A person ran up the porch and knocked. It took a minute, but JoJo let him in."

"Who was it?"

"I couldn't tell. She turned on the light, but the individual wore a hood and baggy pants. He did not want to be seen."

"Yet, she let him in because it was someone she knew."

"And that's why I left." She wiped an eye. "I didn't think…if only I had gone to the door…"

"First off, we still don't know if there was foul play in her death. Even if someone was hiding out before going inside, he or she could've just wanted to talk. A close friend or relative, maybe." Who could it be? "Did you see a car? Or anything to indicate how he got here? Take your time and think."

"That's all I've been doing. Thinking of that night. The only thing I can say for certain is he was carrying something. A bag or a jacket, I couldn't tell."

When we parted ways, I questioned whether Gifty made up the story. It was a tidy way to keep her out of the suspect pool. There was no Alistair to ask, which was convenient. Was she sending me on a wild goose chase?

* * *

I made a beeline for my car, but switched gears after a few moments. The wind carried voices down the hill from the crime scene investigation, which was in full gear. That's where I needed to be.

Half of the team stood around. The other half worked inside a designated perimeter surrounded by yellow and black crime scene tape. A couple of detectives lingered at the top of the hill, retracing Alistair's footsteps and those of the killer. If I figured things out, the experts had to know it wasn't a suicide. Evidence was logged, photographed, collected, sealed, and tagged.

This was the elaborate version of what I did in a pinch. Hank stood, arms folded against his chest, talking to an officer who seemed to hang on his every word.

"Busted," I muttered as Hank pointed to me. Would he be here if he'd played a hand in JoJo's and Alistair's deaths? If he was bold enough, this is exactly where he'd be.

I spit out everything I knew to Homicide Detective Luke Chen. But I restrained myself from offering my take on what happened. I was on an official case and needed to protect my client, even if she played a hand in her sister's demise. At least until I had proof. I did, however, suggest a visit to Means Well Ranch with the hope they would discover something I'd overlooked. I didn't stick around after that. I had an office to break into.

* * *

The town was mostly deserted this time of night. Shops and businesses closed at five. Only a wine-tasting bar and an upscale pizza place welcomed people inside. I parked on Main Street and strolled to the post office. A stocky, middle-aged guy sorted through his mail in the area housing postal boxes. I joined him.

"Hi."

The man's dyed brown hair was brassy; lines ran along his face like a recently plowed field. His low-key denim gear was probably his daily wear. He mumbled something and turned to his box.

"Does Darin live in town?" I had the sudden urge to question him about Alistair before anyone else did.

"He'll be in tomorrow," he replied without turning.

"It's kind of an emergency." I texted Michael:

Find out what the post office supervisor's last name is and anything else worth knowing. First name is Darin.

The man pivoted around to face me. "What kind of emergency?"

"It's confidential." I handed him my business card.

He read my card. "You're a private eye? No way." He stared at me, then regarded my card. He looked up with a smirk. "You're a college student, right? This is a scavenger hunt. Bring in the first person you meet in a government building?"

I spoke low and slow, "I'm racing against the clock to find a murderer. Does that sound like a game to you?" I pushed away the hem of my jacket to display the holster on my belt.

The guy took a step back. "Whoa. I thought—"

"Do me a favor and keep your thoughts to yourself." This is how I worked out my frustration.

Michael texted me:

Darin Reynolds. According to YELP reviews, he's a nice guy. Helpful. Recommends Hank's breakfast burritos. Grew up in Los Ranchos. Search engine shows he lives at 210 Apple Tree Way.

Michael texted me directions, and I headed for the door.

"Nothing personal!" the guy shouted after me.

Darin's small white cottage was brightly lit. Bottlebrush trees, ornamental grasses, and boulders provided drought-tolerant landscaping. Darin seemed like a conscientious fellow. How observant was he? I knocked, and he answered quickly. No peephole, no asking who it was. None of the neighboring homes showed signs of home security either. This town really was far removed from L.A.

Darin blinked a few times, as if to ensure I wasn't a mirage; the TV was muted behind him.

"Sorry to drop by so late. We met today. I'm Corrie Locke."

A serious expression was fixed on his long face. His cheeks were full, his chin square. His silver chain glinted under the exterior light.

"You're the private investigator."

"I work for the Means family. I understand Alistair and JoJo were friendly."

He nodded.

"Did you know he visited her on the night she died?"

"No."

"Anything you can recall about the two of them would be helpful."

His stare pushed past me before recapturing my gaze. "Alistair was worried about her recently. He said they had a problem on their hands."

That was a headline I hadn't seen coming. "What type of problem?"

He shook his head. "Didn't say. I can ask him."

Here was the part I dreaded again. "I'm sorry to inform you that Alistair died tonight."

Darin took a wobbly step back and leaned against the hallway wall. "Died? How?"

"I'm not sure. It's a police matter." I stepped forward. "Would you like to sit down?"

He shook his head as a shiver ran through him. "That's not possible."

"There's a sofa right behind you." His place was sparsely furnished. Museum-style display cases hung on his walls featuring an array of colorful stamps. Framed photos sat on a bookshelf.

Darin's gaze hit the stone walkway. "Can't think right now."

He seemed to be gasping for air. The poor guy was in shock. I pulled out my phone. "Is this Alistair's writing?" I showed him the photo of the suicide note, magnifying a small portion of the words.

Darin glanced at it, turned his head, and exploded in a coughing fit, covering his mouth with his fingers. "Don't know." His coughing grew more frantic.

I reached into my purse and pulled out a small water bottle. "Sorry again. I appreciate your time." Handing the bottle to him, I ran off beneath the moonlight.

I hopped in my car and motored away from Main Street, ambling onto a narrow, pock-marked road. I rolled down my window, sucking in the cool night air and cutting my lights. The pale glow of the moon kept me on track as I crossed an old bridge straddling a dry riverbed, long overtaken by branches from sprawling shrubs and trees, habitat and hideout to all sorts of wildlife, judging by the chirping, twittering, and squealing.

The Community Services Building sat by its lonesome on a corner next to a bare lot and utility poles. Lights on short posts spread down a walkway to the entry. Wall lights provided dim accents. A wrap-around porch surrounded the compact structure. Any dreams of a front lawn had dried up long ago.

I parked a block away near a small mobile home community. Squeezing into an end spot, I popped open my trunk, home to a variety of tools, weapons, and spyware. I switched my cross-body bag for a purse the size of a bathtub. Weapons were already in place inside the bag. Slipping into vinyl gloves, I packed up the rest of my break-in gear. Would the cops check out Alistair's office? Probably, which meant I'd have to be extra smart about where I placed the hidden camera. I wasn't too worried. Even if the cops found it, they'd assume Alistair planted it.

After a quick run around the building, I was relieved to find no security system in place. I doubted there were cameras inside, but I'd check that out, too. The back door was in the perfect spot, out of sight of the road and the parking lot. A perimeter privacy fence ran along three sides of the building.

I climbed through an unlocked double-hung sash window near the door. Pushing the blinds away, I hopped inside. Los Ranchos relied on the Calabasas police force and did just fine. I could see why. Crime was rare. Except for the recent thefts and now, murder.

No sign of any type of interior security was good news. Brass nameplates appeared on the doors of four small offices. The rear office belonged to Alistair. Yet another sign of feeling secure in this town: his office door stood wide open. An antique desk and chair took center stage. A glass-topped table below a window displayed books, a small vintage globe, and a wrought iron cowboy statuette. Plaques expressing appreciation for Alistair's community contributions hung against the walls.

I thumbed through his files and searched inside drawers. Handwritten notes and letters confirmed that Alistair wrote in carefully drawn cursive, bordering on calligraphy. No block letters anywhere. Whoever forged the note assumed block letters were the norm. People closer to my age didn't use cursive so much. Had someone younger played a hand in the phony suicide note?

Alistair's trash pail was half-filled with paper, a food wrapper, and green *No Fresher* gum wrappers. His favorite brand. There were a couple of paper cups and another gum wrapper. The brand was *HiDent*. Only one wrapper meant it belonged to a visitor. Did visitors have to sign in when entering the building? Doubtful in a town this size, where everyone knew each other's names, addresses, and pets.

A desk calendar kept track of Alistair's appointments. On the night of JoJo's death, he'd handwritten the letter "J" and the time: eight o'clock. Gifty's credibility rose to the top of the truth meter. Did I dare grab Alistair's laptop and take off? There could be incriminating information. I reached for the laptop and withdrew seconds later. Stepping on the steely toes of law enforcement during a murder investigation could get me in hot water. Or, more accurately, in a place without hot water, like a jail cell. I was already in trouble just being here, so I flipped open the laptop. A few pushes of a button, and it took me straight to his email.

Most of his communications were business-related. None involved JoJo. I checked his laptop history.

"Bingo."

Almost all recent online searches had to do with habitat conservation plans. General information on the importance of preservation. Was he gathering evidence to convince someone about preserving a habitat?

"Habitat for what?"

I searched some more, and there it was. "Habitat for the California red-legged frog." I skimmed words like "permanent protection" and "effect on the species."

I sat back. Where was this habitat, and why was Alistair interested? More importantly, did it have something to do with his death? And maybe JoJo's? I pictured the vintage conservationist pin I'd found in JoJo's living room. Gifty saw Alistair leaving JoJo's house on the night of her death. All signs pointed to the pin belonging to Alistair. I needed to get into his house.

The whirr of engines roared as the parking lot lit up. Blue and white lights flashed between the slats of the blinds in the hallway. I ran forward and peeked through. Two patrol cars had pulled in.

"Oh boy."

I hustled back to Alistair's desk and shut the laptop. I dove for my purse and pulled out an upright box of tissues. Planting it on the corner of the table beneath the window, I made sure the box faced the desk and the office entry.

A hand-painted poppy decorated the exterior. The box had been a gift to Dad from a happy client. I took a moment to marvel at how perfect it was for this job. Vintage and unique, it looked like something Alistair would have selected himself for that space, especially if he knew the contents. A small camera was hidden inside. Off-center, a hole had been drilled underneath a red flower petal, just big enough for the camera lens to watch and record activities. If anyone entered Alistair's office outside of law enforcement, I needed to know.

Car doors slammed, and voices shook the parking lot. I gathered my goods and opened the window in the office. Thankfully, unlocked doors and windows seemed to be usual around this town.

Bells chimed as the front entry to the compact building opened.

"Check reception for a log of visitors. I'll find his office."

The window gave a soft squeal of protest as I lifted it. I dropped my bag outside, slid through, and jumped to the hard ground.

"Oh boy," I said for the second time in five minutes. The ground was too low for me to reach up and close the window. Keeping in the shadows, I ran like the wind to my car.

Chapter Twenty-One

"We've got a problem," Veera called just before I unlocked my car door.

"Are the police there?" The cops were probably grilling everyone, and no one wanted to answer without a lawyer present.

"They came and went already. It's about toothpaste."

"For a second there, I thought…did you say toothpaste?"

"There isn't any. Not a tube in the house, the garage, or the barn. Bart even checked the attic. Toothbrushes, hand lotion, shampoo, we got plenty. Just no toothpaste. Most of us brought our own, but Marti didn't. She wants to send Hank out to get some just for her."

Was that a ploy to get him out of the house? What was Marti up to? "That's not possible. JoJo had ample supplies of everything. How could she be out of toothpaste?"

"That's the question. Any stores open in town?"

"Are you kidding? It's past ten o'clock. This place shuts down before sunset. Can't she borrow some from Gifty or a neighbor?"

"Marti said she wants a fresh, store-bought tube from someone who's not a murder suspect. She doesn't trust the neighbors."

"Where's Mom?"

"Cleaning up in the kitchen and…" she lowered her voice, "…snooping around. I'll get her."

A minute later, Mom came on the line. "Everything's under control. I'm mixing baking soda, water, and salt. All-natural toothpaste will soon be in a sanitary plastic container. Marti's going to love it."

"You drove yourself to the ranch today, right?"

"I'm parked on the street. Do you need a ride, honey?"

"What's in your trunk?"

"A spare tire, a sweater, shoes, socks, toothbrush—"

"Toothpaste?"

Mom sucked in a breath. "Maybe."

"Please give a tube to Marti."

"I have Cleure toothpaste, gifted to me by the dentist who created the line in return for my helping pick a few outfits for her promotional tour. This is a special line of toothpaste and, at twelve bucks a tube, Marti can afford to buy her own Cleure. I'm not sharing."

"This is an emergency." What happened to JoJo's extra toothpaste?

Mom went quiet, which was highly unusual. "Oh, alright. But I'm also promoting my homemade, all-natural, teeth whitening—"

"Not tonight, Mom. As your lawyer, I advise against it. Marti needs firmly capped, commercial grade toothpaste."

"You know what? You're right. I'm not FDA approved."

"See you soon." I flipped my BMW toward the ranch. Just before I reached JoJo's driveway, red flashing lights kissed my rear windshield. I pulled over, and a squad car bustled by, disappearing past a curve in the road. I was willing to bet he was on his way to Alistair's house, which meant I needed to shadow him.

* * *

Alistair had lived on his own version of Means Well Ranch. The road leading to his pad wound up a gentle hillside surrounded by acres of vineyard. Pepper trees lined the driveway and led to a sprawling Tuscan-style estate, all lit up and ready for a police search. Good timing on my part, except that another round of flashing lights got in my way. A CHP officer blocked ingress through the open wrought iron gates. The investigation had expanded onto Alistair's pad.

I rolled down my window and pulled over. The officer aimed his flashlight at me. An older cop with elfin features, he had a wiry body and quick movements. I wouldn't be surprised if his hand whipped out to flick away a moth drawn to the beam.

"What are you doing here?"

"I was headed to Means Well Ranch, but I decided to drive around the neighborhood, and here I am." I showed him my driver's license.

"What's your business at Means Well?"

"I know the family." His police SUV was parked on the side. This wasn't the guy I'd followed here.

"Saw you at the crime scene. You discovered the body."

"That was me." Was he going to let me through or not?

"You're Monty Locke's daughter. Figured out that much when I heard you give your statement." He peered close enough to examine my pupils. "Following in his footsteps, are you?"

"No, I'm making my own."

He inspected my license and handed it back. "Monty was a world-class P.I. He knew what he was doing, and he did it without clashing with law enforcement. Didn't need to throw his weight around or stick his nose where it didn't belong. His reputation earned him entry into places most P.I.'s can't get into."

"I learned a thing or two from him."

"Oh yeah? You know how to make people talk and say things they prefer to keep to themselves?"

What would Dad do if he were here? "Why don't you let me through, and I'll show you?"

He cracked a half-hearted grin. "Not unless you want to knock me out and face charges for assaulting a police officer."

He had a very strange way of inviting me in. "Tempting, but I want to assist, not assault, you, Officer." My cell phone chimed. Alistair's place had better reception than JoJo's ranch. Mom was looking for me. I grabbed the steering wheel and put my car in reverse. "I hear my mother calling me." I threw a wave, leaving him to ponder my skills. One thing I knew for certain. I'd be back soon, with or without his help.

* * *

I arrived at Means Well Ranch to find everyone gathered in the living room. Marti slumped on the settee. Gifty, Red, and Bart monopolized the couch, and Hank sat on the hearth, chin resting on his knuckles. My team guarded the various exits. Okay, Mom leaned against the wall, filing her nails, but she knew what was up.

Red whittled down a small branch with a jackknife, using shallow cuts. His fingers worked nimbly. "I'm carving a mushroom that's either harmless or poisonous depending on who I gift it to."

"Where's Heidi?" I asked. She was a slippery one.

"I'm taking a time-out." Her high-pitched voice squeaked from behind the couch. She lay flat on her back on the floor, staring at the ceiling.

"She's wallowing." Red grunted.

Marti came over to stand by me. "She overheard a detective say that hers 'was a profession rife with deception.'"

Heidi shot up. "I've never deceived anyone in my life."

There was no arguing that she tended to be a tad dramatic.

Marti turned to me. "Have you figured out who killed JoJo yet?"

I checked my watch. "Not in the past hour, but…" I took my time to scan the room and make eye contact. "I'm getting closer."

Mom slid next to me. "What took you so long to get here? I was worried."

"I had a nice chat with a police officer." I turned toward the others. "Anybody have a theory as to why there's no toothpaste in the house?"

"I do." Gifty stood. "JoJo kept extras in the garage. The same thief that's been robbing from neighbors stole her toothpaste supply."

I should've seen that one coming. "Why toothpaste? There were more valuable items for the taking. Even in the trunk." This whole thing was getting more and more bizarre.

"Maybe it was stolen on a day Aunty Jo left the garage door open when she wasn't home," Bart said. "It was expensive toothpaste."

A toothpaste thief? "What kind of toothpaste was it?"

"Superbe. It costs thirty-five dollars a tube," Bart replied.

Everyone oohed and aahed over the high price tag.

"It was her only splurge," Bart added.

"I have clients who use it. It's a popular French brand created for Marie Curie," Mom said. "Or was it Marie Osmond?"

That reminded me. I needed a writing sample from Bart. "Michael, would you please find a pen and paper?"

He dashed off so quickly, he turned into a blur. How did he do that?

"Is anything missing from the garage besides the toothpaste?" Veera asked.

Heads shook, and murmurs circulated until Hank got to his feet and stroked his beard.

"Took a look around myself soon as I heard about the toothpaste. Mind if I look some more?"

I found that highly suspicious, but I agreed. "Let's go."

Marti started to follow as we aimed for the garage.

I put up a hand. "Everyone else stays put."

Michael dashed back to me and held up a pen and notepad. I turned to Bart.

"Make me a list of Aunty Jo's top three favorite things."

"I'll text it to you."

"I need a hard copy, pronto." Something about him brought out my bullish side. I turned to Michael and whispered, "Tell me if he writes in block letters."

When Hank and I got to the garage, I paused to admire the neatness once more. There were items in my garage that disappeared forever, thanks to my lack of organization. Nothing could vanish in JoJo's clutter-free, neatly labeled garage. Yet, toothpaste had disappeared.

Three rows of open metal shelving held closed plastic bins of everything from detergent and dishwashing necessities to toiletries. The contents were sorted into perfectly organized categories. Hank examined a stack of vintage wine crates while I studied his leather cowboy boots. Size eleven or twelve was my best guess.

"Is that gum on the bottom of your shoes?" I asked.

I scrambled closer as he lifted his boots. The soles were smooth, without any pattern. But he looked like a man who had more pairs in his closet.

"You see gum on this floor?" He squinted at the concrete. "That would be near impossible unless it happened after JoJo–"

"My mistake. It's been a long day."

He shoved his hands on his hips and dropped his gaze. "When I… found JoJo, I couldn't accept that she was gone. Still don't. Now, with Alistair… I'm beginning to think I could be next. You getting a better sense of what happened to JoJo?"

I wouldn't tell him if I did. "I need to take a closer look in here without you."

"I'm not going anywhere. I've got a stake in this game, too."

I slammed my fists on my hips. "I'm investigating possible foul play, and you're a suspect. No suspects allowed while I'm checking out the garage."

"Suspect?" He stood stock still, and so did I. What if he didn't leave?

"Need help, Corrie?"

My sweetie's built-in radar was always tuned into me. Michael showed up whenever he thought I could use a hand. Either that or he was looking for another chance to admire JoJo's Ford Galaxie 500. He stood in the doorway, all six feet of handsome, heart of gold, and enough muscle to get a large man like Hank thinking. Michael's natural habitat may have been in the computer science department at L.A. Tech College, but he rose to the occasion in my investigations. And to let Hank know that he meant business, Michael lifted his shirt just enough to display his toned abs and his gun, a non-lethal weapon that fired pepper spray projectiles. Not a fan of bullets, Michael carried a weapon that looked enough like the real thing to make Hank reconsider. Of course, I could've handled Hank, but Michael was good company all the same.

Hank put up his hands. "That's what I get for trying to be helpful." He turned on his heel and left.

"Wait!" A question was burning the tip of my tongue.

He stopped to face me.

"Do you water the plants in the greenhouse?"

"Why? Was one of them killed off, too?"

I glared at him.

"That's right, I water. And when I can't make it, Gifty handles it. And if she can't, we find someone who can."

Our eyes trailed him out the door.

"What was that about?" Michael asked.

I brought him up to date on the overcrowding in JoJo's greenhouse.

"Doesn't sound like the JoJo I know. She would've kept it tidy like everything else. What's she growing?"

"Cacti, carnivorous plants, and flowers."

"Whoa! That's a whole new side of JoJo."

"The plants were Marti's." She was definitely a plant person, judging by the books in her home library. "What have you got?"

"You want the good news or the bad news?"

"Can you put a good news spin on them both?" I wasn't in the mood for any more bad stuff.

"The old cell phone in the trash belonged to Josephine Means." Michael spoke in a low voice. "She bought a new phone a few weeks ago. Bart told the truth."

I wanted to ask how he'd found that out, but I knew better. Michael was all about doing things the right way, and when he couldn't, he didn't want to talk about it. "And the other good news?"

"Fun fact: Bart writes in curvy letters that slant to the left." Michael beamed. "He didn't write the suicide note."

I wasn't sold on that theory. I slid over to the bin holding the toiletries. There were plenty of toothbrushes, floss, even toothpicks, but no toothpaste, although there was an empty section for the tubes.

Michael poked around the garage, briefly stopping to admire the Galaxie, while I checked my phone's iDetect app for activity inside Alistair's office. My hidden camera was connected to the app. As expected, cops breezed in and out, confiscating the laptop and a few files.

"Michael?"

He slid to my side.

"Would you mind keeping an eye on my iDetect app? I've got a camera in

Alistair's office."

His eyes widened, but his lips curved up in a smile. "Thought you'd never ask."

"I'll text you the password."

Just as I pressed send, the door opened. Red peered inside.

"Charlie Bucket." Red stepped in and closed the door.

Michael and I gathered around him.

"Charlie Bucket is what we used to call Chuck's litter box."

"Chuck?" Michael asked.

"Our childhood feline. We had a special relationship, him and I. My sister put something in his bucket that she wanted a certain someone to figure out. That would be me."

"You?" Why would JoJo want Red to find it?

"Marti was too young to remember. JoJo knew I'd get it, eventually. I'll leave it to you professionals." Red moseyed out of the garage, like he'd done his duty.

"If we split up, we might be done by dawn." Michael climbed up a step ladder.

"Hold on. We're taking for granted that something's hidden when we could be looking right at it." It seemed JoJo suspected someone was after her. I lifted the lid of a bin.

Minutes ticked by until the door opened. Mom stuck her head in.

"Oh, my! It's like an *Architectural Digest* set." She toured the two-car garage like she was at a rare art exhibit.

"It's just a garage," I said.

"Look at how she tamed the clutter and reduced dust."

"Mom, if you wanted to hide something in here..."

"Something really important..." Michael climbed down.

"...where would you put it?" I asked.

"Ooohs" and "ahhhs" punctuated her stroll. After she sauntered full circle, she pointed to a white bucket sitting inside a larger metal bucket near the back. She lifted the white one. It was marked *Fresh N' Clean Cat*. "What's with the kitty litter?"

"Is that what that is?" Michael headed for the bin.

I knelt and opened the top.

"There's no litter box anywhere. Why keep kitty litter?" Mom knelt next to me.

I scooped some litter from the white bucket and poured it in the metal bucket.

"Maybe JoJo was planning to adopt a cat." Michael's face lit up. "Or maybe this belonged to Charlie Bucket."

To move things along, I picked up the bucket and slowly poured the tiny crystals out. Midway through, I struck gold. A rectangular plastic container with a gray lid lay buried inside. Something was stuffed in the container.

Mom knelt next to me. "Who keeps Tupperware inside a tub of kitty litter? Gross."

"Do you seriously think there's food in here?"

Her hand shot to her mouth. "Oh."

Michael stood behind us. "What's that?"

I flipped open the plastic lid and stared at a folded piece of paper.

* * *

JoJo wasn't just a woman of secrets. She enjoyed riddles and hiding notes in odd places. But what if no one found them?

"Does anyone know who this is?" I showed everyone the paper in the kitty litter pail. It had three words written on it: *olivet raid hill*

"I'd say my sister had a child out of wedlock named Olivet," Red said. "Fathered by a man named Raid-Hill. Can we go to sleep now? I get grumpy if I don't get enough zzzz's."

"There's a hamlet in Maryland called Olivet Hill." Michael tapped on his cell phone. "Does that mean anything to anyone?"

"What's a hamlet?" Heidi asked.

"It's a Shakespearean character who goes crazy with revenge and kills everyone." Marti clicked her tongue. "I get punchy when I'm pooped out."

"A hamlet's a place that's too small to list as a town." Hank stared at Marti as if she'd grown horns.

I glanced at an antique bar with copper panels and wrought iron accents. There was a space between the whiskey and bourbon. An empty glass sat on a side table by Marti. Ten to one, she'd had one too many nips. "We're getting off track." We were so off track, we were afloat in the Indian Ocean, clinging to a capsized boat. "Time to get some shut-eye. Michael, go with Red, Hank, and Bart to the office. Mom, you're in charge of Marti and Heidi. Gifty will stay with Veera and me."

"Since I'm the boss of everyone, I'm going with you." Marti hiccupped. "Gifty can bunk with Heidi."

"I'm not bunking with anyone." Heidi was on her feet. "If I go to sleep, evil spirits will enter."

"There's nothing for them here, honey," Mom said. "Not even any leftover dinner."

"JoJo's murderer is in this house. Doesn't anyone get that?" Heidi balled her fists.

No one seemed concerned about Heidi's statement.

Marti turned to me. "You're getting paid to find my sister's killer." She cut the air with her hand, her speech slurred, and her eyes blinked in slow motion. "I'm not paying you to find Alistair's killer, unless it's the same person. Understand?"

"You're paying for our time and expertise." Veera stepped forward. "And for us to find out if something bad happened to JoJo, which means it may be connected to Alistair's death."

Marti swayed, and Red grabbed her arm to straighten her out.

"Righto," Red said.

Michael herded the guys into the office, while the rest of us stayed put. I looked at Heidi.

"Do you have anything to add about JoJo's death?"

"There'll be a visit tonight that will make an impact."

Could she possibly get any vaguer? "A positive or negative impact?"

"Depends on who you ask."

I blew out a sigh that ruffled the curtains. "Let's hit the sack, people."

* * *

Both Heidi and Marti ended up in JoJo's room with Mom. Marti made it clear that Gifty wasn't welcome.

"I won't have Papa's indiscretion keeping me up at night."

"Gifty will be with me," I said. She seemed like the only glimmer of sanity among the Means clan.

Marti claimed first dibs on the king-sized bed, then immediately changed her mind. "That bed's the scene of a crime. No one's sleeping there."

"Unless you can sleep standing, the floor's all yours," I said.

"I'll sit in that chair." Heidi pointed to a comfortable-looking recliner with a thick cushion. "I'm not sleeping anyway."

"Then I'll take the chair," Marti said. "I need to sleep. You take the floor."

"Fine."

Since JoJo wasn't fond of visitors, especially when it came to sleepovers, she had no spare beds, but she had plenty of blankets and quilts, which we piled up to sleep on. Hank carried in the settee for Mom to use, which made her happy.

I sent Veera off with Gifty to collect blankets from her house, while I got everything settled. Michael was organizing sleeping arrangements for the guys in JoJo's office when I stuck my head in.

"Didn't you say you spent the night when you visited?" I asked Bart.

"Yes, ma'am."

I threw him a dirty look. "That's not how you address me."

"What's your point?"

My look got even dirtier. "What do you think it is?"

"You think I killed my aunt."

"Now that you mention it…"

"I'm sleeping in the barn loft."

I blocked his path. "Everyone stays in the house." I was a shepherd keeping potential wolves in sheep's clothing in one place until I could tell them apart.

"Mind explaining why I need to stick around?" Hank asked. "I'm not family, and I had nothing to do with Jo's passing."

They both talked at once, denying any connection to JoJo's death. Michael blew a shrill whistle.

"You're suspects tonight." I focused on Hank. "A word."

I stepped into the living room. He lumbered behind me. "Anything out of place on the day you discovered JoJo?"

His gaze wandered the living room, mentally retracing his steps. If he was the killer, he could have tidied up the scene before anyone else arrived.

"Didn't pay much attention to anything after finding Jo, but as I recall, everything seemed to be right where it should've been."

"Did you notice dishes in the sink or drinking glasses anywhere?" That would indicate a visitor.

"No. Jo always cleaned up before she went to bed." His gaze shifted to mine. "Finding her like that was such a shock…"

"Didn't Gifty join you inside?" That's what she'd said.

"I was in JoJo's bedroom, when she came in. I heard a… squawk, you could say, and there was Gifty in the doorway, hands covering her mouth. I walked her outside. That's where we stayed till the 9-1-1 team arrived."

They could've been in on it together and planned to find her this way. It would make everything more legitimate. But what was their motive?

"When did Marti and Red arrive?" I asked.

"About an hour later." He exhaled and returned his focus to me. "I called Marti; she must've called Red and Bart. Bart showed up later. You know how it is, battling L.A. traffic."

"How'd you feel when you found out Alistair and JoJo were lovers?" Might as well throw sand in his eyes.

His face crinkled. "It wasn't like that. Alistair would be as attracted to Jo as Tom would be to Jerry."

So that wasn't Hank's motive.

"There is one thing though."

Was he trying to change the subject?

"You can check with Marti. Jo liked this house locked up at night. Even when Bart slept in the barn, she kept the house closed till she was ready to let him in." He looked off, unfocused and lost in the memory. "Jo always shut the door of her bedroom closet. That day, when I found her, the closet door stood wide open."

"That struck you as odd?"

Sometimes big revelations rise from small details. Dad's words shot through my head again.

"Jo kept that door closed. Something about boogie man stories she'd heard as a kid. Odd, since nothing ever spooked Jo. She was a woman of courage and conviction. But…" he looked down at his calloused palms. "…I didn't tell the police about the closet door. Didn't think of it."

"Hank?" Bart appeared behind him. "Michael wants to know how many blankets you'll need."

Hank huffed and marched back into the office. Bart regarded me.

"I'm no psychic, but I've got this feeling that Aunty Jo is hoping this awful situation will bring our family closer together. Especially Gifty. She trusted Gifty."

Why was Bart sharing this with me? Either because he was sincere or he was throwing the wool over my eyes. I always carried a sharp knife to cut out eye holes should that happen.

"Thanks for sharing. When did you arrive at the ranch on the day your aunt was discovered?"

He shoved his hands in his pockets. His hair was especially scruffy. His icy blue eyes were rimmed with red, and his breath reeked of bourbon. "To tell you the truth, I don't remember much. I blocked it out. God, I miss her. Aunty Jo was our rock."

"Did she ever lend you money?"

"Lend me? She gave it to me, any time she thought I needed clothes or wasn't eating enough. I didn't really need anything, but it made her happy to take care of me, so I let her." His eyes welled. He dropped his head, mumbled, and left as Veera and Gifty returned with a stack of blankets. Veera even had two sleeping bags.

"You must like camping out," I told Gifty.

"I like to sleep under the stars on clear, warm nights. Reminds me of life in Ghana."

"You were worried when you hadn't seen JoJo in a few days. Why call Hank? Why not investigate yourself?"

"Because if she was hurt or worse, I could be blamed. Marti would see to that."

Fair enough. "Set her up in JoJo's library, please," I told Veera and headed for the door.

"Where you goin', C?"

"To make sure everything's locked up for the night."

I'd parked close to the house. Good thing because I needed items from my trunk tonight. I popped open the lid and rummaged around.

My trunk was a covert operatives' paradise. Besides assorted weaponry locked in a metal box, I carried a mini storehouse of gadgets, field equipment, and enough creative everyday items to make MacGyver giddy with excitement. Everything from night vision binoculars to a noise generator that ensured eavesdroppers would never gain access to confidential conversations. I grabbed a cloth bag and stuffed fishing line, scissors, and keychain alarms inside, along with a hammer and nails. Duct tape was already in the bag.

"You need better watchdogs. Wasn't hard to slip away."

I flipped around. A fleece throw was wrapped around Heidi's shoulders, arms folded across her chest. She gloated smugly.

"Marti conked out thirty seconds after you left. Took your mom a minute later."

"Young lady." Mom snuck up behind her, pepper spray raised and ready. "I never sleep on the job."

Heidi spun around, hands up. "You looked like you were fast asleep. I just wanted to let Corrie know so she could beef up security. The others might not be as awake as you."

"You knew I was her mother?" Mom asked.

"There are photos of us online with Dad, from back in the day." It wasn't rocket science to connect the two of us. "What are you trying to prove, Heidi?"

"I want to catch the killer as much as you do." She shot glances at Mom and me. "Let me help."

Michael bounded toward us from the porch. "Veera's holding down the fort." He pointed to Heidi. "Is there something you want to tell us?"

"A real medium wouldn't have to ask." Heidi stuck a hand on her hip.

Michael looked up and rubbed his chin with his thumb. "You're right, but I'm giving you a chance to tell us your story before I do." He focused on Heidi.

She squeezed her lips tight.

"You were a student in JoJo's high school English class. After you graduated, you became her teaching assistant, until five years ago when you turned to mystical pursuits." He circled his hands in the air.

Our eyes turned on Heidi. I didn't bother with questions. Silence has a way of encouraging the guilty to talk.

"JoJo was my teacher, then my boss, always my friend." She clasped her hands together. "We lost touch for a while when I went off to discover my true purpose, which she fully supported. Well, not in the beginning, but once she got used to the idea…we were good. When I heard JoJo had died, I reached out to Marti and offered my services. She took me up on it, and here I am."

"You didn't tell Marti about you and JoJo, did you? You're milking a grieving family," I said. "Why pretend to have contact with JoJo's spirit?"

"I'm making them think!" She turned to Mom. "If there wasn't an autopsy on your husband, his murder might've been overlooked, like JoJo's. The family has a right to know. All it costs them is a few dollars."

"Dollars that line your pocket." I stepped forward as Heidi stepped back.

"I only get paid if you prove me right. Otherwise, this is a freebie." She turned to Michael. "You believe me. I sense it."

Michael bunched his lips and watched the house. "I believe…" He pivoted toward me. "…we should give her a chance."

I regarded Heidi. "Alistair was murdered because of my snooping."

"You don't know that, honey." Mom stroked my arm. "We don't know much of anything except that Alistair is dead. And…" She thrust her arm toward the house. "…those people are counting on you to find out what happened to a member of their family. One of those same people might be dangerous to the rest of them. If Heidi wants to help, bring her on."

A grin tugged at the corners of Heidi's mouth. I slammed shut the trunk and slung the bag of tonight's supplies over my shoulder.

"You knew about JoJo's Japanese broom because you'd seen her use it," I told her.

"So?" Heidi shot back.

Michael gasped. "That's not exactly psychic work."

"Look who's talking." She snapped at him.

"You also saw the conservationist pin on the floor and didn't tell anyone," I said.

"Because I thought that if you found it, you'd know it was a clue. No one else would care."

Mom cut her hand into the palm of her other hand. "Why didn't you just tell us upfront? We could have worked together to solve this case faster."

"It's not like I know what I'm doing." Heidi dropped her chin.

"Finally!" Took her long enough to admit it.

She slid over to me. "You know my dad's a police detective. I asked him to check with the police officers who were called in about JoJo."

Michael and Mom moved in closer.

"There were broom fibers all over the floor of her bedroom and closet." Heidi waited for that compelling information to sink in.

"Because she'd been sweeping the floor?" I didn't bother to hide my eye-roll.

"Maybe the broom was getting old," Michael said, "and shedding."

"Luxury brooms don't shed," Mom said.

"Why was the broom in the burn pile?" Heidi looked triumphant. "Because the killer's DNA was all over it."

An ounce of sense floated around her words. Was it possible JoJo used the broom to fend off her killer? If there was a killer, which I was nearly certain of at this juncture.

Could we use Heidi to flush out the culprit? If it turned out she was involved…keeping the enemy close is always a good idea. "Here's what I want you to do."

Chapter Twenty-Two

Everyone returned to the house with tasks to complete. Mom and Michael retired to their respective rooms and pretended to sleep. Hopefully, the pretend part wouldn't turn out to be real. Heidi's job was to share sensitive information first thing in the morning and see if anyone cracked. Also, she was going to let the Means family know that the guards would be snoozing soon. That could be an incentive for someone to make a bold play. Meanwhile, my work kept me outside of the house. I texted Veera to let her in on the plan.

It took less than twenty minutes for me to set up booby traps for the front and back doors. In case someone did slip out, they'd trigger an annoyingly loud, chirping alarm that sounded like the descent of an alien spacecraft.

I stretched fishing lines, ankle height, across the front and back thresholds, keeping the lines loose enough to avoid a nasty spill, but tight enough to trigger the noisy keychain alarm. The line was cast between two nails and hooked up to the keychain. It gave me a chance to feel like a real-life *MacGyver.* I texted my team after all was in place.

I took up sentry duty outside, in my car, night vision goggles pressed to my eyes. Minutes later, Michael opened the front door, stepping over the wire. He turned, knelt, and did a quick check before whirling back to me with a discreet thumbs up. In a flash, he was back inside. Reclining my seat back, I rolled my window down a bit and fell asleep in an instant.

A thumping jolted me awake. I automatically reached for the goggles, pressing them to eyes so heavy they felt like little weights pinned down the lids. Fresh air was what I needed. I stepped into the night, as a bushy-tailed fox trotted out of a hedge, dangling something limp and small from its mouth.

The fox scampered away while I peered through my goggles. A shapeless shadow hustled off near the back of the house, headed in the direction of the barn. The escape artist hadn't tripped the fishing wire. How did the runner know about the trap? Heidi must have said something in her zeal to push someone into making a move.

Moonlight gave off enough glow to illuminate movement. I crouched and tailed the skittering silhouette. I wanted to rule out Hank or Red due to their large sizes, but they could've been crouching, or channeling their inner ballerinas. Hard to determine any height or shape at a distance. No legs or arms were visible. A billowy cape seemed to hide the person.

The shadowy figure stopped, and I flattened my back to the barn wall. High-pitched squawks exploded from the chicken coop, and the shadow disappeared.

I tiptoed forward, nearing the barn's back entry. The night was still enough to let me know I was alone. I turned to make my way back when a muffled moan made me freeze. I reached for the barn door.

Darkness and silence poured out as it creaked open. My penlight swept the ground. A howl cracked the stillness. I swooped in and dove behind an empty feed bin. I waited a minute before shining my light. It hovered over a body lying on its side, near the stairs to the loft. I pulled out the pistol strapped to my thigh and shone the light around. Was someone hiding out?

"Help," a voice whispered.

His back was to me, but I recognized the pale clothing and hair. It was Bart.

Stepping forward, I circled my beam until it shone on shattered glass. The bottom half of a beer bottle spread out in jagged pieces. I knelt near Bart and flashed the light by his head. "What happened?"

Bart rolled onto his back and winced. His hand slowly rose to a cut on his forehead that bled in a single drip. "I got hit." He blinked up at me. "It was Hank. He texted me to come outside."

"Wasn't he in the office with you?"

He shook his head. "Doesn't seem like it, does it?"

Why didn't Bart trip the wire? "You just walked out the back door?"

His hand rose to his head, and he moaned again. I took out a bag of alcohol wipes from my pocket.

"This will sting." I pressed it to the cut, and he winced. "There was a wire by the door. Did you see it?"

"I looked down, by my feet, before stepping outside, like Hank told me to."

How did Hank know? I pulled out another wipe. Slipping closer, I pressed it to his cut. "What else do you remember?" I flashed my beam around.

Cringing, he spoke softly, "I went outside. I heard Hank running near the barn. The barn door opened, and I hurried over."

"How do you know it was him?"

"Who else could it be?" Bart lifted his head and cringed some more.

I took off my jacket and tucked it under his head. "I'll call the police." I pulled out my phone. Darn it. No service. "Don't move," I told Bart and ran outside. I found a hotspot and called 9-1-1. I hoped this wasn't becoming a habit.

I turned back toward the barn, as padded steps approached. Veera dashed toward me with a flashlight.

"Don't shoot! It's me!" she yelled.

I held out my hands. "No gun."

"You weren't in your car, and the back door was wide open."

I told her about Bart as we entered the barn. He was sitting up.

"What happened?" Veera asked.

"We're trying to figure that out. See if Hank's in the house."

Veera dashed off, and I returned to Bart. "Where's your phone?"

He fumbled around and finally handed it to me. His phone showed a text from Hank, just like he said. I went through his other texts and didn't find anything. I fixed my stare on Bart. Questions jammed into my brain. "How come you and Hank have service in the house, and I don't?"

Bart massaged the side of his head. "There are parts on this ranch where there's reception. Sections in Aunty Jo's house have reception, too."

"Where in the house?" Why wasn't this information shared before? What was wrong with these people? "Tell me." I leaned over Bart.

Bart lifted his head. "Office." He dropped it again.

Veera dashed inside through the back door. "Hank's inside, snoring away. Doesn't look like he went anywhere. I woke Michael and told him what happened." She turned to Bart. "You snuck past Michael. He was there to protect you, and now look at you."

"Some protection," Bart mumbled, rubbing his head.

"Don't get smart with me," Veera said. "If you'd stayed put, you wouldn't be in any pain right now."

Bart groaned. Bright lights flashed through a barn window.

Veera turned to me and whispered, "Michael checked Hank's phone. No record of any outgoing texts in the past hour. He said someone must've disguised their phone number by using Hank's to fool Bart into responding. It's called spoofing."

I knew all about spoofing. "To get Bart outside. Probably told him about the wire, too." Who knew about that besides us and Heidi?

"Can't block or reply to spoof texts, Michael said. It's easy enough to create. All you need is to set up three computers, and you've got your very own phone system."

"Three computers?" Who would want their own phone system?

The next few minutes were a blur of paramedics and a police officer who briefly questioned Veera and me. Since Bart's injuries were minor and the evidence scanty, the officer lost interest quickly. It didn't help that Bart reeked of alcohol. Of course, that could've been the beer. Had he staged the whole thing? Or had someone else been out there, too?

Chapter Twenty-Three

The smoky-sweet aroma of coffee wafted through the house before the crack of dawn. Mom's energizing brew made it easy to forget the chill inside and out. Banging pots and pans, she made enough noise in the kitchen to scare off any lingering critters lurking around the homestead. The clanging was part of the plan to wake up the inhabitants, bright and early. Everyone seemed to have slept through the incidents in the barn. I waited by the hearth in the living room while Michael and Veera stayed in the bedrooms with the other houseguests. Heidi sat cross-legged on the couch, eyes half closed, trance-like.

"How well do you know Hank?" I asked her.

"About as well as you do," she replied without moving.

One by one, houseguests trickled in. Gifty arrived first, eyes pinned on Heidi. Gifty tilted her head toward me and mumbled,

"What's wrong with her?"

"Heidi's getting in touch with the spirit world."

Gifty huffed. Obviously, Gifty wasn't a believer either.

"If she really wants to contact spirits, she should go into the woods, deep at night, and get kidnapped by dwarves. They'll take her to the spirit world. That's how it's done in Ghana."

And I'd pegged her for the sane family member. "If she's whisked away, how's she supposed to report back to us?"

"They let captives go in two months. No one gets hurt." She sank into a wing back chair.

"Reassuring." I waited, but didn't feel the urge to eye-roll. That's what

I called progress. Even with that odd tidbit, Gifty still seemed the most normal of the Means pack.

Marti rubbed her eyes as she wandered in. "Something smells good." She caught her breath as her gaze stumbled upon Heidi. Marti stared up and around the ceiling. "Is JoJo here?"

"Heidi's working on reeling her in." I leaned against the piano. "She said JoJo has new insights to share."

Marti's eyes widened. "Hurry up, Heidi!"

"Can't rush the spirit world." I squeezed my lips to avoid an outpouring of sarcasm. I'd planned this little activity with Heidi last night. She'd repeat the story I'd heard from Gifty about JoJo's last visitors, with the goal that someone would give themselves away. If we kept chipping at it, something had to give.

Veera side-stepped over to me and lowered her voice. "Should I get going?"

"Yes, please."

Veera took off for the back door. Her job was to nose around the barn and look for signs of what went on last night. Had anyone besides Bart been there? We had to test all angles. The cop had taken the bits of broken glass with him, but I was willing to bet he wouldn't find any fingerprints.

Bart crept in, a large bandage across his forehead.

"What happened to you?" Marti asked.

"He's a sleepwalker." I didn't want to interrupt the flow of things with an incident we had so little knowledge about.

He rubbed a hand against his skull. "I'll be okay." He nearly bumped into the wall as he headed for the kitchen.

Was there a murderer in the house or not?

Marti turned to Gifty. "You're still here? I would have thought you'd leave the day after you arrived, nineteen years ago."

"Why should I leave my family home?" Gifty nestled back into the cushiony chair.

Marti's lips turned crooked. "You know something about JoJo's death, don't you?"

"I know nothing."

Marti turned to me. "She was always hanging around this house."

"If you hardly visited the ranch, how would you know?" I was a little tired of Marti's stray accusations and cranky from lack of sleep.

"You left those nasty messages on my sister's answering machine." Marti refocused on Gifty.

"So did Red. I helped JoJo around the ranch." Gifty sat up. "You never lifted a finger."

"Why you–"

Mom came out with a gravity-defying smile, balancing a tray of hot coffee mugs. "Good morning, everyone! It's almost French toast time."

"No eating yet. We're waiting for Heidi to connect to the spirit world," I said.

"The switchboard must be jammed." Red sauntered in from the hallway, brown hair wetted down and combed into submission. He wore a plaid overshirt and jeans. "I'd like to go for a canoe ride before breakfast. Anybody game?"

"It's cold out there." Marti rubbed her arms. "JoJo liked canoeing on the pond. Maybe you can ask her to go with you, if Heidi ever makes contact."

"No one's going anywhere," I spoke in a voice firm enough to crack a billiard ball.

Hank joined in next, followed by Michael. Hank's hair stuck out in all directions. "Something smells sweet and bold. Nothing like a good kick of caffeine to jumpstart the morning."

Bart returned, nursing a cup of coffee. He plopped down next to Heidi, sitting low, and shut his eyes.

Heidi's shoulders jumped up. She shuddered as her head shook rapidly. "Something happened that last night…"

Marti's fingers tapped the armrest of her chair. Bart opened an eye, and Hank paused mid-squint. Red kicked back and slurped his coffee, arm slung along the back of the sofa. Gifty slapped her leg.

"Get on with it." Gifty's impatience bubbled over.

"JoJo wasn't alone. Alistair arrived about eight. They talked business, but it wasn't the usual business. It was something else…"

Mutters and mumblings circled the room.

"Shhh! I can't hear her." Heidi's shaking stopped.

"Long-distance static," Red said between slurps.

"Frogs." Heidi's eyes opened and rolled upward so that only the whites showed.

"That's spooking me out." Veera stared at Heidi's eyes.

I might as well have been at a poker tournament of champions. No one gave themselves away.

"Was Alistair interested in frogs?" I asked Hank.

"Never came up," Hank replied.

"On JoJo's last night, after Alistair left," Heidi continued, "someone else arrived."

"Who?" Marti sat up.

A few beats passed before Heidi spoke again. "She won't say."

"What was Alistair really doing here?" Hank gazed around the room. "Not that I believe what this girl says. It's just, there's no reason for Alistair to come visiting Jo about frogs."

"Didn't they partner up on projects?" I asked.

"Business-related projects. They handled business during the day, never after hours."

"Because you were her after-hours guy?" Michael moved in closer.

"What if I was?" Hank lowered his chin and flicked his gaze around the room.

"JoJo is protecting someone. She says it's…" Heidi's head rolled forward, and she went limp.

"Just when we were getting to the good stuff." Mom turned on her heel and went back to the kitchen.

Marti jumped out of her chair and shook Heidi's shoulder. "Who is it? You can't stop like that!"

If the killer was here, they were hiding out, right in front of my eyes.

Chapter Twenty-Four

Everyone packed up to return to their homes after breakfast, except for the Nightingale team. Veera and I pondered our next move outside by the porch. Michael and Mom were supervising everyone inside the house.

"Except for the broken glass, I'd never have known anything went down in the barn last night." Veera had come up empty-handed. "I cleaned the rest of it up, by the way. No sense in the floor looking like a shoulder on the 405 freeway."

"Let's review the clues again." Sparse as they were. I scratched my head. Now that we finally had a P.I. agency and a backer who believed in our mission, we needed results.

"A missing broom burned in a mysterious fire," Veera was saying.

"A strange note found in a bucket of kitty litter."

Veera punched the information into her cell phone. "Petty thefts before JoJo's death, angry voicemail messages from Red and Gifty…"

"Alistair's death and the suicide note," I added. "Michael's working on figuring out the meaning of *Olivet Raid Hill*. It must be a riddle." He was an ace at cracking codes and riddles.

"Then there's the missing toothpaste, a yellow towel, and the conservationist pin." Veera's eyes were glued to the notepad on her phone.

"There's a strong possibility the pin belonged to Alistair." I told her about the search I'd conducted on Alistair's laptop last night. "But he didn't strike me as someone interested in conservation efforts." Alistair was more like a mounted moose head and tiger skin rug type of guy. "I've got an idea. Follow me." I climbed up the porch steps and headed inside. Marti leaned into a counter, pouring herself a cup of coffee. She wore the trademark Means family frown, as did Red and Gifty.

"We need to visit Alistair's house." I focused on Marti.

"What for?" Marti spoke in a voice that hadn't gotten out of bed. Flat, disillusioned, and uninterested. Red opened the fridge.

"To pay our respects."

She straightened. "Respects to who?"

I slapped my hand to my temple. Why was Marti so difficult?

"Um, Alistair Wallaby?" Gifty flipped her back to Marti.

"I need a legitimate reason to go to his house." I stepped closer to make eye contact. "Can you make that happen?"

Marti sipped her coffee. "I can demand the return of a ladder he borrowed."

"That won't work. We need to get inside the house." Ladders were usually shed or garage-based.

Red shut the fridge and turned to me. "It was 2008, one hot July afternoon, when I lent Alistair our popcorn cart for a movie night fundraiser he hosted. The cart hasn't been seen since."

"Is that where it went?" Marti thumped the counter with her palm.

"Can you prove it belongs to you?" Veera asked.

We shared a discreet, low, high five, behind our backs. That was smart thinking on Veera's part.

"JoJo's receipts date back to 1999." Red dug a hand into a large glass jar filled with jelly beans. He popped a few into his mouth. "When I couldn't sleep last night, I went through her files. I'll retrieve it." He took off.

"Are you sure the cart's at Alistair's?" Marti cocked her head.

"As sure as I know JoJo would want me to have the Ford Galaxie. Alistair has been holding my cart hostage," Red yelled over his shoulder.

"We'll take my car." I handed the key to Veera. "I'll be right there."

Marti followed Veera out. A minute later, Red flashed the receipt my way, and I pointed Red in the right direction.

"Meet you at the car," I said.

I stuck my head into JoJo's office. Michael was talking to Hank about flipping burgers. Bart was snoozing on a small sofa.

"Hank, please take Michael to Alistair's office in town this morning."

"Why?" Hank gave me a squinty eye.

"So he can take pictures of everything. He doubles as our crime photographer." I slid closer to Michael and whispered in his ear. "My hidden camera is in the black tissue box. Has anyone besides the cops visited Alistair's office?"

His hazel eyes rounded, and he shook his head. "I checked earlier."

The killer should be visiting soon. Word had to have gotten around about the note Alistair supposedly left in there.

Michael shot a glance at Hank, then focused on me. "Can I borrow some sunscreen?"

"Follow me." I hurried out.

The moment we stepped away from the office, Michael took my hand. I trailed him to the living room, where he put his lips to my ear and whispered. Sweet nothings would've been nice, but that's not what he wanted to say.

"Olivet Raid Hill." He looked around before resuming the whispering. "Olivet is an anagram for Violet. Raid Hill is an anagram for Hilliard."

"Violet Hilliard. Excellent work! Now we have to find out who she is."

"I searched the Internet. There are a surprising number of Violet Hilliards. None located close by. More than half are over the age of eighty."

"It's still a start." I squeezed his hand. "Can you find out where Hank lives? Should be walking distance."

He nodded once. I kissed him and headed off to find Mom.

My mother was deep inside JoJo's walk-in closet, sticking her fingers in everything that had a pocket.

"Find anything?" I whispered.

She jumped and whirled around to face me, hand to her heart. "Don't startle me when I'm concentrating."

I had to admit, I really appreciated her taking her role so seriously. She was definitely an asset, which was interesting since she never had much to do with Dad's investigations. That's why they'd gotten a divorce. She wanted him to go back to being a history professor at UCLA. He didn't. He was addicted to case-cracking. He'd passed that addiction down to me. Yet, here was my mother, playing a solid role in my cases. Whatever her reason for changing her mind, I was grateful.

Mom reached into the pocket of her cardigan and pulled out a business card. "I found this inside a shoebox."

My heart leapt as I read the card. It had the name, website, and contact information for a lawyer. "Alexandra Violet Hilliard, Attorney at Law." I caught my breath. The first name is what tripped Michael up. I looked at a bright-eyed Mom.

"Not too shabby for a beginner, wouldn't you say?" She grinned.

I gave her a quick hug. "Not bad at all."

"There's more." Mom put out her hand. "Japanese broom bristles." A couple of fine, honey-colored fibers sat on her palm. "Found these on the floor."

This broom played an important role in JoJo's closet. That's the message I kept getting. I gave Mom a bigger hug. "Thanks for being here."

"Oh, sweetie!"

Minutes later, I wound my way outside and skipped down the porch steps.

It was too early to call Violet Hilliard. Plus, I had a more pressing engagement.

Chapter Twenty-Five

We parked in a circular driveway in front of Alistair's Tuscan-style estate. Set against a backdrop of vast blue sky and verdant rolling hills, Wallaby Ranch was bigger, fancier, and newer than Means Well. It even had its own stone tower.

"Did Alistair live here by himself?" Veera asked.

"Far as we know." Marti lowered her head to look outside the window. "The only family he'd had was a sister back east. Alistair came from money. That's why his place looks so nice. He used to say all the rocks you see were collected from his land."

Red snorted. "That's about all it's good for."

His bushy mustache took up most of my backseat. Apparently, Red wore blinders to the massive vineyard surrounding the property.

Marti slapped his arm with the back of her hand. "Don't be a sore loser." She looked at me. "Our papa sold these fifty acres to Alistair when we were a little low on cash. Worked out for everyone."

Red spread his arms out. "What kind of a man owned all this land and never got his hands dirty? Real ranchers don't get manicures. They've got dirt under their fingernails and calluses on their palms. Heck, they even get dirt behind the ears. Alistair was too city-clean. Man couldn't grow a beard if he tried." Red stroked his thriving mustache.

"Red thinks being called unkempt is a compliment." Marti huffed.

Alistair clearly loved living the ranch life. Horseshoes were embedded in a concrete walkway leading to the entry. A hitching post stood near the door for visiting riders. An elegant two-story structure painted in hunter green, Alistair's barn made the Means barn look like a potting shed. The only things out of place were a squad car and an unmarked vehicle belonging to law enforcement. Had they found something worthwhile?

A uniformed officer waited in the foyer. I hung back and let Marti take the lead.

She dabbed at her eye with a tissue and explained who she was. "Officer, is any member of the family here?"

Veera and I exchanged a glance.

"Only the housekeeper."

"Good old Yvette. Haven't seen her in a while." Marti turned to me. "She was like family to Alistair."

"May we talk to her, Officer…?" I stepped forward.

"Ludwig."

"We'd like to express our condolences." I wiped my eye with a finger and dropped my chin. "It was so sad, so sudden." That much was true.

Veera pitched her head toward me. "She's the one who discovered–"

My elbow shot into Veera's side.

Veera coughed. "—she discovered Alistair had died. News travels fast in these small Southern California, mid-western type towns."

"You wait here." Officer Ludwig's gaze ran over us.

Red's lips tightened in a grimace, and his thick brows nearly met in the middle of his forehead. "I came to collect my popcorn cart." He held out the receipt. "Alistair borrowed it for some charity function and never returned it. We need it back for our own charity."

Officer Ludwig took the receipt. "I'll check."

The moment he left, I rushed into a spacious living room with soaring ceilings. Vivid Navajo rugs, Spanish Colonial artifacts, and elegant antiques made up the decor. Picture windows provided ample natural lighting. A moose head was mounted on the wall above the stone fireplace, and a bearskin rug lay on the wood flooring, just as I'd suspected. Would a conservationist mount animal heads? What about the bear rug?

A woman, sixty or so, shuffled in, gripping two bottles of water. She stopped when she saw me. "Who are you?" Small and plump, she wore a white blouse and dark jeans with a matching jacket.

"Officer Ludwig let me in." I handed her my business card. "I'm investigating Alistair's death on behalf of the Means family. They believe their sister met an untimely death at the hands of whoever killed Alistair."

"Mon Dieu!" Her fingers slapped against her lips, and her stare intensified. She brought my card closer to her eyes. "You are this Corrie Locke?" Despite her heavy French accent, her English was easy to understand.

"Yes. I'm here with my associate and two members of the Means family." She needed to know I was legitimate, so she'd answer my questions.

Yvette placed the bottles on a table.

"Do you know—"

"I know who killed him," she said and sank onto a leather sofa.

That went better than expected. I sat nearby. "You do?"

"I worked here sixteen years. Mister Alistair and I, we talked often. We understand each other. He came home yesterday, agitated." She wrung her hands together. "He's been that way lately. He was a cool-headed man until JoJo Means' death. That changed him."

"How so?"

"Lost his appetite. Became quiet. Jumpier. He worried more."

Did Alistair suspect that JoJo was murdered?

Yvette leaned closer. "He carried his gun with him after she died. Never left home without it. Until…" She pointed to a pearl-handled pistol sitting on the hearth.

It was a rough rider .22 magnum. Good for shooting small game, and for personal defense. "The meeting last night. Why didn't he take it?"

"I ask myself the same question."

Brown suede pillows ran across each side of the hearth to serve as seating for extra guests. An indentation dipped in the center of one pillow. Alistair's favorite seat, no doubt. I took a wild guess that he was sitting on the hearth when he got on the phone with someone wanting a meeting. "Who killed him?"

"Darin."

"The post office guy?" Big, soft-spoken, stamp-collecting Darin? "What makes you say that?"

"He's the one nobody would suspect. Including Alistair. That's why Alistair didn't take the gun."

Someone had been watching one too many TV murder mystery shows. "Did Darin say something that makes you think that?"

"That's the problem. He's too quiet." She shook her index finger at me. "Those types are like dynamite. They blow up when nobody's looking. Darin was jealous of Alistair's money and power."

"Okay, I'll take a closer look at him." Like I had nothing else to do. "Tell me about that night. Alistair got a phone call, didn't he?"

"I sat over there." She pointed to a wingback chair facing the hearth. "Nobody called Alistair." Her eyes grew wide. "But he called somebody. When he talked on the phone, I left to give him privacy."

Too bad she wasn't the nosy sort. "Did you hear anything?"

"It was someone he knew. No hello, no greeting. Alistair just said, 'How about a little walk?' That was it."

"Did he call on the landline?"

She shook her head.

"Where's his cell phone?"

She lifted a shoulder. "The police did not find it. His murderer took it."

"Do you watch *Murder She Wrote*?" That would explain where she was coming up with this stuff.

"*Columbo*."

"You need to rejoin the group." Officer Ludwig interrupted, straight-faced and emotionless.

"Okay." I thanked Yvette with a small smile and followed the officer. He exited first, so I hung back and turned to Yvette. "Have you seen this before?" The conservationist pin sat on my palm. "Found it at the Means Well Ranch house."

She nodded quickly, eyes wide. "It's his. Belonged to his mother."

"Did Alistair ever talk about frogs?"

"Never."

"Thanks." I followed Officer Ludwig.

Yvette tagged along.

"I want my popcorn cart," Red was saying to Marti.

She strolled around the large foyer, turning over vases and bowls that decorated the furnishings. "Made in Spain, made in Portugal, made in Italy…" Marti muttered.

Officer Ludwig peered out the front door while Veera stood near a window. She craned her neck to stare outside.

I turned to Yvette. "Did JoJo Means come over often?"

Everything went quiet, and Yvette took her time, brown eyes skimming the group. "Not too much. Alistair went to her house more."

"Our sister, the homebody," Marti said.

"Have you seen an old-fashioned popcorn cart?" Red butted in. "This officer couldn't locate it. The cart's red with big wheels and a steel cabinet. A large glass container sits on top where you can watch the kernels popping." He held out his cell phone. On it was a picture of a vintage popper.

"It's in the movie room closet, on the other side of the house." Yvette stared at his phone.

Officer Ludwig put up a hand and faced Red. "You can't take it until the crime scene unit is done investigating."

"I'll wait here." Red balled his hands and sat on a wrought iron bench.

"It's not going to be ready to move today."

Marti stepped toward Yvette. "Sorry for your loss. Alistair was a good man." She leaned forward. "Don't you think?"

Yvette stepped back.

"Thank you." I shook Yvette's hand. "Please call me if I can help."

I left with Veera at my side. The others shuffled out after us.

"Did we make any progress?" Veera whispered to me. "Besides Red's locating his popcorn popper."

"The pin belonged to Alistair. Yvette ID'd it."

"He must've dropped it that last night when he visited JoJo. Think it was important?"

"It was meaningful to him and had something to do with the frogs." I stepped out into the cool morning. "Can you keep Marti and Red busy while

I place a call?"

"You know I can." Veera scooted away.

I pulled out my phone. Violet Hilliard's office should be open for business right about now. Why would JoJo go to the trouble of hiding Violet's name in a bucket of kitty litter? Why stash her business card in a shoebox? What was JoJo afraid of?

Chapter Twenty-Six

I'd debated what angle to use when calling Violet. Should I tell her I was a private eye or a family friend of the Means clan? I settled on telling her I was a lawyer. Lawyers paid attention when talking to their own kind. That's what happens in a shark-eat-shark world. If one shark cuts himself and bleeds, and a hungry shark happens by, she'll happily help herself to a chunk of the other guy. Lawyers can be cannibals. Some of them, anyway.

Since Violet answered the phone herself, I figured she wasn't a big operator. I'd be the first to draw blood.

"You're the attorney that prepared the estate plan for Josephine Means." I didn't bother identifying myself.

"Her last two estate plans, actually."

Just how many estate plans did JoJo have?

"Who are you?" Her voice was high-pitched, like a little mouse screaming to be heard.

"Corrie Locke. I'm also a lawyer, calling on behalf of the Means family." Violet didn't need to know that I worked in the entertainment field. Hardly relevant. "The family wants to see a copy of any updated estate documents."

A few beats drummed by while she chewed on that information.

"I just looked you up on the State Bar website," she said. "You work for a movie studio. What's that got to do with estate planning?"

Oh, so she was going to play that game. "Have you ever handled cases outside of your practice area? There's no law against that, is there?" I let that sink in for a minute. "I'm working with the Means' to obtain the most recent will."

"You're a private investigator, too?"

Obviously, she was too busy researching my background on the internet to listen. "You practice estate planning, criminal, and family law. You play pickle ball on Sundays." I'd searched the internet, too.

"It's America's fastest growing sport."

"All I'm interested in is getting a copy of the latest estate documents. I'm representing the siblings and the nephew. If they appear in JoJo's estate plan, they get a copy." That much I knew from my law school days. "This is my informal request." I could hear her fingers pounding the keyboard. She still wasn't listening. "Your website says you're dedicated and compassionate. I'm not feeling those vibes." It turned quiet at her end, except for a clicking. She was probably twirling a pen while she considered her next move. "Are you available for a meeting later today?"

"I've got a three o'clock opening."

Now we're talking. Her office was in Ventura, forty minutes north of Los Ranchos. A stone's throw away, by Southern California standards. "We'll be there." I disconnected and headed for my car, leaving her to ponder who the "we" would be. I didn't even know that part yet.

Marti and Red were arguing in the back seat over the best way to pop corn. Veera was scrolling through our social media accounts. I started the engine and motored down the driveway, away from the home of the late Alistair Wallaby.

Veera leaned toward me. "I'm posting about how we talked our way into a crime scene investigation and interviewed a possible witness."

"I don't know if we want to alert local law enforcement on what we're doing." This was an avoidable stumbling block, provided Veera hadn't posted yet.

"Uh-oh." Veera looked at me wide-eyed.

"You posted?"

"No. We're being followed." She pointed behind her.

I gazed in the rearview mirror. A Ford Explorer tailed us; a hand twirled outside the window, signaling me to pull over. I pulled to a stop.

"Why are we stopping?" Marti stuck her head toward me.

"We're expecting company." I pointed my thumb behind me.

Everyone turned around. A man wearing a dark blue shirt and tan slacks sauntered toward us. His windbreaker matched the shirt. As the wind flapped his jacket back, I spotted a badge clipped to his belt.

"Who's he?" Marti asked.

"A tool of the state." Red chuffed.

Detective Luke Chen stopped by my window, bending his head so he could eye us all. "Heard you dropped by to pay your respects."

"That's what neighbors do," Red said.

Detective Chen straightened. "I need you all to step outside."

"Do we have to?" Marti whispered to me.

"We don't." I was curious to see what he had to say. "But, if he's ambitious, he'll bug us until we talk to him. Might as well get it over with."

Veera was already out of the car. I exited next; the other two took their time.

He probably quizzed Yvette after I left. Did she say something to encourage him to come after us?

"I don't see why we need to speak to you." Marti marched up to the detective. "We have a lot on our plates right now."

Red lingered behind her. "We never left the foyer. Which means there wasn't enough time to do much damage."

The detective's tongue rolled around his cheeks as his gaze swept over us. "Alistair left notes about a meeting with your late sister, Josephine Means."

"So?" Marti's frown was full-blown. The kind of frown that would make a baby cry. "We don't know anything about that."

Here was my chance. "Did he mention the frog habitat issue?" Maybe Detective Chen could help me with my homework.

He turned to me. "Why would you ask that?"

Oh boy. I should have thought my question through a teensy bit more.

"JoJo and Alistair served on a bunch of committees together." Veera was going for the save. "With all these dry creek beds around, they might've formed a committee to save frogs."

"That makes sense." Marti tilted her head and blew a curl out of her face.

The detective pointed to me. "You asked Yvette about frogs. Why?"

"Yesterday, in downtown Los Ranchos, I overheard some talk tying Alistair to frog habitats." Going through Alistair's computer was kind of like eavesdropping. "End of story."

"Who was talking?"

"Don't know."

"Step aside for a moment." He stomped away about ten paces off; I joined him.

Detective Chen regarded the frog clue as an important one. Why?

He stopped at the edge of the expansive lawn that fronted the house. The grass ended at a small hill leading to…what else? A dry creek bed.

"I've been combing through that house for something that might give me a lead on who killed Alistair Wallaby. Frogs kept showing up."

"You think an army of frogs killed him?" I couldn't resist. A group of frogs is called an army, so he practically walked into that joke. But he didn't think so.

His face turned red, and his cheeks puffed out. "Why don't you save us both a lot of trouble by telling me all you know about frogs."

"Okay. Frogs are amphibians with excellent night vision who can leap more than twenty times their body length. Their legs are quite a delicacy in French cuisine." This was my way of letting off steam in a case overflowing with the watery gas.

"You're a comedian. And here I thought you were a private investigator. Like your father." His eyes narrowed, and he leaned his torso forward. "What do frogs have to do with Alistair?" He spoke through clenched teeth.

"If I knew that, I wouldn't need to crack jokes." My hands landed on my hips. "Did he mention a particular type of frog?"

He studied my face before waving an arm. "No."

That was a lie. If I knew about the red-legged variety, so did he. "What makes you think frogs were the reason he met with JoJo Means?"

Detective Chen turned his head and scratched the side of his neck. He was debating how much to share. "There's a wall calendar behind an old desk in Alistair's library upstairs." He stared up at a second-story window. "There are no less than three entries in the past three weeks of meetings with Ms. Means. Below each entry, in parenthesis, he wrote 'frogs.'"

"The frogs keep hopping around your investigation and mine."

"Why were you hired?"

"To confirm JoJo died of natural causes." Were the frogs a threat somehow? Destroying a valuable crop maybe, or were they poisonous frogs? Now I felt like I was playing a role in a Hollywood B movie. I needed to think more logically. Maybe a frog habitat was in danger in Los Ranchos. Was there a big development project planned that the two of them were involved in? I had to find out. "I don't have any other information."

We swapped business cards.

"Did you find anything questionable at the crime scene?" I asked. Would he tell me if he did?

"You got there before we did." His lips turned inward.

The detective wanted me to show my cards first. "There was the alleged suicide note." I doubted he found anything new, but he had a whole team swarming the area. "You?"

"Can't share information on an open investigation."

I should've known.

"But in his office, in town…"

I gulped. They'd found my hidden camera. "Yes?" My voice went squeaky-high.

He looked away for a moment. "It's not much, but there could be a connection."

I gritted my teeth to prevent confessing about the camera.

His gaze turned upward. "Alistair Wallaby liked to chew *No Fresher* gum. He's got boxes of the stuff in his kitchen drawers at home. But there was a different brand of wrapper in his trash pail in town. *HiDent.*"

Why would that stick out in Detective Chen's head? Alistair probably had visitors all day long. Unless… "You found a *HiDent* wrapper near his body."

"Wasn't much of a breeze last night. The crime scene investigator says the wrapper was fresh."

The killer chewed gum. "Did you question anyone about gum chewing at Means Well Ranch?"

It was his turn to shake his head. "It's under wraps for now."

"Why would you trust me with that information?" I could go blabbing to everyone.

"I know you by reputation."

"Really?" I guess that meant my reputation wasn't half bad. "Why didn't you investigate JoJo Means' death?"

"No sign of foul play."

"How about the attack on Bart last night?" I asked.

"No indication anyone else had been present."

"You think he hit himself over the head?"

"I've got nothing to add." Detective Chen stepped toward the house. "Let me know if you find anything."

I gave him a thumbs-up and headed for my car. My trio of passengers watched my return.

"Well?" Marti said. "Is he any closer to finding out what happened?"

I knew why she was asking. If Alistair's killer was found, there was a possibility of linking his death to JoJo's. "Not yet."

Red opened the back door. "I'm ready to go home."

"Good, if you're talking home, as in Means Well Ranch," I said. "We have an appointment this afternoon in Ventura. We're going to meet with the attorney that prepared JoJo's last will."

"I don't need to be there." Red slid inside.

"If JoJo left you something in her will, you get a copy of the document, which we'll need to see." Veera beamed at me. "Law school's teaching me all kinds of things."

I gave her two thumbs up and regarded Marti again. "Bring your copy, too."

"Is there room in the car for all of us?" she asked.

"Of course." Oh no. "Heidi's not coming."

"I'm not going without her."

I'd tackle that later.

Chapter Twenty-Seven

Meanwhile, back at the ranch, Mom had kept herself busy. We found her sitting on the kitchen floor with Heidi, rummaging through the cabinets.

"What do you think you're doing?" Marti walked up to them aghast, like they were freeing gremlins living among the pots and pans.

"We're looking for clues in unexpected places." Mom tossed me a big smile. "Are you hungry, honey?"

"I'm good." I was still full from this morning's breakfast.

"Did you find anything?" Veera asked her.

"Not yet." Mom stood.

In a house filled with snoozy neutrals, Mom had gone full technicolor. A wild graphic print covered her pantsuit. A black turtleneck appeared underneath. Her hair was bigger than ever, and the usual black pumps added elegance to her ensemble.

"Right after you left, we lost power again," Mom said. "It came on about ten minutes ago."

"Either something's wrong with the circuit," Veera said. "Or…" She shuddered.

More like someone was still trying to scare us out of the house.

Marti's hand shot to her mouth. "Heidi, what's happening?"

Heidi shrugged. "The spirits are mad, or impatient, or annoyed, or whatever. They're not responding."

"Is something wrong with your antennae?" Mom asked.

Heidi looked at me. "Your detective daughter should've found something out by now."

"Now listen." Mom shook her finger. "We've got spirits, police, family members, even neighbors, none of which are very helpful. I suggest you step up your game, missy." She turned to Marti. "Ask Heidi about her vision." Mom looked down at Heidi. "Tell them."

Heidi sat cross-legged, eyes on me. She knew that I knew that she knew nothing.

"Say something, Heidi." Marti squatted next to her. "Did my sister tell you to look in these cabinets?" She looked up at me. "JoJo's probably just as bossy in the afterlife."

"I haven't heard a word from JoJo." Heidi massaged her temples. "But I'm sensing we could entice her spirit over by making her favorite meal."

"That would work." Red wandered in, wearing his trademark disgruntled expression. "As long as it's something with meat and potatoes."

"Heidi said JoJo will float in during a happy meal enjoyed by the family and guests." Mom's expression was smug, like she was cooking up her own plan. "When everybody is getting along."

"Did she tell you that?" I asked Mom.

"I know it intuitively." She looked smugger than ever.

Michael joined us. His eyes lit up when he saw me, and he gave me a finger wave.

"What was JoJo's favorite dish?" Marti tapped her lower lip with her finger.

Heidi rose to her feet. "Bart would know."

"Is he still here?" Marti asked.

"He was sleeping in the office last I saw." Michael pointed behind him.

I hustled away to the living room. Bart could be the reason for the blackouts, and who knew what else. I paused by the old piano. A cell phone with a dark green case sat on the bench.

"Bart's cell phone." Michael had followed me.

"How long has it been out here?"

He slid closer. "He'd been napping in JoJo's office. Hank left a few minutes after you did. Said he didn't have time to take me to Alistair's office 'cause he had to get ready to go to the diner. So, I asked if I could borrow a razor.

We walked to his house." He dug into his pocket and pulled out a disposable razor. "He gave me this."

Michael's five o'clock shadow appeared daily at five sharp. Well, almost at five. He hadn't shaved since yesterday, so his face was a bit more stubbly, but still sexy as heck.

"You're not going to use that thing, are you?" I wanted the stubble to stay.

"Not today." He ran his fingers along his face. "Tomorrow may be a different story."

"Was this phone here when you left?"

He shook his head. "It was next to Bart, on the floor in the office. He made a good show of sleeping. But I didn't hang around long enough to find out." He dug a hand into his pocket and pulled out a small post-it note. "Here's Hank's address."

"Now would be a good time to check out Bart's phone." I swapped Bart's phone with the note. "Did he use it to cause the blackouts?"

Michael's finger ran along the phone's screen. "It's password protected. This might take a minute."

Bart yawned and stretched his arms as he slogged over to us. "I needed that nap after last night." His sandy hair fanned out around his head. He pointed to Michael's hand. "That my cell?"

"This?" Michael's brows hit his hairline. "It was on the piano bench. What's it doing out here?"

"Must've left it there when I got water."

"Here, man." Michael handed it over.

"How's your head?" Was Bart putting on an act?

His hand shot to his forehead, and his pale blues shifted to me. "Better. I thought I was a goner after I was hit. What were you doing outside the barn, anyway?"

"I work for your aunt, remember? My job is to keep an eye out for things that go bump in the day and night." I took a step closer. There was another layer of roughness to his face. His eyes were puffy. "Last time I looked, your phone was next to you, in JoJo's office. Now the phone's out here while you say you were sleeping."

"Didn't you hear me?" he asked. "I was thirsty."

"There are water bottles in the office. Why come out to get some?" I squinted at him with a menacing glare that could've burned a hole through his pupils.

Bart blinked a few times. "Guess I forgot about them."

I put out my hand. "I need to look at your cell, to make sure no one was messing with it."

It was Bart's turn to peer at me through narrowed lids, like he was challenging me to a duel. "You think just because you're a pretty face, I'll do whatever you say?"

"I think you'll do whatever I say because if you don't, I'll haul your butt outside and make you do it." I would, too. I was all fired up with nowhere to go. I was a little tired of the Means family. Plus, I needed to keep uppity Bart in line.

His whole demeanor changed from passive, wimpy, injured guy to angry, in-your-face, belligerent punk in less than ten seconds. "You can't touch me!"

Michael inserted himself between us. "Whoa. Look, dude. I need two minutes with your phone. You can keep your eyes on me the whole time. That okay with you?"

"You can't just invade my privacy–"

Michael put up his hand. "We'll get through this. Maybe we'll all go out for a beer later and laugh about it."

"Not happening." Bart jerked his face away.

"Why don't you open up your cell phone and hand it to me. Please." Michael put out his palm. "It'll be quick and painless."

"If you've got nothing to hide, that is." I called him out.

It took a few moments, but Bart handed Michael the phone.

Minutes ticked by. Pots and pans clanged in the kitchen. Red exited out the front door, while Bart sank onto the piano bench. He watched Michael a beat before opening the keyboard cover. He ran a hand up and down the keys before banging out a melancholy, old-style tune. Bart played better than expected. In fact, he played so well, if I hadn't seen him sitting there,

CHAPTER TWENTY-SEVEN

I'd think it was the player piano.

"Where'd you learn to do that?" I slid closer.

Bart didn't miss a note. "Uncle Red."

Is that who Hank heard when he passed by the house yesterday? Or was it Bart? "You were playing the piano that Hank heard early morning."

He stopped playing and hung his head. "So what? Aunty M gave me a key, and I came over. I thought if I played, it would help. It didn't."

"Here you go, buddy." Michael gave the phone back to Bart.

He yanked the phone away and went quiet a few moments. "Sorry if I was out of line." He lifted his head and rolled his gaze my way. "You don't know what it's like to lose the rock in your life. That's what Aunty Jo was for me."

"Hey, it's okay." Michael patted his shoulder.

I was still in simmer mode. I could use a shower, a nap, and a dozen donuts.

"By the way, do you know what your aunt's favorite meal was?" Michael asked.

"Chicken pot pie."

"That's not a meal. That's a badly disguised dessert." Red had returned. It was his turn to glare. "How's your head, Bart?"

"Better, I guess."

"Where'd you go, Red?" I was racing full speed with my suspects.

"Checked on Charlotte in the barn. After what happened to Bart, I thought someone might have it out for me."

Seriously? It was hard to tell when his only expression was a perpetual grimace.

"Was she okay?" Michael asked.

I threw him a dirty look.

"Not a scratch on her."

"You're talking about a car, right?" I was about to scream loud enough to blow the roof off this place.

All three turned to me. "Not just any car," Red said.

"She's sweet," Michael added.

"A very cool ride." Bart yawned.

"No one's going anywhere until I say so. Understand?" I was officially freaked out by the Means family. If what just happened wasn't enough motivation for me to solve this case, there was no hope.

No one said a word as I left the room. "Heidi!" I yelled.

She came running out of the kitchen.

"Come with me."

"Where are we going?" Heidi shadowed me out of the house and into my BMW.

"Don't you know?" I couldn't help myself. She should expect those types of questions. I started my car and took off.

Heidi rolled her lips. "We're going to downtown Los Ranchos."

Duh. That was a giveaway since I was driving in that direction. "Be more specific."

She lowered her shoulders and her brows and stuck out her lower lip. "The post office."

"I'll give you one more guess."

"My wires are a tangled mess. For the spirit world to contact me, I need tranquil surroundings."

"I'm impressed. That's exactly where we're going."

Her head snapped my way. "Huh?"

I pulled up in front of Hank's Place a few minutes later. Trendy, hipster dining spots had popped up on Main Street, but this one wasn't one of them. The wood frame structure looked a tad rickety, but still exuded plenty of personality, thanks to the hitching post-style metal fence and wagon wheel decor. "Here we are."

She regarded the diner. "How is this tranquil?"

"You'll see." I held the diner door open for her and peered inside. The wild west vibe was going strong. All it needed to add more flavor were a spittoon and Marshall Dillon and Miss Kitty chatting in a corner.

The dining room had plenty of open tables, but I aimed for the outdoor patio, where a smoky barbecue aroma tickled my nostrils. Breakfast was still a recent memory, but I wouldn't turn down a strawberry shake.

"Can't get more tranquil than this." The outdoor patio was empty and truly felt peaceful. Potted geraniums dotted the border, and a tall hedge of pink roses bloomed in the back. I selected a shaded table in the corner farthest from the street, next to a small pond with a trickling fountain. If that didn't equal tranquility, I don't know what did. It was nearly ten. Too late for a weekday breakfast and too early for a lunch break, it was just the right time for an uninterrupted chat with a pretend psychic.

"I'm not really hungry." Heidi picked up a menu.

"It's okay. We're not really here to eat. Ever been to Hank's before?"

"Once, long ago."

Within seconds, a server asked for our order. Heidi started right in.

"I'll have the twenty-one-piece shrimp basket, and don't think I won't count 'em. A quarter pounder with fries, a side of onion rings, a taco special…"

She ordered enough to feed a cub scout troop.

I turned to the server. "Scratch everything before the burger and after the fries. We're going to share the order."

"And a beer," Heidi added.

"No beer." I leaned toward Heidi. "You can't conjure spirits when you're buzzed."

She narrowed her eyes. "I know why you're wining and dining me."

"We're not ordering wine."

"I'm here to find out what happened to JoJo. It's important. I don't care what Marti, Red, or Bart say, but JoJo was my friend." She sat back and flashed an unhappy gaze at the street.

I suddenly understood. Heidi was mourning JoJo's death. Probably the only one who truly was. She's worried that someone killed JoJo and desperately wants to know the truth. "Why pose as a psychic?" My tone was gentler this time.

"I'm not a poser. I really do get…" She wiggled her fingers in front of her, "…psychic visions. I'm very sensitive. For instance, you were mad when your parents got a divorce, and you were mad when your dad up and died on you. It was thrilling to spend weekends with him. The two of you solved cases left and right. He taught you everything you know. Oh, and your other job? You'll be leaving sooner than you think."

I sighed big-time. "You're not telling me anything new."

"Why are we here?"

"I need information. The tangible kind."

"I deal in the spirit world."

"Are you and your father close?" I figured her LAPD detective connection might be useful.

She stared at me long and hard before loosening up. "It's not like my dad ever brought *me* to work with him. He doesn't take anything I do seriously."

"Time to change that." I didn't know much, but I did know that everyone had potential if they were given the right opportunity. "I'd like to see the police report regarding JoJo's death."

"No crime unit was involved, remember?"

"Yet an officer noticed broom fibers on the floor of JoJo's bedroom. That's where you got your information, isn't it? Either your father gleaned that from one of the attending officers, or there was something in a police report. The burning of that broom was no accident. And the missing toothpaste is no coincidence." Or the yellow towel and the power outages.

Heidi was paying attention. The wheels in her head were spinning as she twirled a strand of hair around her finger.

"We've got too many unanswered questions and missing items." I was trusting her not to be involved in JoJo's death. My hunch told me she was clean. "Who paid for the upkeep of the ranch? The taxes?"

Her eyes opened wide, not in surprise or fear, but in excitement. "It was all JoJo. Marti and Red don't have her kind of money. JoJo was a saver who did well in the stock market. She'd invested in pharmaceuticals since the beginning of time."

I'd figured JoJo carried the burden. "Your dad would be pleased to know you're interested in police work." I'd say she had more than a passing interest.

"You think?"

Now, who was the psychic? I nodded. "I predict that Marti's going to ask you to come to the attorney's office this afternoon. Tell her you've got an appointment."

"Because I do." Heidi grinned. "I've got questions for Dad."

"And…" Be nice. "I predict you're going to be helpful, after all." I meant it.

"I second your prediction."

Chapter Twenty-Eight

When we got back to the ranch, I traded Heidi for Veera.

"I don't think I've seen that girl smile before." Veera watched Heidi float up the porch stairs. "Your meeting must've gone well."

"We'll soon find out."

"What's next on our list?"

"I need to look around Hank's house."

"You don't want him to be there while you're doing that. That's where I come in." Veera pointed her thumb to her chest. "I'll visit the diner and keep an eye on him while you sneak a peek."

Veera kept step with me down the driveway. She was talented, driven, and smart, which meant she needed more responsibility. "How about getting Hank to fess up to something JoJo and Alistair were involved in together?"

"Because Hank's the third wheel when it came to town business and those two?"

"He didn't seem keen on JoJo's relationship with Alistair." But Hank seemed tight-lipped by nature. "You'll have to work him up so he'll be more likely to spill." The man had a temper that he tried to keep in check.

Veera rubbed her hands together. "I'll tell him Alistair spent more time than we think inside JoJo's house."

"Watch yourself. Hank could be the killer." As could any of them.

Veera stiffened. "My pistol's in my boot, and my pepper spray's always ready."

We bumped fists. "We'll meet back here in about an hour." That would give us plenty of time to hightail it to Violet Hilliard's office.

"Speaking of…" She pointed down the road.

Hank trotted onto the driveway, riding a chestnut horse with a light mane, white socks, and matching blaze. All saddled up, Hank looked like John Wayne, except with fluffy gray hair and scruffy gray beard. He even wore a blue neckerchief.

He stopped near us. "I'm mucho late in getting to the diner. But I wanted to come by." He dismounted.

"That's a fine-looking ride." Veera was stroking the horse's neck. "Good boy." She made little kissy noises.

Hank took off his cowboy hat, running his fingers around the rim. He squinted at me. "Is Bart okay?"

"Oh yeah." Maybe too okay as far as I was concerned.

"He told me about last night in the barn. I didn't lure him in there. I'd never hurt the kid."

"Know anybody who would?" I figured I'd start off with the hard questions to see how he'd respond. Veera appeared next to me.

"No one I know." He yanked the neckerchief off. "First Jo, then Alistair, and now, Bart. I'm grateful he's still with us."

Veera's brow arched. "Why would anyone go after Bart?"

"Can't figure that out. But they didn't want to kill him. If someone wanted to kill Bart, he'd be dead."

Unless Bart was spared because I interrupted. "Like Veera said, why go after Bart? What's your gut feeling?"

"Someone thought Bart knew something about Alistair."

Veera and I shared glances.

"Were Bart and Alistair tight?" Veera asked.

"After Bart's ma died, Alistair and I took him under our wing. Made sense. Bart spent time at the ranch. One of us was often visiting at the same time he was. Maybe Alistair confided something in him."

I liked my answer better. Someone was bent on scaring us off so we'd leave JoJo's death alone.

"Give me a holler if you need anything." Hank took a few steps and turned back to face me. "You ladies spending the night again?"

That was part of my current plan, but sharing that tidbit was off-limits, for now. "Probably not."

He climbed up onto the saddle and ambled off.

"Here I go," Veera whispered to me. "Hank, wait up!" She caught up and matched the horse's steps.

Mom strolled up from down the road, adjusting the top of her pleated pants.

"Where were you?" I asked. She wasn't supposed to leave the house.

"Walking breakfast off. I should've worn something with an elastic waistband. This country air really opens up my appetite." Her gaze landed on Hank.

He threw her a wave and a smile and clip-clopped toward the road. Veera walked back to us.

"I don't trust that man." Mom watched him ride away. "The horse is a different story."

"I like him, too," Veera said. "The horse, I mean. He seems on the up and up."

"And that's why he's not a murder suspect." I turned to Veera. "Did you square things away with Hank?"

"We're meeting in twenty minutes at the diner. Told him I've got questions only he can answer." Veera cracked her knuckles. "I get the feeling he knows something."

"That's why I need to look inside his house."

Mom sauntered up the driveway.

"You don't have to stick around, Mom." Crimes were being committed left and right since we'd arrived. What if she walked right into one? "And no walks." She wasn't familiar with the territory, and a killer was on the loose.

Mom waved me off. "I'm not leaving till we're done."

I was about to hand my car keys to Veera when a lone figure shot through the shrubbery at the edge of the pasture. Gifty raced toward us. Was someone chasing her?

"What's up with her?" Veera shielded her eyes from the sun.

Veera and I met Gifty halfway. She stopped, breathing hard and heavy. Her hair fell around her face in a messy frizz.

"Are you okay?" I placed a hand on her arm.

"Someone broke into my home," she spoke between breaths. "You come and see before I telephone the police."

We dove into my BMW and motored next door.

Gifty's home was a disaster. Chairs overturned and cushions sliced open. A drop leaf table was flipped over.

"I walked to town to buy stamps. I returned to find this atrocity." Her accent grew thicker.

Veera led her to a corner chair while I took photos.

"What's the most valuable thing you have?" I asked.

"I have nothing, no jewelry, no cash."

I peered into Gifty's bedroom. The covers were pulled off, drawers ransacked; even a plant was overturned. Was someone angry or on the hunt for something? I returned to Gifty. "Anything here that belongs to JoJo?"

"A wrench and a pie plate."

"Our criminal-at-large has kept busy," Veera said. "That's because he spends normal times eating a meal with us and has plenty of energy to spare. Are we dealing with a psychopath?"

"We're dealing with someone who thinks he's pulling the wool over our eyes by acting like a regular person." I turned to Gifty. "How long were you gone?"

"Twenty, thirty minutes, maybe."

Marti was with Mom…except when she went for a walk. Why didn't Mom follow instructions? Heidi was with me. But none of the guys were accounted for. "Call the police."

Gifty grabbed her phone and made the call.

"The rifle's gone." Veera pointed to the corner. "Who'd want that?"

Gifty disconnected and turned to me. "Any one of the family." She moved closer to me. "Last night, I told Red I have a copy of JoJo's will with papers that say I can stay here permanently. Maybe they are trying to scare me out of my home."

"You've got JoJo's will?" Veera asked. "Where?"

Gifty led the way to the kitchen. Cabinets hung open, as did drawers. Gifty pulled out an open drawer and placed it on the tile counter. She reached into the empty space and yanked out an envelope secured in place beneath the counter. It would be easy to miss if you weren't looking for it. She held it out to me.

"The will." I held my breath. "When was this written?"

"About one year ago. It says JoJo's ten acres and a smaller house go to Bart." Gifty said. "The rest is divided equally."

Veera blew out a low whistle.

I skimmed the six-page document. "Marti says there's a newer will. Have you seen it?"

"How would Marti know?"

"JoJo told her. Where would JoJo hide it?" We'd already found some of her hiding places.

"She once said to hide anything valuable where no one would expect to find it. Paperwork should be taped above the inside of a drawer. That's what I did."

"I'll text Michael to take a look around again." Veera stepped away to call him.

Maybe this wasn't the time to pose this question, but sometimes, the best time to ask is when the heat is turned up.

"Gifty, do you have a criminal record?" I knew the answer.

She nodded. "I shoplifted once. I'm not proud of it."

"Is that all?"

She closed her eyes. "There is more."

Chapter Twenty-Nine

Gifty sat us down and gave us the short version of her criminal history.

"When I was sixteen, Ma's boyfriend moved in with his pet, Dodzi. I was put in charge of cleaning Dodzi's cage, a large plastic container with no wiggle room."

"That's animal abuse right there," Veera said.

"True. Especially if the animal is a fifteen-foot-long African rock python," Gifty told us. "Dodzi and I got along very well, but Ma's boyfriend was another matter. He abused Ma and Dodzi, cramming him into his tiny quarters. One day, when the boyfriend took Dodzi out, Dodzi decided to express his displeasure. He bit the man, then squeezed him to death."

"That snake had been holding it all in," Veera said.

"The man's family brought charges against me for not properly caring for Dodzi. But the court found in my favor."

"That's good news," I said.

Marti had mentioned a murder charge against Gifty, but Marti had put her own spin on it. The death of the boyfriend had nothing to do with Gifty. Even so, Gifty stayed on my suspect list. There was no sign of forced entry, nothing missing except the rifle, and no witnesses. Did Gifty set up the break-in to make us think someone had been in her home? That's what my highly suspicious mind told me.

Moments later, a squad car roared up the driveway. Two officers stepped out. While the police checked Gifty's house, Veera and I slipped outside.

"Gotta say this for Gifty. She didn't have to tell us about the charges against her," Veera said. "Since it happened in Ghana, chances were we'd never find out."

"Yes, we would." Michael was running the background check on Gifty as I spoke. I'd texted him the low-down. "Michael's thorough." We'd heard Gifty's version. Now, we needed validation.

"You're saying she's sly and cunning and would stoop to any means to stay in her home?" Veera was mulling over that possibility.

That's not exactly what I'd told Veera, but we'd somehow landed on the same page.

"I'm kicking that thought around in my head, C. Being an associate P.I. makes me suspect everyone of everything and anything."

"Truth." I studied Gifty's front door. No door knocker, just an average doorbell. JoJo kept her spare key in an electric socket cover made for hiding a key. Where did Gifty hide her spare?

I checked under the mat.

"What are you looking for?"

"A spare key." I eyed pots around me.

Veera overturned large rocks along the walkway. She veered onto a small patch of lawn against the house. "Sweet." She stared at a wooden birdhouse firmly planted between the limbs of a walnut tree. The little house was the same milk chocolatey shade as the tree limbs, blending right in.

I moved closer. "Gifty likes color, but she didn't paint the birdhouse. Why?"

Veera peered in the little round entry hole. "Maybe she hasn't gotten around to it. Looks unoccupied, but it's not exactly springtime." She walked around the tree to the back of the birdhouse. She ran a finger across the wood. "Aw, would you look at that?" Here's a place that opens up to clean out the birdhouse floor. This bird has maid service." Veera smiled and just as quickly gasped. "You're gonna want to see this."

Veera's thumb was holding up a back flap that opened to a small area at the bottom of the house, separated by a board where the bird could build its nest. Two silver hooks were attached to the flap. One held a key.

"Gifty's spare key," I said.

"You think this was used to break into her house?"

Would a thief return a key to its usual spot? Not unless he was a thoughtful thief or knew his way around. "We have no proof this was used to get in."

Minutes later, the police took off. We found Gifty sitting in a corner of her sofa, two balls of yarn, yellow and red, next to her, spiraling tightly around her needles. Her lips formed one tight line, her gaze intense on her knitting, fingers pulling, pushing, and twirling rapidly. We had to watch ourselves around those sharp metal points.

The police had located the missing rifle in the back of the kitchen pantry. Gifty denied putting it there. Her face sagged. "Who would do this to me?"

I gently touched her arm. She slowed her pace and dropped her hands in her lap.

"The recent events have been overwhelming. Why don't we help tidy up?" I asked.

There's no rule that says you can't help a murder suspect straighten up their home and coax information out of them in the process. Veera pulled out her cell phone and punched in some notes on that very point.

We straightened, swept, and got Gifty to loosen up enough for us to learn that when she first arrived in Los Ranchos, she worked as a server at Hank's, eventually becoming part-time assistant manager.

Veera sneezed again and again. "I need some air after all that dusting." She stepped outside.

"Do you lock your doors when you leave?" I asked.

She huffed and tried to stare me down.

I stared right back without blinking. "The spare key's in a birdhouse."

Her eyes rounded. "You found it?" She hustled out the front door. I followed her.

"They came inside using the spare?" Gifty stared at the birdhouse.

"Did you give a key to anyone?"

She nodded. "JoJo had one. And Bart. I trust him."

Back to square one. "Did JoJo give you a key to her house?"

"She did not. But she told me where to hide mine. She even gave me the birdhouse."

My cell phone rang. It was Marti. "Talk later," I told Gifty and headed down the driveway. I answered the call.

"I've got bad news," Marti's voice crackled. "That's all I've been getting lately."

Had someone else gotten hurt? Was Mom okay? "What happened?"

"Sally Martino called on the house landline. JoJo's realtor."

Where was this going? "Is she okay?"

"Of course not. Sally said the buyer backed out of the deal."

"Why?" I had to drop everything for that?

"Oh, I don't know. Something about not being able to develop the property. Get back here now."

"Wait! Who's the—"

She disconnected.

"...buyer?"

Before I could budge, Veera cut through a hedge and jetted my way.

She panted. "Follow me."

She ran toward the back of the home and stopped near a patch of dirt where Gifty grew lettuce and other greens.

"The ground's dry everywhere but here," she said. "If I were to break into this cottage, I'd come around the back and stick to dry ground, wouldn't you?"

"But you don't always stick to a plan when you're in a hurry." I'd been scanning the edges of Gifty's garden. That's when I saw a partial print with the same zig-zag boot pattern as the prints we're hunting down. "That's fresh."

"I know it."

"Nice work, Veera. If the boots were worn by Alistair's killer, the same person broke into Gifty's." We were getting closer. I handed Veera my car key and walked backwards. "Go on ahead for your meeting with Hank. See you at the ranch when you're finished. Don't forget we've got an appointment with Violet Hilliard."

"I won't."

I took a photo of the boot print and texted it to Mom, asking her to check everyone's soles, then I wound my way to JoJo's house. Someone had buried a pair of boots near a trough on JoJo's land. Boots with the same soles. My little voice told me JoJo's death was linked to greed and decisions that didn't sit well with one person in particular. Who? I felt certain the person was close by.

Chapter Thirty

om waved her hands over her head the moment she laid eyes on me. She raced down the porch steps.

"I thought you'd never get here. None of their soles matched your picture. It wasn't easy getting them to cooperate." She pointed behind her with her thumb. "They're going crazy in there."

"They expected a big payout from the sale of this property."

She shrugged. "So, they wait a little longer for another buyer. What's the big deal?"

"Let's find out." I opened the door to the house.

"Wait!" She grabbed my arm and pulled me over to a towering Magnolia tree. She pointed to the ground, and there they were: faint bootprints with portions of the same zig-zag pattern leading to the driveway.

"They could've been here for days." The prints were in the perfect spot to keep an eye on the house. I bent closer. They looked fresh.

"Come in, already!" Marti yelled from the door.

Mom and I trudged inside.

"Finally." Marti handed me a card. "Call Sally and demand to know why the buyer backed out. She won't tell me."

Red and Bart murmured their agreement. Heidi leaned against the wall with her arms crossed.

The buyer could've had any number of reasons, from cold feet to finding a better property. I turned to Heidi. "How does JoJo feel about the deal falling through?" Might as well let this play out.

"She thinks it's for the best."

"When did she say that?" Mom walked in from behind me. "Because I didn't hear anything from you or her."

"Me neither." Marti folded her arms over her chest. "You didn't say JoJo contacted you."

"I made contact intuitively when you were on the phone with the realtor. I'm the medium, remember? That's why I know mystical things, and you don't." She turned to Mom. "How was anyone supposed to get a word in with all the racket made by these three?" Heidi waved a hand toward the Means family members.

"You've got a point." Mom nodded.

"I need help with some heavy lifting." Heidi crooked her finger toward me.

I followed her down the hall to JoJo's closet.

She lowered her voice, "I talked to the officer who came here after JoJo's death. Dad told him to answer all my questions."

"That's exciting." I meant it. "Go on."

"No sign of foul play meant no investigation. But right after JoJo died, as a favor to Dad, one officer came back and talked to neighbors since a few thefts had been reported. A couple of residents saw a tall guy with a big nose and—"

"A black baseball cap."

"How'd you know?"

"I talked to a neighbor, too." I didn't tell her about the mask.

Heidi stomped her foot. "This case is going to go unsolved, isn't it?"

"I'm bringing in the killer, dead or alive. I mean, alive."

She stormed out and yelled over her shoulder, "I'm officially taking my supernatural powers home."

I checked my phone and headed for the living room in time to see Heidi skip down the porch stairs.

"Where's she off to?" Marti asked.

"She's sitting the rest of this case out."

"Victoria called the realtor." Marti pouted.

"The buyer didn't give a reason for canceling the deal," Mom said. "It's possible her psychic advised her to back out."

"Where's Michael?" I asked. He didn't respond to my text about verifying Gifty's record. Winged creatures flitted around in my mid-section. Not butterflies, but bats and crows and vultures.

Everyone looked around. Apparently, no one noticed him missing.

"He said something about going to his car." Mom chewed on a finger, which is what she did when she was worried.

"Excuse us." I took Mom's arm and led her outside. We trotted down the porch steps and walked toward her Volvo.

"Where'd he go, Mom?"

"After we finished prepping the pot pies, there wasn't much happening, so he thought he'd take a look around."

"Where?" Why didn't he tell me?

"Hank's house." She handed me her car key.

I pulled out Michael's note with directions to Hank's. "A Nightingale team member needs to stay here to keep an eye out. That means you."

"I'll hold them hostage." She made her way up the porch.

I dove into Mom's Volvo. Hank wasn't the type who'd keep a welcome mat outside his front door. There was a hard edge to him, which made me certain he kept some form of security at his place.

I slammed on the gas until I hung a left down a long, unmarked driveway between two well-maintained homes. The driveway started out as smooth asphalt, but deteriorated into broken-up pieces mixed with dirt. Other homes dropped out of sight. A grove of thirsty trees appeared, hunched over with dead branches. I parked the car before reaching Hank's pad. I'd notice more on foot.

I hurried ahead, taking long strides and crouching slightly. A dog barked furiously nearby, a series of deep, low, gruff barks. I sprinted onto a rough driveway patterned with holes and ridges. The barks grew louder, suddenly stopping when I reached a tiny house on a narrow strip of land. It was more like a manufactured, modular home trying to turn into a real one. A one-rail fence fortified with chicken wire guarded a dry patch in front. A small porch balanced on a slightly raised platform. Not a security camera in sight.

Tall wooden gates ensured no one could get into the back portion. I overturned a nearby pail and hopped up on it, peering over the gates at a ramshackle shed. Traces of alfalfa scattered around a weathered feed bin.

JoJo's place looked like Versailles compared to this tin can. Plant life was scarce except for a couple of gnarly oaks. A weathered picnic bench and an empty flagpole tried desperately to give the place character. Hank's home didn't fit in the neighborhood.

The furious barking started again, louder. It came from inside the house. "Oh, no." Why didn't Michael let me handle this?

I jumped over the fence and onto the porch. Beer bottles and coffee cups littered the table and floor. I turned the knob on the front door. Locked. How did Michael get in? Was he inside?

I raced around the house and tried a window. Locked. I tried a few more and put on the brakes near a kitchen window that was slightly pushed open. Lifting it all the way, I climbed inside, sitting half on the ledge and half on the frame, about to wiggle in when a big dog jumped up on the counter with a snarl, front paws scratching the tile. I jerked back.

"Are you the welcoming committee?" My heart beat at a hummingbird's tempo.

The large Rottweiler growled. Handsome in a James Cagney type of way, he was the kind of dog who could turn from sweetie-pie into ugly in two seconds. "Anyone here with you?" He quieted long enough for me to listen. Except for a humming fridge, all was still. Michael must have left. I reached into my handbag and pulled out a small pouch that contained something of vital necessity. Something I always brought with me, designed for exuberant canine friends. Unzipping the bag, I pulled out a tube and uncorked it.

"You're such a good boy." I muttered as many sweet nothings as I could, but he wasn't falling for it. He showed his fangs and snarled. "I'll bet females try to flirt with you all the time, don't they?"

He sat back on his haunches and licked his lips. Either he was expecting a treat or planning to bite my arm off.

I slipped out a mini blow gun from the pouch, courtesy of Dad, as was nearly everything in my bag of tricks. I inserted a lightweight dart tipped with just the right meds for convincing a large dog to take a short nap, with no harm to the pooch, except a little grogginess upon waking. A veterinarian pal of Dad's supplied these for him and now for me.

"Steady." I placed the blow gun in my mouth and aimed at the dog's shoulder. Two more darts sat ready and waiting in the pouch. Would I get the red-tipped dart in on my first blow? It had been a while. I blew hard and quick and missed. "Darn." Nothing like a little pressure to get a job done. I inserted the next one, aimed, and puffed. This dart hit the target, a little lower than planned. In about ten minutes, the pooch would be snoozing. He flinched and craned his neck, jaws open to grab me as soon as I got close enough. "Good luck with that." I checked my watch. "Be back in a few."

Grabbing a chair from the porch, I headed for the backyard. I stood on the seat and peered over the privacy fence. The yard was bone dry and dusty. Another large, dilapidated shed and that was it for backyard ambiance. I jumped down and ran to the opposite side of the house, chair in tow. I stopped to peek at the dog. He was lying on the floor, eyes still on the window.

"See you soon." I carried the chair to a gate at the opposite end and stood on it. I pulled out a pair of binoculars and peered. There wasn't much to see.

A pounding nearby quickened my heartbeat. Footsteps padded the dirt by the front of the place. I leapt down and rocketed to the side of the house. Pulling out my pistol, I inched closer.

Chapter Thirty-One

A tall guy hopped over the one-rail fence in a single bound and onto the dirt driveway. The lean, muscular physique was comfortingly familiar. He sprinted toward the road.

"Michael!" I yelled as loudly as I dared, trying not to attract attention. Not that there were any neighbors close by.

He froze and turned. "Corrie?" His expression switched from frantic to puzzled to uncertain. "I can explain."

"No time." I headed back to the house, chair in tow again. Michael caught up. "I need to get inside."

"You can't do that. There's a fierce dog. Though, he's a deep sleeper. I snuck right past. The poor guy must be exhausted after all that barking."

"I need a quick look." I guessed Michael didn't have a chance to nose around with the dog on his tail.

"But he's vicious."

"Not when he's asleep." I gave Michael the nutshell version of my canine encounter and lifted the window.

"I got in through that window, too." Michael pointed at it. "Didn't see any dog. But then I walked down the hall, and there he was, barreling toward me. I ducked into the bathroom and shut the door."

"This window was unlocked?"

"Yeah. Hank must've thought the big guy would handle intruders."

I climbed inside. The dog didn't budge.

Michael leaned his torso over the window ledge and pointed his finger at the sound sleeper. "How long do we have?"

"Fifteen minutes. Maybe twenty." I checked my phone. Veera had texted me five minutes ago to say she and Hank were going to Alistair's office. "Veera's with Hank. Come on in. Hank's computer is all yours."

Michael slid in snakelike, head first. It was like he'd gone boneless.

"How did you do that?" I had to stop and marvel at his finesse.

"I practice sliding in and out of my office window at the college."

"Really?"

"No one's the wiser. The window faces shrubbery. Pretty good, huh?"

"Really good, but we need to discuss why you broke in here on your own." He opened his mouth, and I put up my hand. "Afterward."

Michael shot off toward the back of Hank's home. The inside was surprisingly orderly. The compact kitchen was all stainless steel, white walls and cabinets. Even the dishes were white. JoJo must've loved what he'd done with the interior. A quick glance in each drawer and cabinet revealed nothing extraordinary. Same with the living room. Well-kept and tidy all the way. There wasn't much to the place. Just a short hallway leading to the kitchen, a bathroom, and two bedrooms. Hank used the smaller one as his office. Brown carpet edged out the vinyl flooring in the kitchen and bathroom. I checked my watch. Eleven minutes till wake-up time.

The closets were mostly empty. Cabinets and drawers housed the barest necessities. Hank hardly had any stuff, not counting the overflow on the porch.

"Corrie!" Michael half-shouted.

As I entered the office, Michael stared at the screen of a large monitor, slowly scrolling through the pages. He sat behind a large desk on a chair with a bucket seat and wingback. A recliner was the only other furniture in the room.

"Hank spends a lot of time in this chair."

I moved closer. "How do you know?"

"He does his own bookkeeping daily and makes bank deposits."

"Does he seem tech-savvy?"

"Very."

I leaned over his shoulder. "Is he a good businessman?"

"His eatery brings in enough money to keep him well in the black. And judging by his accounts, Hank's a saver. I'm going through his monthly bills now."

I looked around the room. "Maybe he plopped a mobile home down here to live in while he builds a real house somewhere else."

"He owns his business, but not the land. He switched lenders about six months ago, and his payments are..." he gave a low whistle. "...higher."

"Who's the lender?"

Michael pounded the keyboard, while staring at the screen. "The first one was a bank. Now it's a private party lender. JoJo Means."

"Do I smell motive?"

"The odor gets stronger. A balloon payment is due in less than ninety days." Michael flipped around to face me. "Have you seen the garage? I took a quick detour before hunkering down in here."

Intrigued, I shut Michael's door and hurried down the hall, peering into Hank's bedroom on the way. Spartan, as expected. The hallway ended with a door leading to a packed garage. Wall-to-wall plastic storage bins and antique furnishings covered in sheets and bubble wrap filled every space. Black plastic covered items that were rolled up on the floor in a pile. I knelt next to one and ripped a small piece open. A colorful tapestry shown underneath, thick and soft. A Persian rug, judging by the tiny knots on the bottom; hand-knotted wool. Must have cost a pretty penny. Where did Hank get the rugs and antiques?

Fortunately, the garage windows provided enough light to make nosing around easy. I knelt to remove the lid off a plastic bin, when a thin silver chain caught my eye. It dangled from the corner of a marble-topped table. I lifted the flimsy chain with my fingers. The clasp had come undone. Two keys dangled from the chain.

A low growl prevented me from taking a closer look.

"Uh-oh." I slowly turned.

There he was, in the doorway, teeth bared, ears pushed back.

"Why didn't I close the door?" I bent over slightly. "We've never been properly introduced. What's your name? Rex? Spike, maybe? How about

Cookie?" I kept talking, slow and sweet, while I reached into my handbag for my last dart and blowgun.

Michael's head stuck out, behind the dog. Eyes rounded, he held his bomber jacket in both hands and slowly tiptoed forward.

"I can't let my handsome boyfriend cover your head with that nice leather jacket of his. What if you shred it to pieces? Or worse?"

Rex replied in a series of full-blown barks. So much for his feeling groggy after his nappy-poo. I raised the dart blower to my lips and aimed for the dog's upper left shoulder. I puffed. He barked. And I missed. Now what?

"Michael, do you have any snacks on you?" I asked sweetly.

"Never leave home without them." Just a foot or so behind Rex, Michael's forehead was moist. He dropped a corner of his jacket as his hand reached inside a pocket. "M&Ms, energy bars, here we go. Will mini pretzels work?"

"I know a certain someone who might like those. What a good boy." I kept my voice low and dripping with sugar as I took out my pepper spray and stepped forward. Fingers crossed that Rex was food-motivated.

"He...here, boy. I've got a yummy snack for you." Michael's voice rose two octaves. He ripped open the package with his teeth and dropped a pretzel on the floor, walking backward slowly.

Rex flipped around, barked, and sniffed. In the next moment, his whole demeanor changed. He gave a small whine and lunged forward. Michael jumped back against the wall while the dog scooped up the pretzel, wagging tail curling upward. He munched and crunched. I moved forward, through the doorway, into the hall.

"He likes it." Michael wore a small grin.

Rex looked up, expecting more.

"Trail to the kitchen?" Michael's eyes were on the dog.

"And to freedom." I took a few quick photos of the garage and carefully stepped past a chomping Rex.

Michael slid up on the counter, window wide open behind him. "I only have four pretzels left."

I waited on the opposite side of the kitchen. I spoke in a gentle, high voice, "Hold a pretzel up in your hand so he sees it. As I move toward you, toss each pretzel, one at a time, till we are out of his range."

It took nearly a minute for Michael and me to jump back outside, seconds away from Rex's front paws landing on the counter.

We hightailed it down the driveway, back to the Volvo.

"We work better as a team, wouldn't you say?" I panted.

"I won't be flying solo for a while." Michael held out his palm for a high five.

I obliged. "I know."

We sat in my car. Michael turned to face me.

"There's something you're going to want to see."

Chapter Thirty-Two

As I motored back to the ranch, Michael held up his phone screen. "There's new video footage from the camera you planted in Alistair's office."

I stopped the car in JoJo's driveway. Michael started the playback.

"Hank went in twice today." He fast-forwarded. "First time, he looked through the drawers, and the second time...wait for it..."

Hank rushed inside Alistair's office and settled on the desk chair. He opened the top file cabinet drawer, thumbed through, and pulled out a folder. Stuffing it inside his jacket, he shot out the door.

"Did you see that?" Michael's excitement shook the car. "Happened this morning. What did he take?"

"Something incriminating." The office workers probably didn't blink an eye because Hank visited regularly.

"I went to his house to find that something, but..." He threw up his hands.

"He could still have it on him. But I found a little something." I held up the silver chain.

Michael lifted the keys and peered closer. He held up one of them. "Does this look familiar?"

"It's the twin of the key to the Means' main house." I examined my cell phone photos of the key we'd found on JoJo's porch. "The original key."

"The other one could be to Gifty's..."

"If JoJo gave Hank this key, why would he call a locksmith to get inside? And why go into Gifty's?" How would Hank explain? I stared at the round-headed key and sucked in a wad of air. "This isn't Gifty's key. Her key had a different shape to its head."

"Then whose is it?"

"I'll find out." I dropped the chain in my purse, and we stepped outside.

"Hold on." Michael grabbed my hand. "Gifty's story about the trial in Ghana checked out. It was in the *Ghanaian Chronicle*."

"That's good news." She couldn't have made that stuff up.

When we entered the Means' home, all was quiet. Where was everyone?

"Hear that?" Michael's brows dipped as he faced me.

Airy laughter floated out of the kitchen. The talk was gentle and light.

"Are we in the right house?" Maybe they'd all dipped into the booze.

"It sounds like polite conversation between people who enjoy each other's company." Michael stared at me, mouth open.

We drifted into the kitchen. The Means family, including Gifty, sat around the table, smiling like they were celebrating a happy occasion. Mom held court at the head of the clan, all sugary sweetness.

"What's going on?" Michael asked.

"We're enjoying a delightful lunch." Mom tapped the corners of her mouth with her napkin. "Pull up some chairs."

"Chicken pot pie should be a staple in every home." Red held a spoon in his hand filled with flaky crust and creamy filling.

His usual scowl had eased some; his cheeks slightly flushed. Was he wasted?

"Red's right." Marti leaned back in her chair. Her broad smile erased the frown off her face.

"I'd like a piece, please." Michael sat, grin firmly in place.

"Your mother kindly shared her recipe," Gifty said to me. "I'm going to bake one myself tomorrow."

"Oh, let's make it together," Marti said. "Won't that be fun? Please pass the mashed potatoes."

"I got it." Bart stood and lifted the bowl. He plopped a good portion onto Marti's plate.

"Thank you, love bug." Marti dug in.

I nearly fell over just standing there. This was not the Means family I'd come to know and not like very much. "Mother, may I see you outside?"

"As soon as we're done eating, honey."

"Now, please." I turned and left the room. I scooted down the porch stairs and waited.

Mom showed up a minute later. "Did you need something, sweetie?"

"Why does everyone at the table sound just like you?" What did she put in the chicken pot pie?

She threw her hand. "They're just looking at life through a different lens."

"You know that's not possible." They were the same old Means clan this morning.

"If you see a change in them, that means it is possible."

"Mom, what did you do?" What was she not telling me?

"Nothing, except I reminded them firmly that JoJo's spirit was in the house, and if they wanted more answers and less house haunting, they'd better play nicely. I convinced them it's why Heidi failed to make contact. Perfectly logical, right?" Her eyes glittered as she gestured with her hands in front of her. "And I might have said that if we didn't pass around the olive branch, something bad could happen."

"What does that even mean?"

"It means we're making progress. I'm glad you brought Michael back in one piece."

"Don't change the subject." I watched her closely. That's what I got for putting Mom in charge. "Why can't you just be straight?"

She patted my arm. "I don't do crooked. Crooked causes wrinkles. By the way," She slapped my arm with the back of her hand, "Bart and Red made the creamed corn. It's tasty." She headed for the door.

I followed her in and plopped down next to Michael. Mom could be convincing when she wanted to be. Maybe she *was* being straight with me.

Michael held out the pot pie for me to try. I added some onto my plate and a forkful into my mouth. The flaky, buttery crust was warm and delicious; the creamy herbed gravy nearly lifted me out of my seat. This definitely had something to do with the smile on everyone's face.

* * *

When all the plates and food were cleared, we gathered into the living room. Veera arrived right after clean-up and polished off some pot pie. The dreamy look on her face said it all.

I made an announcement as soon as Veera was done. "We're leaving in ten minutes to drive to the attorney's office. It'll be Marti, Red, Veera, and me."

"I'm coming."

Gifty's Ghanaian lilt was so pleasing to the ears today. Any hardness had vanished.

"I mean…" Gifty shifted in her chair, "…I would very much like to join you, if that is not a problem." Gifty folded her hands in her lap and managed to smile at Marti.

All eyes were on Marti.

She bit her lip before turning to Gifty. "I think you should come. After all, you're a legitimate beneficiary of my…of our dear late sister's estate."

"What?" What was wrong with Marti?

"It warms my heart to see the Means family act this way." Michael pounded his fist over his heart. "I'm amazed by all of you."

"What is going on?" I tried again.

Red stood. "This is what JoJo would've wanted."

Bart was next to stand. "We're family. This is how it should be."

Right then and there, I decided there was one thing left for me to do. I'd go with the flow. "If you want to act like the model family you've never been, I'm all for it."

"Nothing can stop us because we're going to hold each other up." Marti got to her feet.

"Arthritis, back pain, and tendonitis be damned," Red said.

"Okay, fine. Designated Means family members, grab your copy of the will, take a potty run 'cause there are no bathroom breaks along the way, and meet me at my car in five minutes."

They scattered. Michael and Veera slid over to me.

I turned to Michael. "All is not what it seems." Was I right about that? "Can you find out what happened here while we were in Hank's house? Mom did something." He could finesse information out of Mom better than Veera. Veera fell for her tricks.

"I'll get to the bottom of it." He gave me a small salute and scooted away.

Veera kept up with me as I stepped outside.

"What have you got?" I stopped midway down the driveway and faced the house.

"Hank's Place was so jammed, they had me serving and bussing tables. Never made it to Alistair's office. Have to admit, it was kinda fun. Made some good tips and got information at the same time."

Now we were getting somewhere. "Go on."

"Hank wasn't there when I first arrived. Tucker, the cook, said Hank was at the cemetery, taking care of business. Something about bench removal."

"Hank visited Alistair's office this morning." I told her about the camera footage.

"Think he's our man?"

"Looks that way."

"When he finally walked into the diner," Veera said. "He wore sneakers. Did he wear boots on the horse?"

"Cowboy boots with smooth soles."

"He must've changed. I pretended to go to the restroom, but I snuck into Hank's office. He should expect such things when he's got a junior P.I. working his tables."

"Truth." Veera was climbing up the P.I. ladder right in front of me.

"Two pairs of boots were in his office closet, including a pair of work boots. Take a look." She scrolled through her phone and showed me a photo of the soles.

The patterns were different. "Did you get the size?"

"One was eleven. The other a twelve."

"Well done, Veera."

"What makes you think I'm done? I went to the cemetery next. Took me three minutes to walk there. It's small and filled with fancy old headstones. I asked the caretaker about Hank coming by." Veera pulled back and looked around. "Said he hadn't seen him in days."

"Which means he had time to visit Alistair's office." What was he after? And why lie about going to the cemetery?

* * *

We were going to be a little late to the appointment with Violet Hilliard. Both Red and Marti were big on taking bathroom breaks, or so they said. I discovered they liked playing the lottery in different towns, at different gas stations along the way.

"Improves the odds," Red said. "There's a Mobile station coming up on your right."

"No more stops till we reach our destination." I regarded him in the rearview mirror.

"We'll include you in our split of the winnings."

Red was a desperate man.

"Seems reasonable to me," Marti said.

"We're not feeding your gambling habit." Veera turned and gave them a stern stare. "You should be focusing on questions you've got for the attorney. They charge by the hour, you know."

"That's your job," Marti said. "Are you doing okay, Gifty?" Marti caught my gaze in the mirror. "She gets car sick."

"I am not too unwell," Gifty said.

Gifty did look a little woozy. Michael cleaned out my car interior last weekend. I planned on keeping it spotless.

"Want some ginger candy?" Veera held up a small wrapped piece.

Gifty shook her head.

"Row, row, row your boat gently down the stream," Marti started singing. "Merrily, merrily, merrily, merrily, life is but a dream."

Red joined in, and after a bar or two, so did Gifty. They sang at the top of their lungs. On the upside, no one requested a bathroom stop or threw up. On the downside, Red sang way off-key. Thankfully, it only took another ten minutes to reach County Square Road and the law office of Alexandra

Violet Hilliard.

I turned into the lot and parked, gazing up into a gray sky tinged with orange. The half-hearted sun had lost interest in showing up this afternoon. Tall, vertical panels containing limo-tinted windows ran along the office building's front side, alternating with vertical columns of mustard-colored stucco. The names of three law firms appeared on the outside. Violet's firm wasn't one of them.

I couldn't get the Means sibs to stop singing until my palm blasted the horn. I shut the engine as peace and quiet were restored.

"That's my favorite nursery rhyme," Marti said. "Mama used to sing it to us."

"Papa sang it to me," Gifty said.

Hard to picture that scene since Gifty didn't even meet Papa till she was in her twenties. Silence filled the back seat.

"Here we go." Veera opened her door.

I knew the peace wouldn't last.

"That is a sweet memory," Marti said. "Isn't it, Red?"

"Sweet as my favorite chewing gum."

I sat up and gripped the steering wheel. "I'd love a piece of gum." I looked at Red.

He reached into the pocket of his pants, pulled out a piece, and handed the wrapped stick to me. Slightly bent and pliable, there was no name on the silver wrapper.

"What kind of gum is this?" My heart thumped against my chest.

"Double mint." He passed pieces to Marti, Gifty, and Veera.

"What brand?" Was it the brand found in Alistair's office? More importantly, was it the one found near Alistair's body?

Red leaned forward and dug deep into a back pocket. "Come to think of it, sitting on the pack of gum the whole way here didn't provide me with a stick of comfort." He froze as his lips broke into a smile, most of which was covered by his thick mustache. "Get it?"

Marti patted his arm and chuckled. Gifty stared a few moments, then grinned. I had to admit, I liked the civility among the siblings.

CHAPTER THIRTY-TWO

"The brand?" I spoke through gritted teeth. Veera tapped her boot.

Red pulled out a hard plastic, protective case filled with sticks of gum.

"How much gum does that thing hold?" Veera asked.

"A treasure chest of thirty-five pieces. Only twenty-one left."

Was he ever going to show me the brand? I put out my hand.

He dropped a piece in my palm. The wrapper was green and white.

"Hi-dent." I faced Veera. "Yummy." The same brand that was found in Alistair's office and at the crime scene. I focused on Red. Was I staring into the goofy, bloodshot eyes of a killer? Were he and Hank in cahoots?

Chapter Thirty-Three

I walked behind the group as we made our way to Violet's second-floor office, my gaze fixed on Red. Not that I was certain of his role in Alistair's death. Gum wrappers weren't exactly the proof I had in mind. Plus, there was the problem of JoJo's key on Hank's chain. Did JoJo give him the key? And why didn't he bother using it to get inside? What did Hank take from Alistair's office?

With those questions swirling in my mind, we stopped in front of suite 210. Veera held open the door, and the family filed in.

Violet sat behind a cherry wood desk whose drawers faced her clients instead of the main occupant. On the corner of the desk closest to us, a brass lamp with a black shade burned brightly. Business cards, a brass nameplate, and a silver globe sat in the opposite corner. A six-inch ceramic woodpecker didn't quite fit in, but maybe that and the backward desk were conversation starters for someone not great at small talk.

A small, expressionless, nail-biter of a woman, Violet's beady eyes flicked from us to the folder in front of her. Her office was surprisingly large for a solo practitioner. Silver wall frames displayed her diplomas. A tall chrome fan was wedged in the corner behind her, ensuring she'd never break into a sweat. The fan didn't stand a chance of messing with her hair. Piled in a high, coiled bun, her black tresses were lacquered with enough hairspray to withstand a blizzard.

Red stopped in front of the desk. "Are these drawers for your clients' benefit?" His itchy fingers reached out to the top drawer.

"They are not," she replied.

He pulled back, his harsh stare linked to hers. "It's a clever decorative piece, Miss Hilliard. Do you sit on this side often?"

Was he flirting with her?

Violet looked like she was about to pass gas. "I sit on the client's side when I'm alone to enjoy the view."

Veera and I exchanged glances. What view? Wasn't much to see out the window, other than a tree trunk and an office building decked out in muddy-colored stucco.

Red sat in one of two matching low-backed chairs in front of the desk, eyes fastened on Violet. Marti landed on the other chair while Veera and Gifty took over a small couch near the entry. I perched on the armrest.

"My priority is to provide superior representation. That's what I did for Ms. Means." Her hands touched her chest. "I was sad to hear she'd died."

Violet spoke without a trace of emotion. I stepped forward, introduced everyone, and handed her my card.

"We have copies of JoJo's trust." I stood by Marti. "We need to confirm they're the latest."

Violet's squirrely eyes rolled over us before she glided to a metal filing cabinet. Pulling out a drawer, she removed a file and slapped it on her desk. "Do your documents have my name on them?"

"No, they don't," Marti said. "We found out about you in an envelope buried in a container of kitty litter."

"Funny thing is, our sister didn't have a cat." Red's expression didn't shift.

Violet stretched out her hand. "Your documents?"

Gifty gave me her envelope. I collected the other one from Red and placed them on Violet's desk.

"Did JoJo come to your office?" Marti asked.

"Once, to sign and review. She gave me explicit instructions on the phone prior to our meeting." Violet lowered her head and pored over the documents. "Outdated, both of them." She held a different document up in her hand. "The one I wrote supersedes."

Both Marti and Red perked up in their seats. Gifty stood behind Red. I guided her closer to my side. I didn't expect Red to make any sudden moves, but you never know. Veera rose and took her place behind Red, one hand in a pocket that bulged with the shape of her pepper spray can.

"Want me to read the will to you?" Violet asked.

"Of course we do." Marti looked around, and the rest agreed with her.

Everybody fidgeted and frowned as Violet read until she got to the last part.

"She left the entire estate to…" Violet paused.

I stood and moved closer. Marti gripped her armrest, Red cleared his throat, and Gifty bowed her head.

"…Martinique Means…"

Marti gasped and held her chest. "Yes!" She looked around as all the eyes turned her way. "Can't a girl express herself?"

"The entire estate is being split up, as you will see, if you allow me to continue." Now Violet looked really cranky. "Martinique Means, Redmond Means…"

Red's lips squeezed together so tightly, they were completely hidden by his mustache. His brows fell hard, nearly covering his eyes.

"…Barton Means Lansing, and Gifty Carmichael. You all inherit equally." Violet looked up at them. "With the exception of the ten acres designated as the Pond Property."

"Don't tell me Bart's getting that?" Marti asked.

Violet tossed her an uninterested glance, before continuing, "The ten-acre property will be turned into a wildlife habitat with particular concern for red-legged frogs. The house on said property will be designated as a center for science and research pertaining to local wildlife."

"What?" the group asked in unison.

Violet held up her hand. "There's more." She read from the document, "If Josephine Means' death should be proven to be a criminal act by law enforcement, the named heirs will receive nothing."

Marti's mouth stayed open. "We didn't kill her. At least, I didn't."

"What are you insinuating, sister?" Red got to his feet.

"I'm not finished." Violet's stink eye nearly sent me reeling out the door. She continued, "Should the foregoing occur, Henry Ramos shall inherit the ranch in its entirety, minus the ten acres as described. Any and all blood relatives will be excluded from inheritance, unless Henry Ramos determines otherwise. Gifty Carmichael will vacate the cottage residence at Henry's discretion."

Red's face turned four different shades of crimson. Marti grabbed the nearest object, the ceramic woodpecker, sharp beak pointing skyward. And Gifty charged the desk, gripping her purse in both hands.

"This is shocking," Gifty said.

"My sister died in her sleep. Everybody knows that." Marti turned to Red.

"She seemed sickly to me." His fists were balled.

"You're fired." Marti fixed her steely blues on me.

"With all that's happened since you hired us, it's not looking like JoJo died in her sleep," Veera said. "Doesn't that mean anything to you?"

"You don't work for me anymore." Marti lifted her chin.

I didn't care what Marti said. JoJo suspected someone of wanting to snuff her out. Her relatives were her prime suspects. "My team will continue as independent contractors." All I had to do was prove criminal activity. That alone made the job worthwhile.

Gifty stared at Violet. "What about the other trust documents?"

"It's like they never existed," Violet replied.

"Who's the executor?" Veera asked.

"Alistair Wallaby," Violet replied.

"But he's—" Marti said.

"Who's next after him?" I stepped forward.

"Henry Ramos."

An uneasy shudder crept over me. JoJo picked two men she trusted to handle her affairs. One of them was murdered. Was Hank next? Or was he the killer? If he knew he stood in line to inherit, he had a motive. Did he know? And was he clever enough to hide his part in it?

"After Mister Ramos, I'm the executor. The estate is to be divided among four charities if anything should happen to him." Violet slid the document across the desk to Marti. "You can keep this copy."

"Why weren't you the first choice as executor?" That made the most sense to me.

"The two men were trustworthy friends of Ms. Means. They understood her intention, and she said they'd stand up to anyone who objected." Violet took out a small notepad from the folder.

Marti stood. "That's not fair."

"There's nothing more to be said." Violet turned her back to us.

Anticipating an outburst and possibly more, I asked Veera to escort everyone back to my car. I tossed her the keys, herded them out, and shut the door. Why did JoJo make Hank a beneficiary?

Violet whirled around and slapped her hands on her desk.

I faced her. "You said you'd prepared more than one trust for JoJo."

"I did what I was told."

"When and why?"

Violet chewed on her pen and dropped her gaze. "You no longer represent the heirs."

It was my turn to slap my palms on her desk. "JoJo's executor was murdered two days ago. The next in line could be in danger." Or could be the cause of danger. "Keep in mind you're in that queue." I let that fester a few beats. "You don't want to be accused of withholding valuable information that could save a life." Would my Jedi mind trick work?

Violet turned toward the fan and pulled it closer to her. "I helped Ms. Means prepare a trust over a year ago, but she made her own changes and removed my name. She left everything to her relatives, plus the ten acres to Barton. The document I provided today was created more recently." She pressed her lips together.

I perched onto a chair, planting my elbows on the desk. "Did she tell you the reason for the change?"

"You should know better than to ask such a question."

"Why would she hide the new will and trust from her family?" Why leave a jumbled-up clue to find Violet? A clue that might never be found?

"How would I know?"

"You know why. JoJo thought that whoever played a hand in her demise would take you out, too."

Violet looked like she was holding her breath.

I turned to leave, then flipped around. "I may have more questions. The police will have questions as well."

"Police?"

"There was a break-in on JoJo's property earlier today." I headed for the door.

"Wait."

I slowly turned.

"JoJo might have said a few things." She inhaled a deep breath. "Her siblings and nephew were pressuring her to sell the twenty-nine acres, and JoJo refused. She said they'd squander the money and end up with nothing."

"They were always running to her to bail them out." That much I was sure of.

"The last few months, JoJo called every week to let me know she was 'alive and kicking', as she said."

"What were you supposed to do if you didn't hear from her?" I asked.

Violet reached into JoJo's file and pulled out a piece of paper. On it was a handwritten note that said, *Call Alistair Wallaby 805-555-5554*

"I called him, but I never heard back."

Alistair knew something. Was that what got him killed?

Chapter Thirty-Four

Islipped into a stairwell where the air sat heavy with dampness and the stench of rusty metal. Skipping down as fast as I dared, I called Michael. He answered on the first ring.

I told him about Hank and the will.

"He's looking more and more like the killer," Michael said.

"He's no killer unless we prove he's one."

He quieted his voice, "Victoria convinced the Means family she's got psychic abilities."

"Like she did with us in eighth grade." Mom's simple parlor tricks convinced Michael and me that she had mystical powers. "The old secret matching trick?" I could see it now. Mom tore up a piece of paper into quarters, then smaller quarters, making every scrap distinct. Then she gave each Means family member a piece, asking them to write a secret, fold it, and give it back to her.

"Your mom gave Marti a scrap with a short, untorn side, Red's piece with two untorn sharp sides, Bart got a long, untorn side, and Gifty had all torn sides. Then Victoria matched the secrets to each person."

"And they fell for it?"

"Victoria told them JoJo helped her find where each secret belonged. She said the way to get their inheritance was to prove that they could all get along."

I bit my lip. "Glad Mom kept herself busy." And kept a sharp eye on the family.

"Bart slipped out a minute after you left, but I tailed him."

I pushed open the stairwell door and sucked in the fresh air. "Where'd he go?"

"To Gifty's."

"Hmmm. When he knew she wouldn't be home."

"He slipped in her backdoor. I hid in some shrubs and watched."

Gifty said he had a key. Was Bart responsible for the break-in at Gifty's?

"Out he came, two minutes later." Michael took a breath. "He headed for the ranch. But, get this. He was holding something. I couldn't tell what, so I took a picture. I'm going to blow it up."

"Awesome work."

"I had to make up for sneaking into Hank's bachelor pad without you. I'm going to make you proud."

I could practically see his grin through the phone. "You've already done that, many times over."

"I can't do it enough. You think Bart and Gifty are up to something?"

"That's a new angle we'll need to explore. Gotta go." I disconnected as a text rolled in from Darin. I shielded my eyes from the afternoon glare to read the phone screen. Darin asked me to call him. What did he want? Crisp, yellow leaves whooshed around my suede booties. I tried Darin's number, but was sent straight to voicemail.

When I slipped behind the wheel of my car, the atmosphere inside was tense; my backseat passengers were pensive and squirming, like they were sitting on a bubbling pot.

"What's going on?" I scanned their faces.

"We agree that if there's more to JoJo's death, Hank shouldn't be allowed to inherit everything," Marti said. "How do we know he didn't kill JoJo? I'll pay you if you prove it's him."

"He could've done her in just as easily as Marti or Gifty could." Red stroked his mustache.

"If Hank hurt her, he will get his comeuppance," Gifty said. "I am positive."

And I was positive that the same person killed Alistair and JoJo. I was even more positive I'd catch the killer soon.

* * *

When we arrived at the ranch, Marti, Gifty, and Veera bounded inside. But I quick-stepped in front of Red, blocking his way. "Something's bugging me." How could I ask my question without arousing suspicion? "When I counted your sticks of gum, I got a different number."

He reached into a pocket and pulled the container out. "There should be twenty pieces."

"Why don't you check?"

He looked at me with a grimace. "You think I don't know how to count?"

"You tell me." If Hank knew about the will, it was possible he killed JoJo and was trying to pin it on a family member. "What's with counting your sticks of gum, anyway?"

"Are you asking if I have a sticky problem?" He cracked a crooked grin. "I've been known to chew two and a half packs by noon. I can't resist that clean, tingly feeling. My doctor says it's not a problem, but I'm cutting back, anyhow. Counting keeps me from becoming an addict."

"Okay, then."

Red counted out loud, running his fingertips over each stick. "…sixteen, seventeen." He started over again and never got past seventeen. His arched brows rose higher. "Somebody stole my gum. How did you know?"

"I'm a speed counter. When would they have a chance to get into your stash? Seems like you keep a close eye."

"Not while I'm sleeping."

Red and Bart arrived yesterday afternoon around the same time. Could Bart have taken the gum? Did Bart kill JoJo to speed up the inheritance he thought he was getting? And then killed Alistair because he found out?

"I'm no greenhorn. A piece of my gum was found in Alistair's mouth, wasn't it? Well, he didn't get it from me," Red said.

"I believe you." Did I?

Michael zipped out of the house and down the steps. He slowed when Red turned to face him.

"Hey." Michael waved to Red.

Red regarded him with a harsh stare. "We were in the same room last night. Did you see anyone steal from me?"

"I was sleeping. Sorry, man." He gave me a nervous smile. "Was it… important?"

"Extremely." Red's stare never wavered.

"Oh, uh, well…" Michael pointed a finger back at the house as his brows dropped. "I'll ask…"

"Red, you look. You'll recognize the missing gum sticks faster." I was done with Red, for now.

"Gum?" Michael stuck out his neck.

Red's bulging eyes flicked over Michael before he headed for the porch. We watched until the door closed behind him. Michael showed me his phone screen.

"This is what Bart was carrying away from Gifty's house."

I bent forward and squinted. Bart gripped a long, pole-like object; the back portion ended in a gradual tail fin-shape. It was the stock of a gun, the part that serves as the handle. He was carrying away Gifty's rifle. Why?

Chapter Thirty-Five

There was no question that Bart walked out with the vintage rifle. But why? And what was I going to do about it?

I texted Veera and told her about Bart lifting Gifty's rifle.

Find out why.

Her reply came instantly:

Give me five minutes.

I tried calling Darin again. Didn't postal employees take breaks? He finally answered.

"I can't talk. I'm sorting the mail."

Background noise nearly swallowed his words. A loud crunching sound, along with a steady whoosh, made me think he was outside in the breeze. Maybe sorting mail in Los Ranchos happened outdoors.

"I need to find the person behind Alistair's murder." His killer could lead to JoJo's. "I'm looking for evidence. You have something for me?"

A few beats later, and the noise gradually diminished to the squeak of rubber soles.

"Hold on." Darin's slow breaths puffed between his steps. "That day we met you, Alistair opened up after you left the post office. He told me JoJo had confided in him about something important."

"What was it?" Did she share a secret with Alistair? She'd obviously trusted him if he was her executor.

"Alistair was a man of honor. He would never divulge a confidence. But I already knew…"

The last words came out in a whisper so low, I could barely make it out. "I

232

didn't get that. What did you know?" Did worry make Alistair confide in Darin?

"JoJo felt threatened. She thought she was being… poisoned."

My heart skipped a beat. "Okay, Darin, I have a strange request. Throw back your head and laugh."

"What?"

"Act like you're talking to an old buddy. In fact, call me Buddy. Loudly. Just in case someone's watching you, we want them to think this call is no biggie."

Was I paranoid? Absolutely. One needs to be paranoid when there's a killer on the loose in a town the size of a shoebox. What if Darin was being watched? At least he could cover himself.

He chuckled. "That's a funny joke, Buddy." He laughed harder.

"Any idea of when JoJo and Alistair had this talk?" Why hadn't Darin mentioned the meeting sooner?

"About a week before she died."

"Laugh."

A few beats passed before Darin chuckled some more. Birds tweeted and chirped in the background. "JoJo was inside the post office when she talked to Alistair." Darin lowered his voice again.

"And Alistair told you about the conversation afterward?"

"He never told me." Darin went quiet again. "I was on the other side of the wall, organizing the mail to fill the boxes. I didn't mean to eavesdrop. A postal box near the bottom was open. They didn't know I could hear them."

The two areas housing the boxes were closed in on three sides. A wide hallway took up the fourth side and led to the entrance. I guessed that JoJo and Alistair were standing in a spot where they could see anyone entering. But if Darin stood on the other side, behind the postal boxes, no one would know he was there. "There's more, isn't there?"

"Hold on." Darin's panting told me he was on the move. "JoJo told Alistair that she'd felt a burning sensation in her gums that morning. She rinsed her mouth, but she had a terrible headache afterward."

"Did she mention toothpaste?" Did she throw the toothpaste away? Was

JoJo poisoned? Did she suspect that she was being poisoned? Now I knew the reason why no toothpaste was found in JoJo's house. Someone got rid of it all.

"Toothpaste? She never said."

The new will confirmed that JoJo felt threatened. A clever killer had buried traces of his wrongs, but my radar was getting stronger signals. "Thank you, Darin."

"There's one more thing." He paused like he was debating what to say. "When they left, I moved to the next room of boxes. When I opened the top one, I saw—"

"Who?" Someone else had overheard the conversation.

"Hank."

*　*　*

Did Hank kill Alistair because he knew about the poisoned toothpaste? It made sense. Sort of. Veera waited for me at the foot of the porch. Bart leaned against the magnolia tree a few feet away from her. He inched closer when he saw me.

"Bart says Gifty texted and told him to go to her house, get the rifle, and hide it in JoJo's barn. I called Gifty and checked his story. She confirmed. I asked her to show her phone to Michael, and he double-confirmed. Bart's telling the truth."

"I don't tell lies." Bart scratched his head.

I turned to Bart. "Why would anyone want that rifle?"

"It's a Winchester, produced in 1890. It belonged to my grandfather. Aunty Gifty thinks Uncle Red's after it. I agree that he wants it, but would he steal it?"

Veera's phone chimed. "Michael texted that he's in the barn. He found the rifle hidden in the loft, just like Bart said."

"Can I go now?" Bart moved toward the house.

"What was Aunty Jo's favorite toothpaste called again?" I needed to be sure.

CHAPTER THIRTY-FIVE

"A designer brand. Superbe. It was a big splurge for her."

"Does the Los Ranchos General Store carry it?"

"She bought it online. Does this have to do with the missing toothpaste?"

"I didn't want to say anything, but..." I had to lie. After all, Bart was still on the suspect list. "I want to pay tribute to your aunty by creating a basket filled with her favorite things." Creating a basket as a thank you was a definite possibility.

"It's our way of showing we care," Veera added. "And it'll comfort the family, don't you think?"

I appreciated Veera's jumping right onto the moving wagon.

"That's nice." Bart flashed a small smile.

"You can go." I was done with him, for now.

"Okay." He shoved his hands in his pockets and strolled toward the house.

"Wait!" I thought of something else.

"What?" Bart turned on his heel.

"Red's missing some gum."

Bart shrugged. "I took a few sticks in the middle of the night. I needed a sugar fix."

"Let Red know, okay?" Did Bart take all the pieces, or did someone else dip in, too?

Veera started texting.

I turned to her to make sure we were on the same page. "You're checking in with–"

"Michael. He'll take a look at JoJo's computer to see when she last ordered toothpaste online." Veera moved closer to the porch.

She'd progressed by leaps and bounds in this investigation. "You are on fire, Veera." I pulled out my phone. "Calling my mother."

Mom answered, but instead of talking, she laughed heartily. "Oh, Red, you do all that?"

"I kill and prepare the fowl myself, too," Red was saying.

"Yuk." I didn't like to think about the killing of innocent animals. "You have any information, Mom?"

"I'll be back, Red. Don't you go anywhere."

Heels clicked against the wooden floor, and Mom disconnected. I turned my gaze to the front door in time to watch her fly out.

"Get anything out of Red?" I asked.

She narrowed her gaze. "He asked whether I'd seen anyone in the house chewing gum. What kind of question is that?"

"He takes his gum seriously. Can you buy Superbe toothpaste in any stores?"

"Sure. If you live in Florida or New Jersey." She pointed her thumb to her chest. "We can only buy it online. Cleure is a much better brand." She turned and sashayed back to the house.

"That wasn't helpful."

Veera rejoined me. "According to Michael, JoJo Means ordered two tubes of toothpaste at a time. Her last order was a month ago."

"Which means she shouldn't have run out of toothpaste." I updated her on my talk with Darin.

"JoJo knew something was going on." Veera shut her eyes. "And Hank overheard her suspicions. Then, he got rid of the tubes after inserting poison in them. That sound about right?"

"Maybe. We don't know if JoJo figured out that the toothpaste contained a toxin. But if she did, did she tell anyone about it?"

Chapter Thirty-Six

My phone rang just as I was about to tail Veera through the front door of the Means Well Ranch house. I gulped. "It's Lacy." I did an about-face and skipped down the porch stairs.

Veera hurried after me. "Don't answer that."

Our studio boss never called unless she was inebriated or incensed.

"Send her to voicemail." Veera nipped at my heels. "We got a job to finish."

"We're not cowards. Besides, she knows what we're up to." I answered the call and put her on speaker. "Lacy, we're on a case that's right up your alley. There's a psychic—"

"You're fired. I'm calling to tell you myself because I'm not a diva. Is that clear?"

"Which part?" I stalled while I considered whether to try to keep my studio job and Veera's.

"I need fresh blood…"

I muted the phone as she rattled on. I turned to Veera. "When did we start working for her?"

"About four months ago."

"And how much time has she spent in the office?" Lacy was one of the last living legends from Hollywood's glory days. She did what she wanted and didn't care what anyone thought.

"Five days, maybe."

"Do you think I'm unnaturally calm for someone who's going to be without a paycheck soon?"

"You are exactly as you should be. We just got fired twice in one day. And it's cool. Not like we don't have something better to do."

I unmuted the phone and put it on speaker.

"—go ahead, be honest with me." Lacy finished her speech.

Veera and I exchanged a glance.

"You find me intimidating, don't you?" Lacy squawked like she was a hen about to lay an egg.

"Somewhat." That was a safe answer. Since when did I play it safe?

"I had studio security pack up your things." Lacy disconnected.

"Am I fired, too?" Veera asked. "Does she know we're a package deal?"

"Let's confirm." I pushed a few buttons on my phone and placed the call on speaker again. I felt surprisingly tranquil.

"What part didn't you understand?" Lacy answered.

"This is Veera Bankhead, Miss Halloway." Veera leaned close to my phone. "Am I fired, too?"

"I have no idea who you are, but it's obvious you have a deep awareness of what I was saying."

"I think she just paid me a compliment," Veera whispered.

"Fresh blood." Lacy disconnected again.

"No amount of fresh blood is ever going to change that woman." Veera huffed.

"It's not like we didn't see that coming. Let's finish this job."

* * *

Veera and I nearly made it to the front door when Bart came barreling around the corner of the house.

He stopped at the bottom of the porch stairs and stared up at Veera, panting. "Gifty's rifle, it's not there."

"Not in the barn?" Veera asked.

"Maybe Gifty took it back," I said.

"The only people who knew about it were you two and the tall, nerdy guy."

"Michael?"

"He took it." Bart straightened and wiped his nose with the back of his hand. "No one else knew it was there."

Veera tapped her phone keys. "You can't go around accusing people like that."

He pointed to me. "She does it all the time."

"We're private investigators. That's part of our job." Veera stuck her lower lip out and rolled her eyes over him. "I don't like your tone. Are you playing with us?"

He straightened. "Why would I?"

"So that you can keep the very valuable gun for yourself," I said.

Bart froze. "Maybe Uncle Red got to it. He's in the barn right now."

Veera and I skipped down the porch steps.

"Stay here!" I told Bart.

"This is what I call one active family." Veera jogged with me.

We burst through the front doors. The hood of Red's old car was propped open; he stuck his head out from the side.

"The fashionable, highly talented cook told me I could check in on my car."

"Mother," I muttered through clenched teeth. She was supposed to keep an eye on him.

"Know anything about a missing vintage rifle?" Veera asked.

He froze beneath the hood, pale blue eyes darting between us. "You're implying that I ought to know." He turned back toward the engine. "I don't."

I strolled around, looking for possible hiding places. I checked inside a couple of cabinets. Empty. I peered around a smallish armoire near the stables. The handsome piece looked hand-carved. Empty again. Veera manned the main entry like she expected Red to bolt.

"Michael texted me that the last time he saw the rifle, it was in the loft. I'll take a look." Veera rushed up to the loft and returned a minute later. "Nothing there."

Right by the entry to the stables stood a large pine cabinet. A dark wood carving of a horse head in profile was nailed to the cabinet's barn style double doors. They were padlocked.

"That's a tack locker I built." Red lumbered to my side. "For housing a saddle, fly spray, and shampoo. Hides the clutter of horse gear. Mice and dustproof, too. Mother was an avid rider."

"Why is it locked?"

He strolled over and lifted the lock. "Don't know. Marti might have a key."

Veera moved close enough to hear us.

"I need a screwdriver," I said. The standard metal padlock would be simple to open.

Veera shot off toward the tools and returned with three different-sized screwdrivers. I inserted a small one in the keyhole until I hit the lock's barrel. Jiggling it, I shook the lock. I continued jiggling for another minute.

"Why are you so interested in looking inside this locker?" Red's gaze flew to mine.

"No stone left unturned." I enjoyed breaking and entering even more than I enjoyed dessert. It was no surprise that I popped open the lock thirty seconds later. I pulled the padlock off and opened both sides. A pair of boots slumped on the floor. Gifty's antique rifle rested behind the boots.

Veera gasped.

Red's eyes popped out of their sockets. "Is that what I think it is?" He reached for the rifle.

I cut in front of him, pistol drawn. "Don't touch anything." I handed Detective Chen's card to Veera.

"I'll call him." Veera pulled out her phone, muttered about poor reception, and ran outside.

I turned to Red, pistol in hand.

His eyes were glued to my gun. "What are you doing?" He spoke low.

"Why did you hide the rifle in here, Red?"

His brows made a slow ascent. "Why did I…" He backed up. "Someone's paying you to frame me, is that it? Marti fired you, and you got someone else to hire you right away. It's Hank, isn't it? You planned this with him."

"Are those your boots?"

"They are not." He didn't even bother looking at them.

Veera raced back in. "Police are on the way."

"Cinderella," Red said.

Was he trying to distract me?

"I'll bet you my inheritance that if I try to pull on the boots, they won't fit. I have double wide feet." He lowered himself onto the concrete floor and unlaced the boot he wore.

Veera pointed her pepper spray at his face when he turned to look at her. "You're obviously a bootman."

"True, but the ones in the locker belong to a wannabe bootman. I wear lumberjack, semi-dress boots, or I go bare." Red turned to me.

"What about the rifle?" I asked. "Everyone knows you wanted it."

He did a lazy, slow blink. "I've been lusting after that baby for a long time. But I'm no thief."

I picked up a boot and froze. Behind it sat a red and black box the size of a brick. A box holding fifty rounds of .380 auto ammo. "Those are the same bullets used in the gun found next to Alistair's body."

"That's what I call incriminating evidence." Veera's mouth dropped open. "Might as well be holding a smoking gun."

Red leaned forward. "I'm no gunman. Look inside my house; you'll find no weapons."

"You expect us to believe that? You know your way around firearms, growing up on a ranch." I was willing to bet over half of the Los Ranchos residents had firearms.

"Nothing inside that locker is mine."

"Hands to the ceiling." I nodded toward Veera.

"You're kidding." His hands reached for the sky.

Veera lowered her pepper spray and did a slow frisk of Red's person, standing back moments later. "He's clean."

"You forgot to check behind my ears." There was no wiping away his permanent scowl.

I placed a boot in front of him. "Put it on."

The zig-zag pattern on the sole matched the prints that had tailed me and the boots Michael found buried behind the trough. The pattern had shown up near Alistair's body, Gifty's garden, and Means Well Ranch.

Red looked pretty smug. "I'm telling you they don't..." It only took one try for him to pull the boot on smoothly.

"Oh, they fit fine," Veera said.

"That's not possible," Red mumbled. His voice rose as his eyes caught my stare. "I'm telling the truth."

He drank, he gambled, and had a thing for antique firearms. "We know you're up to your ears in gambling debt." I let that sink in. Yet, why would Red choose this time to steal the rifle? He'd had plenty of chances without a P.I. team breathing down his neck and cops on the hunt for suspects.

He shook his head. "Somebody set me up as the fall guy."

The door burst open as Detective Chen stormed in, followed by two officers. The rest of the Means gang joined in moments later.

"What's going on?" Marti asked. "Red?"

He stood. "Which one of you is responsible for framing me?" His sharp gaze raked over Marti, Bart, Gifty, Michael, and Mom.

"Don't look at me." In one giant step, Mom stood on my side, drawing an imaginary line on the floor with the toe of her pump.

"No, he couldn't have!" Marti's hands shot to her face, and she regarded Red. "Did you kill JoJo? That means we won't get…"

Her brother faced arrest, and her only concern was the money?

Detective Chen took the lead, asking everyone but Red and me to step back. He motioned me forward with two fingers. I gave him the low-down.

Marti's hand shot to her chest. "This can't be happening. Red? Say something!"

"That's mine." Gifty pointed to the rifle.

"We're taking it in as evidence, ma'am," Detective Chen told her. "We'll return it when we're done."

"This is not good," Gifty mumbled.

"Oh, honey." Mom moved closer to her and stretched an arm around her shoulders. "Everything will be all right."

Within the next ten minutes, Red was handcuffed and led to a patrol car.

Detective Chen approached me. "We're going to question him in greater detail. We'll get prints from the antique rifle and wrap things up. Thanks for your help." He exited the barn.

Marti marched up. "I've lost two sisters, my brother's a murder suspect, and my family money is about to be flushed down the toilet. You've only made things worse." She dropped her head in her hands and shuffled outside.

I turned to Veera, handed her my car key, and whispered, "Find out if Hank's at his diner."

"Sure thing, boss." She lowered her face to mine. "You think someone set Red up?"

My head was muddled with too much information. "Why would Red kill Alistair?" The motive eluded me. Did he kill JoJo?

"Alistair took Red's popcorn maker," Veera said. "Revenge could be the motive."

I clicked my tongue and headed out the door. Veera hustled out right behind me, phone pressed to her ear.

"Hank's been at the diner," Veera said a minute later. "But he left about five minutes ago."

"Are his boots double wide?"

"I'll find out." She zipped away.

Marti slumped in the driveway, watching Red being carted off. I raced over to the detective.

"I have a question for Red."

Detective Chen pitched his chin in Red's direction, and I headed over. Red stood cuffed near a squad car.

"Who helped pay off your gambling debt?" I asked.

He stared at me a few beats and turned away. I considered threatening him.

"We'll get you the answer." Detective Chen stood next to me.

I tramped away from the car. Where was Gifty? She had a way of coming and going undetected. I spotted her on the porch, watching the activity from afar. Michael leaned against a wall behind her. I made a beeline toward them.

Michael moved to the top of the stairs. "Gifty's got something to say."

Gifty's hands gripped the wooden railings, gaze pinned on mine. Her serious expression was riddled with worry. "A few days ago, I went inside the barn," she said. "I looked everywhere for something to show that JoJo had been…murdered. I searched the locker. It was easy to open. The rusty padlock never worked right. What happened to that padlock? Who put the new one on? No boots or bullets were in the locker when I opened it up, just the saddle, fly spray, and grooming tools."

"She doesn't think Red did it," Michael added.

My gut instinct was to agree, but my confidence level sagged around my knees. For the first time in my P.I. career, I lacked direction. I wished my father was here.

Clues can be messy and hard to recognize.

Really? His voice was as clear as if he stood right next to me. I jumped as my phone buzzed. Was I standing in a hotspot? I hopped down the stairs and answered.

"Hank's M.I.A.," Veera said. "Tucker said Hank rode home to get his truck, but get this: Hank wears size eleven extra, extra wide."

"Same as Red." Same as the boot prints. What was I missing? Gifty's house was ransacked. Bart was lured to the barn. Red was framed. What about Marti? Was she next? Or was she the culprit?

Chapter Thirty-Seven

I switched into my black op duds, a.k.a. my sweats and combat boots, and crammed my pockets with snacks for Rex. Leaving Michael and Mom to pack up so we could vacate the ranch, I hightailed it to Hank's residence. Although it looked as if Alistair's killer had been arrested, I wasn't buying it. In my book, someone else had done the dirty deed. Veera was meeting me at Hank's pad. I needed to find something linking Hank to Alistair's and JoJo's deaths. I jogged down the road and didn't stop until the tiny residence came into view.

I hid behind an oak and peeked out. Hank's truck was parked at the top of the driveway; his dog barked, deep and menacing. Why wasn't Hank at the diner? Should I storm inside or wait? He was bound to leave again.

I slid to the ground, leaning my shoulder against the rough, scaly bark of an old oak. I texted Veera, asking her to wait to hear from me before coming to Hank's house. That was my way of ensuring her safety. I muted my phone and tucked it inside a snack-filled pocket.

An engine rumbled. Hank was on the move. I crawled to the opposite side of the trunk to hide as he motored past.

The moment his truck left my sight, I jetted to the house. Lifting the kitchen window, I fingered the first of many treats just as the rottweiler scampered into view. He leapt up, jaws snapping, large paws scratching against the tile counter. I pitched a treat over his head, and he lurched toward it, crunching and munching. I climbed inside the house.

Tossing a trail of treats for him to gobble, I dashed in the garage and shut the door. Time to switch to my inspector hat.

I tackled a plastic bin hosting vintage tools, from forged iron hammers with wooden handles to mallets, wrenches, and files. Other bins held everything from jewelry boxes to stock certificates.

I peeled away thick bubble wrap that revealed antique furnishings, intricately carved and carefully restored. Why were they here? What had Marti said about JoJo taking valuables away from the family home? Did she hide them in Hank's garage? Or was this Hank's doing?

I opened the drawer of a small dresser. My heart pounded in my ears when I viewed the content. "Toothpaste." A tube of JoJo's favorite brand, Superbe, rested inside.

The door flew open behind me. Hank's hulky form filled the doorframe. The dog's snarling snout poked out between Hank's knees.

I slowly straightened; my heart beat double-time. "What's all this?" My hand gestured over the bins.

"What the hell do you think you're doing?"

The dog growled.

Could I pull out my shuriken and hurl it fast enough to hit my mark? "What are you doing with the Means family antiques?"

His gaze narrowed, and his nostrils flared. "What does it look like? I'm storing them here."

"Until you sell them off? Is that why you killed Alistair? He found out and–"

Hank put up a large, calloused hand. His stare blazed into mine, and his face burned crimson. "Alistair was my friend. JoJo was more than a friend. I didn't hurt either of them. You have one minute to get out." He hooked a finger under the dog's collar and stepped aside. The pooch growled again.

Hank didn't behave like a killer. Or did he? Would he ambush me as I flitted by him?

I didn't budge. "Why did you come back to the house? I watched you drive off."

He gestured for the dog to lie down and, in two long strides, he swept up to a piece of furniture covered by a moving blanket. He flicked it away to reveal a mahogany bookcase whose shelves brimmed with old books. He tossed a green-covered volume to me.

"*My Special Garden*?" I read the title.

He stuck his hand inside the pocket of his jacket and extracted a small plastic bag filled with dark blue flower petals. "I searched Alistair's office yesterday. Found nothing. These miraculously appeared today in his desk drawer. That book will tell me what kind of plant these belong to."

I'd rummaged through Alistair's drawers, too. There were no flower petals. Snatching the bag, I peered inside. There was very little about poisonous plants that I didn't know. I'd educated myself after I learned that my father's last cup of coffee had been laced with ricin. "The petals belong to a monkshood plant. All parts of monkshood are poisonous to the heart and nerves." I strode to the dresser and pulled out the tube. "You had the toothpaste here all the time." I held it up and pointed my gun at him.

He shook his head. "You put that there."

"Not me. I'm betting JoJo's toothpaste was laced with parts from the pretty blue petals."

He opened his mouth to speak, but his voice was hoarse, barely above a whisper. "JoJo…" He sank onto a bench behind him, breathing heavily.

"You poisoned her." Could I get a confession out of him?

His head snapped up. "It was Marti. Had to be. She has that greenhouse–"

I pulled the silver chain out of my purse and held it up. "You had the key to Means Well Ranch all the time."

"No, I didn't. Jo would never give me–"

"That's what you want me to believe." I was losing steam. Something didn't feel right.

Hank continued babbling his denial while my phone buzzed with texts, including one from Veera telling me she waited outside and four from Michael asking me to call. I dialed his number, pressing the phone to my ear.

"Hank wasn't the only one that went into Alistair's office. Video footage shows a janitor there this afternoon. A strange-looking dude in blue coveralls."

"How strange?"

"His nose is big, and his brows are like tumbleweeds. He wore a black baseball cap. I'll text the photo."

Was it the masked guy I saw by the pond?

"The weird part was that when he saw the tissue box you planted, he raced out." Michael continued, "Who does that?"

Had he spotted the camera in the box? I put Michael on speaker and caught my breath when I saw the photo. "This guy tailed me yesterday to the pond. He's wearing a mask."

"That explains his gargantuan facial features. But the dude's big," Michael said. "His head nearly reaches the doorframe."

I regarded Hank. Was he behind the mask? I ran a hand through my hair, staring at the photo. "It's someone who's been in Alistair's office enough times to know what didn't belong." In one quick move, my pistol was in my hand, my gaze on Hank. "You lied about going to the cemetery."

His slowly raised his hands. "Didn't want anyone to know I was going to Alistair's office."

"Where you took a file."

His dry lips parted. "How did you…I've been storing Jo's antiques here, at her request. I've got the paperwork to prove it. And the file's in my kitchen. Planned on giving it to you. I knew you'd want to see it. It contains a letter from Jo explaining she couldn't sell her home because of an endangered frog habitat near the pond. Jo was in the process of setting aside ten acres just for those frogs, so it wouldn't affect other Los Ranchos property values. She and Alistair worked on that together. They never bothered telling me."

That explained Alistair's research on habitats. JoJo wanted to sell the ranch, but the frogs kept getting in the way. "You watered the greenhouse plants. So did Gifty."

"That's right."

"Who else helped water?"

"My cook, Tucker, did once when I couldn't make it, but he returned my key. Then there was…"

"Yes?"

Hank's gaze was on the silver chain in my hands. "Where'd you get that?"

"Hanging at the edge of that piece." I gestured toward the marble-topped table and held up the chain. Where had I seen this chain before? Marti had one. Who else? "Where's your key to the greenhouse?"

Hank fumbled around in a pocket and pulled up a leather keyring. He held out a key that matched the mystery one on the chain.

Was it possible the chain was planted in Hank's garage to frame him? The toothpaste, too? The fog in my head cleared. "Darin had a key to the greenhouse."

"I gave him one. He watered a few times. I trust him. Everyone does. He and Alistair were close. Wait a second…you're not saying…Alistair was like a father to him." Hank slapped his hand to his head. "Darin spent the night here when I slept at the ranch. Said he was painting his walls and couldn't get any shut-eye, it smelled so bad." Hank's jaw dropped.

How could I be so dumb? I raced out of the house. Veera hopped out from behind a shrub near the driveway.

"Where are we going?" She trotted next to me.

"To catch a killer."

Chapter Thirty-Eight

Veera and I motored to town and parked near Darin's small white bungalow, clothed in darkness tonight.

"Veera, go back to the ranch. Make sure Mom's okay."

"I'm not going anywhere. She's got Michael to watch her back. Who's watching yours? This guy may be lying in wait."

"All the more reason to stay out."

"Good idea. I'll go 'round back and sneak in so we can surround him. He won't be expecting me." She raced off before I could stop her.

I pushed out a sigh and called Detective Chen. "Pick up, pick up." I left a voicemail and edged toward the entry. The door was unlocked, so I let myself in, slow and steady.

My gaze raked across the dark room. No food odors, no paint smell, no open windows. Quiet reigned. I ducked behind a small sofa. Was he hiding inside?

Minutes ticked by with no sign of Darin. And no sign of Veera. I tip-toed along the perimeter of the compact living room using my penlight. I faced a closed door near the kitchen. Turning the knob, I eased inside. The constant hum of machinery muffled other sounds in a room the size of a spacious walk-in closet. Two desks held three computers. Why would Darin need three? I sucked in a breath. What was it Michael had said to Veera? Three computers would create a system to spoof phones. That system was in this room. What else was Darin up to? I backed out and closed the door.

The rustic furnishings in the living room looked hand-hewn. A small, rectangular wood table rested on two chunks of matching wood. A side table looked to be crafted from pine. Was this Darin's handiwork?

An old-school rotary phone sat on a Shaker-style bookcase. Framed photos lined the shelf below and included a faded picture of a blonde woman and a large, unsmiling, younger Darin. There were photos of the blonde at the beach, in a garden, then two newer photos of Darin and some guy. I peered closer, expecting to see Alistair. But it wasn't Alistair in the picture. I held my breath. "I didn't see that coming."

The door behind me burst open. I spun around, gun raised. Using Veera as his body shield, Darin pressed his revolver against her temple. His eyes glittered; veins on his forehead and neck were prominent. He may have been angry, but I had my own Mount Vesuvius itching to erupt inside.

"You don't want to do this, Darin." Did I have a clear shot?

"Listen to what he's got to say, C." Her voice was steady. Her chin pressed down against his arm. She knew what she was doing.

I nodded. "Go on."

"I was paid to poison JoJo by one of her relatives." Darin's monotonous voice was deep, low, and suddenly very familiar.

"Who paid you?" I inched closer.

"He doesn't know. It was his life or hers." Veera was positioning herself as an ally. She spread her feet wider. "Darin had no choice."

Oh, boy. Don't be a hero, Veera. There wasn't an iota of truth to his words. "Don't tell me it was your father, Darin." My mind flashed to the photos on his shelf. The man in the pictures smiled in the first photo. An uncharacteristic smile, but he looked like his usual self in the next picture. How to get to Darin without triggering a response?

Veera's gaze darted from me to the gun.

"Your dad made your furniture, didn't he? He sure knows his way around a piece of wood."

Darin's gaze slightly widened; he breathed out of his mouth. His grip on Veera loosened as his focus turned on me.

I steadied my arm. "You killed JoJo and Alistair."

He shook his head.

"Did Red have anything to do with it?" I was going for it. "Your father, I mean."

Veera's eyes popped open. Darin's Adam's apple bobbed, and his pale blue eyes fluttered toward the front door.

"Red was happy to have you in his life, in the beginning," I put the pieces together as I went along, "after you helped him pay off part of his gambling debt. But he lost interest when you refused to give him more."

"I didn't have more to give!" He shoved Veera forward, tightening his grip on her.

I stepped back. Was he headed out the door with her? "Is that why you framed Red for Alistair's murder? Because he lost interest? You tried to frame Hank for JoJo's death."

"He and JoJo were always talking behind my back. He convinced her to shut me out."

"That was mean," Veera said.

"Why kill JoJo?" If he talked long enough, could I make a move?

"She wouldn't recognize me as her nephew. I showed her the DNA report. She had her lawyer contact me after that and threaten me with a lawsuit."

"That was even meaner." Veera bit her lip and stiffened. "Why'd you kill Alistair?"

"He figured it all out after we met you." Darin glared at me. "He wanted to know why the family hired a P.I. You ruined everything!"

Darin's snarl was worse than Rex's. And I had a strong feeling snacks wouldn't divert his attention like they did for Rex.

"I overheard JoJo talking to Alistair about her mouth burning and her head hurting, but I never thought he'd put it together. Then you walked into the post office that day. Alistair knew I'd watered the greenhouse plants. He knew about the monkshood. It was why JoJo kept the greenhouse locked."

"Alistair confronted you about JoJo's death." I side-stepped toward the small sofa. "And all this time, you thought he was your friend."

In one swift move, Veera elbowed him hard in the ribs and dove behind the sofa. Darin fired a shot that blew past me. I fired two before hitting the floor and rolling behind the side table. Blood poured from his shoulder.

In a blast sounding like a thousand popping balloons, bullets from his revolver sprayed the room in a staccato of flashes. Glass shattered with a tinkling and crash, as Veera and I crawled at record speed toward the kitchen.

Veera helped me up while Darin fired out of a broken window into the night. Shouts and shrieks cut up the quiet outside. I hurled myself forward, grabbing him by the back of his hair as he howled in pain. Sliding forward on her stomach, Veera clutched his ankles and yanked back. Darin hit the ground hard, face first, dropping his gun. Veera landed with a thump on top of him and pulled his arms behind him in a death grip. I grabbed the gun and banged it over his head till he became still. Cuts bled in bright red drips along his skull. Panting, I checked his soles. I'd finally found the zig-zag patterned boots.

Moments later, Detective Chen and a few uniforms stormed in.

"That's a lot of blood." Veera panted furiously.

"I might have hit him harder than I'd planned." My breath came out in short bursts.

"I'm not talking about him."

I looked around. Was Veera bleeding? "Are you okay?"

"It's you I'm worried about." She pointed to the back of my head. I pressed my fingers against my skull and stared at my bloody hand. Funny, I didn't feel any pain.

Chapter Thirty-Nine

A bouncy gurney carried me outside, where I sucked in enough air to fill the lungs of a dozen coalminers.

"You're one lucky girl." A paramedic cleaned me up.

"The bullet went through the table before grazing the back of her head," Veera told him.

She spoke like I'd planned it that way.

"You really are hard-headed." Hank stood over me. "The detective arrived right after you left my house. Seems your psychic guy thought I was the villain. Can't believe Darin tried to push the blame on me. There were rumors that he was taking too many breaks at the post office lately. I should've paid attention. Looks like we figured things out too late."

"Probably wouldn't have figured things out at all if it wasn't for Corrie." Veera handed him a business card. "You know who to call when you need a P.I."

"Sure do." Hank saluted me before ambling away.

* * *

It didn't take long before Michael drove up, Mom in tow. Marti and Gifty tumbled out of the back seat. Mom gasped when she saw me; Michael knelt by my side.

"I should've been here." He gripped my hand.

"You're wounded!" Mom said.

"Her head's like a natural helmet. Paramedics said it's a surface wound."

Veera beamed. "Corrie took Darin out before he did any real damage."

"Couldn't have done it without Veera." That was the truth. "She deserves a medal for tonight."

Veera glowed as she gave them the rundown.

"Darin poisoned JoJo? Using my monkshood? It's practically my fault. This is too much." Marti sank to the ground. "Red never said anything about Darin. Are you sure he's Red's kid?"

"Red told me once," Gifty said, "he had a child out of wedlock, like our daddy. I pictured a small boy, not an overgrown man-killer."

Two officers exited out the front door, dragging Darin away in cuffs.

"Darin visited JoJo that last night," I said. "He watched Alistair leave and made his move."

"My sister suspected something," Marti said. "That's why she wrote the will the way she did. But she thought it was one of us. Does this mean Heidi was right?"

"Looks that way," Mom said.

Hank and Detective Chen joined us.

"Jo knew I'd handle things," Hank said. "She talked to me about the trust and swore me to secrecy. She didn't explain much, but it makes sense now."

"What about your loan with JoJo?" Michael asked.

"What about it?" Hank ran his fingers along his belt. "I'm going to pay it off. My credit's not great, and JoJo was good enough to make me a short-term loan so I could open a second diner up north. I appreciated that."

"The accused's mother told him about Redmond Means before she died a few months ago," Detective Chen said. "We still have questions. We'll find some answers in there." He pointed to the house before turning to me. "We appreciate your assistance, Miss," he told me. "I'll be sure you get the reward money."

Veera jumped up. "Reward money?"

"Wait a minute!" Marti shot to her feet. "Does Darin count as a relative?"

She was ever focused on the family funds. "Violet Hilliard may be able to point you in the right direction," I said.

Marti scampered away, probably running all the way back to the ranch.

She had no plans to go quietly.

Detective Chen turned to Veera. "Alistair's sister put up reward money, which will be yours once the paperwork is completed."

"How much?" Mom asked.

The detective looked at me. "A hundred thousand."

Mom gripped my wrist and Veera's.

Veera let out a low whistle. "That's a whole lot more than Marti's going to pay us. Don't think I won't send her a bill."

Michael helped me to my feet. Not that I needed help; I was feeling light as a feather.

"I have many questions still." Gifty stared at me.

"I'll pack it up, neat and tidy for everyone, just the way JoJo liked things." I was grateful Darin wasn't running around loose in the world. For the first time, I felt the full impact of the murders. "Bart played the piano that Hank heard in the wee hours of the morning. It helped relieve his sadness. He didn't think anyone would hear him. And he wanted us to back off the case."

"Darin must have spent hours watching the house," Mom said. "I saw those bootprints all over the place this afternoon. I showed Detective Chen. He can confirm."

"I can do better." Chen stepped forward. "A pup tent was found inside a grove of trees, not far from the house. Inside were a pair of binoculars, a set of keys, and a funny-looking mask. Looks like Darin Reynolds spent a lot of time in there. Two cell phones were buried behind the tent. We'll be contacting the service providers shortly."

"They must belong to JoJo and Alistair," Michael said.

"We'll find out soon. You'd better believe we'll find prints and a DNA match. Not that we need it now." Chen shot me a grin.

"Darin knew where to find JoJo's spare key. He watched the house for a while." I worked through the facts in my mind. "He stole JoJo's antiques when she wasn't home."

"That's why she asked to store them in my garage. She didn't know who was behind it." Hank blew out a huff. "She thought it was Bart."

"Darin was a bad, bad man." Gifty's eyes glinted.

"He tried to spook us away from investigating JoJo's death," I said, "on the chance we'd solve it and implicate him."

"Which we did because we don't spook easily." Veera slapped high fives on everyone present. "When we sink in our teeth, there's no shaking us off." She slammed her hands on her hips like she was ready for more action. "He's the one that messed with the electrical panel and burned the broom."

"What about the neighborhood robberies?" Gifty asked.

"Darin thought things through." More puzzle pieces were slowly fitting together. "If someone smelled foul play in JoJo's death, the police could look at it as a robbery gone wrong. JoJo already reported antiques missing."

"Red blabbed to everyone about Marti's carnivorous, poisonous, and spiny plants. I'd heard him." Gifty rubbed her forehead. "He must've told Darin."

"And she used the Japanese broom to fight him off that last night," Michael added. "She'd been keeping it in her closet."

"I should never have borrowed it," Gifty said.

"Good thing you did," Mom said. "She used it to wallop Darin. He might still have bruises on him from that encounter, thanks to you." She patted Gifty on the arm.

"That explains why the closet door in Jo's room was open. Darin didn't close it." Hank swayed, like he was going down. Mom took his arm to steady him.

"But the person I saw go inside JoJo's house that last night carried a bag," Gifty said.

"With the yellow face towel. He was planting evidence, removing toothpaste, and who knows what else," I said.

"Why did he come into my house?" Gifty asked.

"Maybe he thought you had a copy of JoJo's updated will." Veera dove right in. "Alistair might've mentioned it since he was the executor. Darin wanted to see if he was a beneficiary."

I turned to Gifty. "I'm betting on Red telling Darin about your rifle and how valuable it was. Darin planned to steal it, but then you came home. You startled him, and he changed his mind and hid it in the pantry. He was watching the house and got wind of Bart stashing the rifle in the barn. That's when Darin discovered a perfect way to make sure Red was implicated in Alistair's death."

"Revenge was his motive," Veera said. "He sure snuck around a lot."

"I'm ready to go home now." Mom released Hank and marched to Michael's car. Veera and Gifty followed her.

"What about Red's missing chewing gum?" Michael held my shoulders.

"Had to be Darin's handiwork," I said. "He knew his father's favorite brand and used it against him, dropping wrappers by Alistair's body and in his office."

"You know what this means?" Michael's face lit up a night flooded with darkness.

"You can turn the boots you found by the trough over to the detective."

"Done already."

"I can finally pay you for your services?"

"We can go on that date we've been postponing." Michael's grin lit up the night.

"Truth." I closed my eyes. "All we have to do is decide where to go."

"I wouldn't say no to a double-decker taco supreme at Tacolicious, but more importantly…"

"Yes?" What was more important than deciding what to eat? I was hungry.

"Case-cracking is off limits during our date, promise?"

"But you're so good at it."

"That's just my excellent acting skills. No hunting down criminals. Agreed?"

"It'll be a criminal-free date." Why did I find that so hard to believe?

Acknowledgements

The author gratefully acknowledges:

Grace Topping, talented *USA Today* bestselling author, for generously sharing her time and eagle eyes with me, and her valuable feedback.

Marilyn Metzner whose loving friendship, ever-present encouragement and wisdom mean so much to me.

The remarkable Level Best Books' publishing team of Verena Rose and Shawn Reilly Simmons, experts in pulling together all necessary pieces to create just the book I'd been hoping for. And the ever-responsive Deb Well for handling my author requests so seamlessly.

My Sleuths & Sidekicks sisters and fellow authors: Jen Collins Moore, Tina deBellegarde & Carol Pouliot. Our joining forces to spread our writing wings has been splendid in too many ways to mention. Who are the Sleuths & Sidekicks? Find out here: www.SleuthsandSidekicks.com

Lorie Lewis at *Kings River Life* magazine for her tireless support of us authors, and my fictional characters' namesakes: the real-life Heidi Honeyman, bookstore manager extraordinaire, and the real-life Caleb Wiseblood, ace journalist, who both so willingly lent me their unforgettable names. And to savvy journalist Pamela Dozois for listening when it really mattered.

The bright stars who add so much shine to my writing life – my husband, sons, and daughters-in-law. Thank you for indulging my technical, grammatical, fanciful, and medical questions. This particular story couldn't have been written without my hubby's planting the idea seeds which, when watered and nurtured, sprouted into an entire novel!

My darling sister, my sweet Aunt Flora and Uncle Andy – your support and enthusiasm mean so very much.

All the marvelous booksellers, librarians, journalists, podcasters, bloggers, reviewers, and readers – gratitude once more for all the time and energy spent reading, spotlighting, and supporting my books. And many thanks for reading the acknowledgements, dear readers, with extra, extra thanks to special readers and friends, Wayne & Ruth Norman.

About the Author

Lida Sideris' first stint after law school was a newbie lawyer's dream: working as an entertainment attorney for a movie studio…kind of like her heroine, Corrie Locke, except without the homicides. Lida is a recipient of the Helen McCloy Mystery Writers of America Scholarship Award and a 2x Silver Falchion Award finalist. She lives in the northern tip of Southern California with her family, rescue dogs, and a flock of uppity chickens.

SOCIAL MEDIA HANDLES:
   Facebook: https://www.facebook.com/lidasideris
   Twitter: @lidasideris
   Instagram: @lida_sideris
   Book Bub

AUTHOR WEBSITE:
   www.lidasideris.com

Also by Lida Sideris

The Southern California Mysteries (in order of appearance):
Murder & Other Unnatural Disasters
Murder Gone Missing
Murder: Double Or Nothing
Slightly Murderous Intent
Gambling With Murder

And don't forget the picture book for kids - *The Cookie Eating Fire Dog*